Madam Crowl's Ghost &
Other Stories
J. Sheridan Le Fanu

GRAPEVINE INDIA

Published by

GRAPEVINE INDIA PUBLISHERS PVT LTD

www.grapevineindia.com
Delhi | Mumbai
email: grapevineindiapublishers@gmail.com

Ordering Information:
Quantity sales: Special discounts are available on quantity
purchases by corporations, associations, and others.
For details, reach out to the publisher.

First published by Grapevine India 2023
Copyright © Grapevine 2023

PROLOGUE

Joseph Sheridan Le Fanu, who died just fifty years ago, was in his own particular vein one of the best story-tellers of the nineteenth century; and the present volume contains a collection of forgotten tales by him, and of tales not previously known to be his.

There have always been readers and lovers of Le Fanu's works, though not so many as those writings deserve. To these I know that the addition which I bring to their stock will be welcome. But the larger public, which knows not this Joseph, may be glad to be told what they are to expect in his stories.

He stands absolutely in the first rank as a writer of ghost stories. That is my deliberate verdict, after reading all the supernatural tales I have been able to get hold of. Nobody sets the scene better than he, nobody touches in the effective detail more deftly. I do not think it is merely the fact of my being past middle age that leads me to regard the leisureliness of his style as a merit; for I am by no means inappreciative of the more modern efforts in this branch of fiction. No, it has to be recognized, I am sure, that the ghost-story is in itself a slightly old-fashioned form; it needs some deliberateness in the telling: we listen to it the more readily if the narrator poses as elderly, or throws back his experience to "some thirty years ago."

I digress. Ghost stories and tales of mystery are what this volume contains, and, in order to lure the reader on, I have placed the most striking and sensa[viii]tional of them at the beginning of it. These are also the most recent in date; for, as was natural, Le Fanu made improvements in the proportions and in the conception of his short stories as time went on. If the reader likes *Squire Toby's Will and Madam Crowl's Ghost*, as I think he must, he will go on to the earlier stories and find in them the same excellent qualities, only slightly overlaid by the mannerisms of the forties and fifties.

I hope he will then inquire what other work of Le Fanu's is accessible. To aid him in his search, I have put together in an epilogue or appendix what I know of the order and character of Le Fanu's novels and tales.

I need only add that the stories in this volume have been gleaned from extinct periodicals. They are the result of a fairly long investigation, but I am sure that some anonymous tales by my author must have eluded me, and I shall be very grateful to any one who will notify me of any that he is fortunate enough to find.

M. R. James.

PROVOST'S   LODGE,
ETON, *July*, 1923.

NOTE:—I have omitted three other stories of a similar nature, viz: *The Mysterious Lodger* (*Dublin University Magazine*, Vol. 50) which, though it contains some excellent detail, is more in the nature of a religious allegory than a ghost story proper; *My Aunt Margaret's Adventure* (*ibid.* 1864) which belongs to a class of which I disapprove—the ghost-story which peters out into a natural explanation; and also a fragment called *Hyacinth O'Toole* which appeared posthumously in *Temple Bar* (1884).

1

MADAM CROWL'S GHOST

Contributed anonymously to *All the Year Round* in 1870-1, but afterwards incorporated bodily into *Chronicles of Golden Friars* (1871, vol. i.) in the story of «Laura Mildmay,» where it is put into the mouth of an old north-country nurse, Mrs. Jolliffe.

I'm an old woman now; and I was but thirteen my last birthday, the night I came to Applewale House. My aunt was the housekeeper there, and a sort o' one-horse carriage was down at Lexhoe to take me and my box up to Applewale.

I was a bit frightened by the time I got to Lexhoe, and when I saw the carriage and horse, I wished myself back again with my mother at Hazelden. I was crying when I got into the "shay"—that's what we used to call it—and old John Mulbery that drove it, and was a good-natured fellow, bought me a handful of apples at the Golden Lion, to cheer me up a bit; and he told me that there was a currant-cake, and tea, and pork-chops, waiting for me, all hot, in my aunt's room at the great house. It was a fine moonlight night and I eat the apples, lookin' out o' the shay winda.

It is a shame for gentlemen to frighten a poor foolish child like I was. I sometimes think it might be tricks.[2] There was two on ‹em on the tap o› the coach beside me. And they began to question me after nightfall, when the moon rose, where I was going to. Well, I told them it was to wait on Dame Arabella Crowl, of Applewale House, near by Lexhoe.

"Ho, then," says one of them, "you'll not be long there!"

And I looked at him as much as to say, "Why not?" for I had spoke out when I told them where I was goin', as if 'twas something clever I had to say.

"Because," says he—"and don't you for your life tell no one, only watch her and see—she's possessed by the devil, and more an half a ghost. Have you got a Bible?"

"Yes, sir," says I. For my mother put my little Bible in my box, and I knew it was there: and by the same token, though the print's too small for my ald eyes, I have it in my press to this hour.

As I looked up at him, saying "Yes, sir," I thought I saw him winkin' at his friend; but I could not be sure.

"Well," says he, "be sure you put it under your bolster every night, it will keep the ald girl's claws aff ye."

And I got such a fright when he said that, you wouldn't fancy! And I'd a liked to ask him a lot about the ald lady, but I was too shy, and he and his friend began talkin' together about their own consarns, and dowly enough I got down, as I told ye, at Lexhoe. My heart sank as I drove into the dark avenue. The trees stands very thick and big, as ald as the ald house almost, and four people, with their arms out and finger-tips touchin', barely girds round some of them.

Well, my neck was stretched out o' the winda, looking for the first view o' the great house; and, all at once we pulled up in front of it.[3]

A great white-and-black house it is, wi' great black beams across and right up it, and gables lookin' out, as white as a sheet, to the moon, and the shadows o' the trees, two or throw up and down upon the front, you could count the leaves on them, and all the little diamond-shaped winda-panes, glimmering on the great hall winda, and great shutters, in the old fashion, hinged on the wall outside, boulted across all the rest o' the windas in front, for there was but three or four servants, and the old lady in the house, and most o' t'rooms was locked up.

My heart was in my mouth when I sid the journey was over, and this, the great house afore me, and I sa near my aunt that I never sid till noo, and Dame Crowl, that I was come to wait upon, and was afeard on already.

My aunt kissed me in the hall, and brought me to her room. She was tall and thin, wi' a pale face and black eyes, and long thin hands wi' black mittins on. She was past fifty, and her word was short; but her word was law. I hev no complaints to make of her; but she was a hard woman, and I think she would hev bin kinder to me if I had bin her sister's child in place of her brother's. But all that's o' no consequence noo.

The squire—his name was Mr. Chevenix Crowl, he was Dame Crowl's grandson—came down there, by way of seeing that the old lady was well treated, about twice or thrice in the year. I sid him but twice all the time I was at Applewale House.

I can't say but she was well taken care of, notwithstanding, but that was because my aunt and Meg Wyvern, that was her maid, had a conscience, and did their duty by her.

Mrs. Wyvern—Meg Wyvern my aunt called her to herself, and Mrs. Wyvern to me—was a fat, jolly lass of fifty, a good height and a good breadth, always good[4]-humoured, and walked slow. She had fine wages, but she was a bit stingy, and kept all her fine clothes under lock and key, and wore, mostly, a twilled chocolate cotton, wi' red, and yellow, and green sprigs and balls on it, and it lasted wonderful.

She never gave me nout, not the vally o' a brass thimble, all the time I was there; but she was good-humoured, and always laughin', and she talked no end o' proas over her tea; and, seeing me sa sackless and dowly, she roused me up wi' her laughin' and stories; and I think I liked her better than my aunt—children is so taken wi' a bit o' fun or a story—though my aunt was very good to me, but a hard woman about some things, and silent always.

My aunt took me into her bed-chamber, that I might rest myself a bit while she was settin' the tea in her room. But first she patted me on the shouther, and said I was a tall lass o' my years, and had spired up well, and asked me if I could do plain work and stitchin'; and she looked in my face, and said I was like my father, her brother, that was dead and gone, and she hoped I was a better Christian, and wad na du a' that lids.

It was a hard sayin' the first time I set my foot in her room, I thought.

When I went into the next room, the housekeeper's room—very comfortable, yak (oak) all round—there was a fine fire blazin' away, wi' coal, and peat, and wood, all in a low together, and tea on the table, and hot cake, and smokin' meat; and there was Mrs. Wyvern, fat, jolly, and talkin' away, more in an hour than my aunt would in a year.

While I was still at my tea my aunt went up-stairs to see Madam Crowl.

"She's agone up to see that old Judith Squailes is awake," says Mrs. Wyvern. "Judith sits with Madam[5] Crowl when me and Mrs. Shutters»—that was my aunt›s name—» is away. She›s a troublesome old lady. Ye›ll hev to be sharp wi› her, or she›ll be into the fire, or out o› t› winda. She goes on wires, she does, old though she be.»

"How old, ma'am ?" says I.

"Ninety-three her last birthday, and that's eight months gone," says she; and she laughed. "And don't be askin' questions about her before your aunt—mind, I tell ye; just take her as you find her, and that's all."

"And what's to be my business about her, please ma'am ?" says I.

"About the old lady? Well," says she, "your aunt, Mrs. Shutters, will tell you that; but I suppose you'll hev to sit in the room with your work, and see she's at no mischief, and let her amuse herself with her things on the table, and get her her food or drink as she calls for it, and keep her out o' mischief, and ring the bell hard if she's troublesome."

"Is she deaf, ma'am?"

"No, nor blind," says she; "as sharp as a needle, but she's gone quite aupy, and can't remember nout rightly; and Jack the Giant Killer, or Goody Twoshoes will please her as well as the King's court, or the affairs of the nation."

"And what did the little girl go away for, ma'am, that went on Friday last? My aunt wrote to my mother she was to go."

"Yes; she's gone."

"What for?" says I again.

"She didn't answer Mrs. Shutters, I do suppose," says she. "I don't know. Don't be talkin'; your aunt can't abide a talkin' child."

"And please, ma'am, is the old lady well in health?" says I.[6]

"It ain't no harm to ask that," says she. "She's torflin' a bit lately, but better this week past, and I dare say she'll last out her hundred years yet. Hish! Here's your aunt coming down the passage."

In comes my aunt, and begins talkin' to Mrs. Wyvern, and I, beginnin' to feel more comfortable and at home like, was walkin' about the room lookin' at this thing and at that. There was pretty old china things on the cupboard, and pictures again the wall; and there was a door open in the wainscot, and I sees a queer old leathern jacket, wi' straps and buckles to it, and sleeves as long as the bed-post, hangin' up inside.

"What's that you're at, child?" says my aunt, sharp enough, turning about when I thought she least minded. "What's that in your hand?"

"This, ma'am?" says I, turning about with the leathern jacket. "I don't know what it is, ma'am."

Pale as she was, the red came up in her cheeks, and her eyes flashed wi' anger, and I think only she had half a dozen steps to take, between her and me, she'd a gov me a sizzup. But she did give me a shake by the shouther, and she plucked the thing out o' my hand, and says she, "While ever you stay here, don't ye meddle wi' nout that don't belong to ye," and she hung it up on the pin that was there, and shut the door wi' a bang and locked it fast.

Mrs. Wyvern was liftin' up her hands and laughin' all this time, quietly in her chair, rolling herself a bit in it, as she used when she was kinkin'.

The tears was in my eyes, and she winked at my aunt, and says she, dryin' her own eyes that was wet wi' the laughin', "Tut, the child meant no harm—come here to me, child. It's only a pair o' crutches for lame ducks, and ask us no questions mind, and we'll tell ye no lies;[7] and come here and sit down, and drink a mug o› beer before ye go to your bed.»

My room, mind ye, was up-stairs, next to the old lady's, and Mrs. Wyvern's bed was near hers in her room and I was to be ready at call, if need should be.

The old lady was in one of her tantrums that night and part of the day before. She used to take fits o' the sulks. Sometimes she would not let them dress her, and other times she would not let them take her clothes off. She was a great beauty, they said, in her day. But there was no one about Applewale that remembered her in her prime. And she was dreadful fond o' dress, and had thick silks, and stiff satins, and velvets, and laces, and all sorts, enough to set up seven shops at the least. All her dresses was old-fashioned and queer, but worth a fortune.

Well, I went to my bed. I lay for a while awake; for a' things was new to me; and I think the tea was in my nerves, too, for I wasn't used to it, except now and then on a holiday, or the like. And I heard Mrs. Wyvern talkin', and I listened with my hand to my ear; but I could not hear Mrs. Crowl, and I don't think she said a word.

There was great care took of her. The people at Applewale knew that when she died they would every one get the sack; and their situations was well paid and easy.

The doctor come twice a week to see the old lady, and you may be sure they all did as he bid them. One thing was the same every time; they were never to cross or frump her, any way, but to humour and please her in everything.

So she lay in her clothes all that night, and next day, not a word she said, and I was at my needlework all that day, in my own room, except when I went down to my dinner.[8]

I would a liked to see the ald lady, and even to hear her speak. But she might as well a'bin in Lunnon a' the time for me.

When I had my dinner my aunt sent me out for a walk for an hour. I was glad when I came back, the trees was so big, and the place so dark and lonesome, and 'twas a cloudy day, and I cried a deal, thinkin' of home, while I was walkin' alone there. That evening, the candles bein' alight, I was sittin' in my room, and the door was open into Madam Crowl's chamber, where my aunt was. It was, then, for the first time I heard what I suppose was the ald lady talking.

It was a queer noise like, I couldn't well say which, a bird, or a beast, only it had a bleatin' sound in it, and was very small.

I pricked my ears to hear all I could. But I could not make out one word she said. And my aunt answered:

"The evil one can't hurt no one, ma'am, bout the Lord permits."

Then the same queer voice from the bed says something more that I couldn't make head nor tail on.

And my aunt med answer again: "Let them pull faces, ma'am, and say what they will; if the Lord be for us, who can be against us?"

I kept listenin' with my ear turned to the door, holdin' my breath, but not another word or sound came in from the room. In about twenty minutes, as I was sittin' by the table, lookin' at the pictures in the old Æsop's Fables, I was aware o' something moving at the door, and lookin' up I sid my aunt's face lookin' in at the door, and her hand raised.

"Hish!" says she, very soft, and comes over to me on tiptoe, and she says in a whisper: "Thank God, she's asleep at last, and don't ye make no noise till I come[9] back, for I›m goin› down to take my cup o› tea, and I›ll be back i› noo—me and Mrs. Wyvern, and she›ll be sleepin› in the room, and you can run down when we come up, and Judith will gie ye yaur supper in my room.»

And with that away she goes.

I kep' looking at the picture-book, as before, listenin' every noo and then, but there was no sound, not a breath, that I could hear; an' I began whisperin' to the pictures and talkin' to myself to keep my heart up, for I was growin' feared in that big room.

And at last up I got, and began walkin' about the room, lookin' at this and peepin' at that, to amuse my mind, ye'll understand. And at last what sud I do but peeps into Madame Crowl's bed-chamber.

A grand chamber it was, wi' a great four-poster, wi' flowered silk curtains as tall as the ceilin', and foldin' down on the floor, and drawn close all round. There was a lookin'-glass, the biggest I ever sid before, and the room was a blaze o' light. I counted twenty-two wax-candles, all alight. Such was her fancy, and no one dared say her nay.

I listened at the door, and gaped and wondered all round. When I heard there was not a breath, and did not see so much as a stir in the curtains, I took heart, and I walked into the room on tiptoe, and looked round again. Then I takes a keek at myself in the big glass; and at last it came in my head, "Why couldn't I ha' a keek at the ald lady herself in the bed?"

Ye'd think me a fule if ye knew half how I longed to see Dame Crowl, and I thought to myself if I didn't peep now I might wait many a day before I got so gude a chance again.

Well, my dear, I came to the side o' the bed, the curtains bein' close, and my heart a'most failed me. But I took courage, and I slips my finger in between the thick curtains,[10] and then my hand. So I waits a bit, but all was still as death. So, softly, softly I draws the curtain, and there, sure enough, I sid before me, stretched out like the painted lady on the tomb-stean in Lexhoe Church, the famous Dame Crowl, of Applewale House. There she was, dressed out. You never sid the like in they days. Satin and silk, and scarlet and green, and gold and pint lace; by Jen! ‹twas a sight! A big powdered wig, half as high as herself, was a-top o› her head, and, wow!—was ever such wrinkles?—and her old baggy throat all powdered white, and her cheeks rouged, and mouse-skin eyebrows, that Mrs. Wyvern used to stick on, and there she lay grand and stark, wi› a pair o› clocked silk hose on, and heels to her shoon as tall as nine-pins. Lawk! But her nose was crooked and thin, and half the whites o› her eyes was open. She used to stand, dressed as she was, gigglin› and dribblin› before the lookin›-glass, wi› a fan in her hand, and a big nosegay in her bodice. Her wrinkled little hands was stretched down by her sides, and such long nails, all cut into points, I never sid in my days. Could it ever a bin the fashion for grit fowk to wear their finger-nails so?

Well, I think ye'd a bin frightened yourself if ye'd a sid such a sight. I couldn't let go the curtain, nor move an inch, not take my eyes off her; my very heart stood still. And in an instant she opens her eyes, and up she sits, and spins herself round, and down wi' her, wi' a clack on her two tall heels on the floor, facin' me, ogglin' in my face wi' her two great glassy eyes, and a wicked simper wi' her old wrinkled lips, and lang fause teeth.

Well, a corpse is a natural thing; but this was the dreadfullest sight I ever sid. She had her fingers straight out pointin' at me, and her back was crooked, round again wi' age. Says she:[11]

"Ye little limb! what for did ye say I killed the boy? I'll tickle ye till ye're stiff!"

If I'd a thought an instant, I'd a turned about and run. But I couldn't take my eyes off her, and I backed from her as soon as I could; and she came clatterin' after, like a thing on wires, with her fingers pointing to my throat, and she makin' all the time a sound with her tongue like zizz-zizz-zizz.

I kept backin' and backin' as quick as I could, and her fingers was only a few inches away from my throat, and I felt I'd lose my wits if she touched me.

I went back this way, right into the corner, and I gev a yellock, ye'd think saul and body was partin', and that minute my aunt, from the door, calls out wi' a blare, and the ald lady turns round on her, and I turns about, and ran through my room, and down the back stairs, as hard as my legs could carry me.

I cried hearty, I can tell you, when I got down to the housekeeper's room. Mrs. Wyvern laughed a deal when I told her what happened. But she changed her key when she heard the ald lady's words.

"Say them again," says she.

So I told her.

"Ye little limb! What for did ye say I killed the boy? I'll tickle ye till ye're stiff."

"And did ye say she killed a boy?" says she.

"Not I, ma'am," says I.

Judith was always up with me, after that, when the two elder women was away from her. I would a jumped out at winda, rather than stay alone in the same room wi' her.

It was about a week after, as well as I can remember, Mrs. Wyvern, one day when me and her was alone, told me a thing about Madam Crowl that I did not know before.[12]

She being young, and a great beauty, full seventy years before, had married Squire Crowl of Applewale. But he was a widower, and had a son about nine year old.

There never was tale or tidings of this boy after one mornin'. No one could say where he went to. He was allowed too much liberty, and used to be off in the morning, one day, to the keeper's cottage, and breakfast wi' him, and away to the warren, and not home, mayhap, till evening, and another time down to the lake, and bathe there, and spend the day fishin' there, or paddlin' about in the boat. Well, no one could say what was gone wi' him; only this, that his hat was found by the lake, under a haathorn that grows thar to this day, and 'twas thought he was drowned bathin'. And the squire's son, by his second marriage, by this Madam Crowl that lived sa dreadful lang, came in for the estates. It was his son, the ald lady's grandson, Squire Chevenix Crowl, that owned the estates at the time I came to Applewale.

There was a deal o' talk lang before my aunt's time about it; and 'twas said the step-mother knew more than she was like to let out. And she managed her husband, the ald squire, wi' her whiteheft and flatteries. And as the boy was never seen more, in course of time the thing died out of fowks' minds.

I'm goin' to tell ye noo about what I sid wi' my own een.

I was not there six months, and it was winter time, when the ald lady took her last sickness.

The doctor was afeard she might a took a fit o' madness, as she did, fifteen years befoore, and was buckled up, many a time, in a strait-waistcoat, which was the very leathern jerkin' I sid in the closet, off my aunt's room.

Well, she didn't. She pined, and windered, and went off, torflin', torflin', quiet enough, till a day or two before[13] her flittin›, and then she took to rabblin›, and sometimes skirlin› in the bed, ye›d think a robber had a knife to her throat, and she used to work out o› the bed, and not being strong enough, then, to walk or stand, she›d fall on the flure, wi› her ald wizened hands stretched before her face, and skirlin› still for mercy.

Ye may guess I didn't go into the room, and I used to be shiverin' in my bed wi' fear, at her skirlin' and scrafflin' on the flure, and blarin' out words that id make your skin turn blue.

My aunt, and Mrs. Wyvern, and Judith Squailes, and a woman from Lexhoe, was always about her. At last she took fits, and they wore her out.

T'sir (parson) was there, and prayed for her; but she was past praying with. I suppose it was right, but none could think there was much good in it, and sa at lang last she made her flittin', and a' was over, and old Dame Crowl was shrouded and coffined and Squire Chevenix was wrote for. But he was away in France, and the delay was sa lang, that t'sir and doctor both agreed it would not du to keep her langer out o' her place, and no one cared but just them two, and my aunt and the rest o' us, from Applewale, to go to the buryin'. So the old lady of Applewale was laid in the vault under Lexhoe Church; and we lived up at the great house till such time as the squire should come to tell his will about us, and pay off such as he chose to discharge.

I was put into another room, two doors away from what was Dame Crowl's chamber, after her death, and this thing happened the night before Squire Chevenix came to Applewale.

The room I was in now was a large square chamber, covered wi' yak pannels, but unfurnished except for my[14] bed, which had no curtains to it, and a chair and a table, or so, that looked nothing at all in such a big room. And the big looking-glass, that the old lady used to keek into and admire herself from head to heel, now that there was na mair o› that wark, was put out of the way, and stood against the wall in my room, for there was shiftin› o› many things in her chambers ye may suppose, when she came to be coffined.

The news had come that day that the squire was to be down next morning at Applewale; and not sorry was I, for I thought I was sure to be sent home again to my mother. And right glad was I, and I was thinkin' of a' at hame, and my sister, Janet, and the kitten and the pymag, and Trimmer the tike, and all the rest, and I got sa fidgetty, I couldn't sleep, and the clock struck twelve, and me wide awake, and the room as dark as pick. My back was turned to the door, and my eyes toward the wall opposite.

Well, it could na be a full quarter past twelve, when I sees a lightin' on the wall befoore me, as if something took fire behind, and the shadas o' the bed, and the chair, and my gown, that was hangin' from the wall, was dancin' up and down, on the ceilin' beams and the yak pannels; and I turns my head ower my shouther quick, thinkin' something must a gone a' fire.

And what sud I see, by Jen! but the likeness o' the ald beldame, bedizened out in her satins and velvets, on her dead body, simperin', wi' her eyes as wide as saucers, and her face like the fiend himself. 'Twas a red light that rose about her in a fuffin low, as if her dress round her feet was blazin'. She was drivin' on right for me, wi' her ald shrivelled hands crooked as if she was goin' to claw me. I could not stir, but she passed me straight by, wi' a blast o' cald air, and I sid her, at the wall, in the alcove[15] as my aunt used to call it, which was a recess where the state bed used to stand in ald times, wi› a door open wide, and her hands gropin› in at somethin› was there. I never sid that door befoore. And she turned round to me, like a thing on a pivot, flyrin› (grinning), and all at once the room was dark, and I standin› at the far side o› the bed; I don›t know how I got there, and I found my tongue at last, and if I did na blare a yellock, rennin› down the gallery and almost pulled Mrs. Wyvern›s door, off t›hooks, and frightened her half out o› her wits.

Ye may guess I did na sleep that night; and wi' the first light, down wi' me to my aunt, as fast as my two legs cud carry me.

Well, my aunt did na frump or flite me, as I thought she would, but she held me by the hand, and looked hard in my face all the time. And she telt me not to be feared; and says she:

"Hed the appearance a key in its hand?"

"Yes," says I, bringin' it to mind, "a big key in a queer brass handle."

"Stop a bit," says she, lettin' go ma hand, and openin' the cupboard-door. "Was it like this?" says she, takin' one out in her fingers and showing it to me, with a dark look in my face.

"That was it," says I, quick enough.

"Are ye sure?" she says, turnin' it round.

"Sart," says I, and I felt like I was gain' to faint when I sid it.

"Well, that will do, child," says she, saftly thinkin', and she locked it up again.

"The squire himself will be here to-day, before twelve o'clock, and ye must tell him all about it," says she, thinkin', "and I suppose I'll be leavin' soon, and so the best thing for the present is, that ye should go home this[16] afternoon, and I›ll look out another place for you when I can.»

Fain was I, ye may guess, at that word.

My aunt packed up my things for me, and the three pounds that was due to me, to bring home, and Squire Crowl himself came down to Applewale that day, a handsome man, about thirty years aid. It was the second time I sid him. But this was the first time he spoke to me.

My aunt talked wi' him in the housekeeper's room, and I don't know what they said. I was a bit feared on the squire, he bein' a great gentleman down in Lexhoe, and I darn't go near till I was called. And says he, smilin':

"What's a' this ye a sen, child? it mun be a dream, for ye know there's na sic a thing as a bo or a freet in a' the world. But whatever it was, ma little maid, sit ye down and tell us all about it from first to last."

Well, so soon as I med an end, he thought a bit, and says he to my aunt:

"I mind the place well. In old Sir Oliver's time lame Wyndel told me there was a door in that recess, to the left, where the lassie dreamed she saw my grandmother open it. He was past eighty when he telt me that, and I but a boy. It's twenty year sen. The plate and jewels used to be kept there, long ago, before the iron closet was made in the arras chamber, and he told me the key had a brass handle, and this ye say was found in the bottom o' the kist where she kept her old fans. Now, would not it be a queer thing if we found some spoons or diamonds forgot there? Ye mun come up wi' us, lassie, and point to the very spot."

Loth was I, and my heart in my mouth, and fast I held by my aunt's hand as I stept into that awsome room, and showed them both how she came and passed me by, and[17] the spot where she stood, and where the door seemed to open.

There was an ald empty press against the wall then, and shoving it aside, sure enough there was the tracing of a door in the wainscot, and a keyhole stopped with wood, and planed across as smooth as the rest, and the joining of the door all stopped wi' putty the colour o' yak, and, but for the hinges that showed a bit when the press was shoved aside, ye would not consayt there was a door there at all.

"Ha!" says he, wi' a queer smile, "this looks like it."

It took some minutes wi' a small chisel and hammer to pick the bit o' wood out o' the keyhole. The key fitted, sure enough, and, wi' a strang twist and a lang skreeak, the boult went back and he pulled the door open.

There was another door inside, stranger than the first, but the lacks was gone, and it opened easy. Inside was a narrow floor and walls and vault o' brick; we could not see what was in it, for 'twas dark as pick.

When my aunt had lighted the candle the squire held it up and stept in.

My aunt stood on tiptoe tryin' to look over his shouther, and I did na see nout.

"Ha! ha!" says the squire, steppin' backward. "What's that? Gi'ma the poker—quick!" says he to my aunt. And as she went to the hearth I peeps beside his arm, and I sid squat down in the far corner a monkey or a flayin' on the chest, or else the maist shrivelled up, wizzened ald wife that ever was sen on yearth.

"By Jen!" says my aunt, as, puttin' the poker in his hand, she keeked by his shouther, and sid the ill-favoured thing, "hae a care sir, what ye're doin'. Back wi' ye, and shut to the door!"[18]

But in place o' that he steps in saftly, wi' the poker pointed like a swoord, and he gies it a poke, and down it a' tumbles together, head and a', in a heap o' bayans and dust, little meyar an' a hatful.

'Twas the bayans o' a child; a' the rest went to dust at a touch. They said nout for a while, but he turns round the skull as it lay on the floor.

Young as I was I consayted I knew well enough what they was thinkin' on.

"A dead cat!" says he, pushin' back and blowin' out the can'le, and shuttin' to the door. "We'll come back, you and me, Mrs. Shutters, and look on the shelves by-and-bye. I've other matters first to speak to ye about; and this little girl's goin' hame, ye say. She has her wages, and I mun mak' her a present," says he, pattin' my shoulder wi' his hand.

And he did gimma a goud pound, and I went aff to Lexhoe about an hour after, and sa hame by the stagecoach, and fain was I to be at hame again; and I never saa ald Dame Crowl o' Applewale, God be thanked, either in appearance or in dream, at-efter. But when I was grown to be a woman my aunt spent a day and night wi' me at Littleham, and she telt me there was na doubt it was the poor little boy that was missing sa lang sen that was shut up to die thar in the dark by that wicked beldame, whar his skirls, or his prayers, or his thumpin' cud na be heard, and his hat was left by the water's edge, whoever did it, to mak' belief he was drowned. The clothes, at the first touch, a' ran into a snuff o' dust in the cell whar the bayans was found. But there was a handful o' jet buttons, and a knife with a green handle, together wi' a couple o' pennies the poor little fella had in his pocket, I suppose, when he was decoyed in thar, and sid his last o' the light. And there was, amang the squire's papers,[19] a copy o⟩ the notice that was prented after he was lost, when the old squire thought he might ⟨a run away, or bin took by gipsies, and it said he had a green-hefted knife wi⟩ him, and that his buttons were o⟩ cut jet. Sa that is a⟩ I hev to say consarnin⟩ ald Dame Crowl, o⟩ Applewale House.

2
SQUIRE TOBY'S WILL

A GHOST STORY

Anonymous in *Temple Bar* (1868, vol. xxii.). This story was written, it seems, contemporaneously with the novel *The Wyvern Mystery* (1868-9), and the old Squire in that book intimately resembles Squire Toby.

Many persons accustomed to travel the old York and London road, in the days of stage-coaches, will remember passing, in the afternoon, say, of an autumn day, in their journey to the capital, about three miles south of the town of Applebury, and a mile and a half before you reach the old Angel Inn, a large black-and-white house, as those old-fashioned cage-work habitations are termed, dilapidated and weather-stained, with broad lattice windows glimmering all over in the evening sun with little diamond panes, and thrown into relief by a dense background of ancient elms. A wide avenue, now overgrown like a churchyard with grass and weeds, and flanked by double rows of the same dark trees, old and gigantic, with here and there a gap in their solemn files, and sometimes a fallen tree lying across on the avenue, leads up to the hall-door.

Looking up its sombre and lifeless avenue from the top of the London coach, as I have often done, you are struck[21] with so many signs of desertion and decay,—the tufted grass sprouting in the chinks of the steps and window-stones, the smokeless chimneys over which the jackdaws are wheeling, the absence of human life and all its evidence, that you conclude at once that the place is uninhabited and abandoned to decay. The name of this ancient house is Gylingden Hall. Tall hedges and old timber quickly shroud the old place from view, and about a quarter of a mile further on you pass, embowered in melancholy trees, a small and ruinous Saxon chapel, which, time out of mind, has been the burying-place of the family of Marston, and partakes of the neglect and desolation which brood over their ancient dwelling-place.

The grand melancholy of the secluded valley of Gylingden, lonely as an enchanted forest, in which the crows returning to their roosts among the trees, and the straggling deer who peep from beneath their branches, seem to hold a wild and undisturbed dominion, heightens the forlorn aspect of Gylingden Hall.

Of late years repairs have been neglected, and here and there the roof is stripped, and "the stitch in time" has been wanting. At the side of the house exposed to the gales that sweep through the valley like a torrent through its channel, there is not a perfect window left, and the shutters but imperfectly exclude the rain. The ceilings and walls are mildewed and green with damp stains. Here and there, where the drip falls from the ceiling, the floors are rotting. On stormy nights, as the guard described, you can hear the doors clapping in the old house, as far away as old Gryston bridge, and the howl and sobbing of the wind through its empty galleries.

About seventy years ago died the old Squire, Toby Marston, famous in that part of the world for his hounds, his hospitality, and his vices. He had done kind things,[22] and he had fought duels: he had given away money and he had horse-whipped people. He carried with him some blessings and a good many curses, and left behind him an amount of debts and charges upon the estates which appalled his two sons, who had no taste for business or accounts, and had never suspected, till that wicked, open-handed, and swearing old gentleman died, how very nearly he had run the estates into insolvency.

They met at Gylingden Hall. They had the will before them, and lawyers to interpret, and information without stint, as to the encumbrances with which the deceased had saddled them. The will was so framed as to set the two brothers instantly at deadly feud.

These brothers differed in some points; but in one material characteristic they resembled one another, and also their departed father. They never went into a quarrel by halves, and once in, they did not stick at trifles.

The elder, Scroope Marston, the more dangerous man of the two, had never been a favourite of the old Squire. He had no taste for the sports of the field and the pleasures of a rustic life. He was no athlete, and he certainly was not handsome. All this the Squire resented. The young man, who had no respect for him, and outgrew his fear of his violence as he came to manhood, retorted. This aversion, therefore, in the ill-conditioned old man grew into positive hatred. He used to wish that d——d pippin-squeezing, hump-backed rascal Scroope, out of the way of better men— meaning his younger son Charles; and in his cups would talk in a way which even the old and young fellows who followed his hounds, and drank his port, and could stand a reasonable amount of brutality, did not like.

Scroope Marston was slightly deformed, and he had the lean sallow face, piercing black eyes, and black lank hair, which sometimes accompany deformity.[23]

"I'm no feyther o' that hog-backed creature. I'm no sire of hisn, d——n him! I'd as soon call that tongs son o' mine," the old man used to bawl, in allusion to his son's long, lank limbs: "Charlie's a man, but that's a jack-an-ape. He has no good-nature; there's nothing handy, nor manly, nor no one turn of a Marston in him."

And when he was pretty drunk, the old Squire used to swear he should never "sit at the head o' that board; nor frighten away folk from Gylingden

Hall wi' his d——d hatchet-face—the black loon!"

"Handsome Charlie was the man for his money. He knew what a horse was, and could sit to his bottle; and the lasses were all clean *mad* about him. He was a Marston every inch of his six foot two.»

Handsome Charlie and he, however, had also had a row or two. The old Squire was free with his horsewhip as with his tongue, and on occasion when neither weapon was quite practicable, had been known to give a fellow "a tap o' his knuckles." Handsome Charlie, however, thought there was a period at which personal chastisement should cease; and one night, when the port was flowing, there was some allusion to Marion Hayward, the miller's daughter, which for some reason the old gentleman did not like. Being "in liquor," and having clearer ideas about pugilism than self-government, he struck out, to the surprise of all present, at Handsome Charlie. The youth threw back his head scientifically, and nothing followed but the crash of a decanter on the floor. But the old Squire's blood was up, and he bounced from his chair. Up jumped Handsome Charlie, resolved to stand no nonsense. Drunken Squire Lilbourne, intending to mediate, fell flat on the floor, and cut his ear among the glasses. Handsome Charlie caught the thump which the old Squire discharged at him upon his open hand, and[24] catching him by the cravat, swung him with his back to the wall. They said the old man never looked so purple, nor his eyes so goggle before; and then Handsome Charlie pinioned him tight to the wall by both arms.

"Well, I say—come, don't you talk no more nonsense o' that sort, and I won't lick you," croaked the old Squire. "You stopped that un clever, you did. Didn't he? Come, Charlie, man, gie us your hand, I say, and sit down again, lad." And so the battle ended; and I believe it was the last time the Squire raised his hand to Handsome Charlie.

But those days were over. Old Toby Marston lay cold and quiet enough now, under the drip of the mighty ash-tree within the Saxon ruin where so many of the old Marston race returned to dust, and were forgotten. The weather-stained top-boots and leather-breeches, the three-cornered cocked hat to which old gentlemen of that day still clung, and the well-known red waistcoat that reached below his hips, and the fierce pug face of the old Squire, were now but a picture of memory. And the brothers between whom he had planted an irreconcilable quarrel, were now in their new mourning suits, with the gloss still on, debating furiously across the table in the great oak parlour, which had so often resounded to the banter and coarse songs, the oaths and laughter of the congenial neighbours whom the old Squire of Gylingden Hall loved to assemble there.

These young gentlemen, who had grown up in Gylingden Hall, were not accustomed to bridle their tongues, nor, if need be, to hesitate about a blow. Neither had been at the old man's funeral. His death had been sudden. Having been helped to his bed in that hilarious and quarrelsome state which was induced by port and punch, he was found dead in the morning,—his head hanging[25] over the side of the bed, and his face very black and swollen.

Now the Squire's will despoiled his eldest son of Gylingden, which had descended to the heir time out of mind. Scroope Marston was furious. His deep stern voice was heard inveighing against his dead father and living brother, and the heavy thumps on the table with which he enforced his stormy recriminations resounded through the large chamber. Then broke in Charles's rougher voice, and then came a quick alternation of short sentences, and then both voices together in growing loudness and anger, and at last, swelling the tumult, the expostulations of pacific and frightened lawyers, and at last a sudden break up of the conference. Scroope broke out of the room, his pale furious face showing whiter against his long black hair, his dark fierce eyes blazing, his hands clenched, and looking more ungainly and deformed than ever in the convulsions of his fury.

Very violent words must have passed between them; for Charlie, though he was the winning man, was almost as angry as Scroope. The elder brother was for holding possession of the house, and putting his rival to legal process to oust him. But his legal advisers were clearly against it. So, with a heart boiling over with gall, up he went to London, and found the firm who had managed his father's business fair and communicative enough. They looked into the settlements, and found that Gylingden was excepted. It was very odd, but so it was, specially excepted; so that the right of the old Squire to deal with it by his will could not be questioned.

Notwithstanding all this, Scroope, breathing vengeance and aggression, and quite willing to wreck himself provided he could run his brother down, assailed Handsome Charlie, and battered old Squire Toby's will in the Prerogative[26] Court and also at common law, and the feud between the brothers was knit, and every month their exasperation was heightened.

Scroope was beaten, and defeat did not soften him. Charles might have forgiven hard words; but he had been himself worsted during the long campaign in some of those skirmishes, special motions, and so forth, that constitute the episodes of a legal epic like that in which the Marston brothers figured as opposing combatants; and the blight of law costs had touched him, too, with the usual effect upon the temper of a man of embarrassed means.

Years flew, and brought no healing on their wings. On the contrary, the deep corrosion of this hatred bit deeper by time. Neither brother married. But an accident of a different kind befell the younger, Charles Marston, which abridged his enjoyments very materially.

This was a bad fall from his hunter. There were severe fractures, and there was concussion of the brain. For some time it was thought that he could not recover. He disappointed these evil auguries, however. He did recover, but changed in two essential particulars. He had received an injury in his hip, which doomed him never more to sit in the saddle. And the rollicking animal spirits which hitherto had never failed him, had now taken flight for ever.

He had been for five days in a state of coma—absolute insensibility—and when he recovered consciousness he was haunted by an indescribable anxiety.

Tom Cooper, who had been butler in the palmy days of Gylingden Hall, under old Squire Toby, still maintained his post with old-fashioned fidelity, in these days of faded splendour and frugal housekeeping. Twenty years had passed since the death of his old master. He had grown lean, and stooped, and his face, dark with the peculiar[27] brown of age, furrowed and gnarled, and his temper, except with his master, had waxed surly.

His master had visited Bath and Buxton, and came back, as he went, lame, and halting gloomily about with the aid of a stick. When the hunter was sold, the last tradition of the old life at Gylingden disappeared. The young Squire, as he was still called, excluded by his mischance from the hunting-field, dropped into a solitary way of life, and halted slowly and solitarily about the old place, seldom raising his eyes, and with an appearance of indescribable gloom.

Old Cooper could talk freely on occasion with his master; and one day he said, as he handed him his hat and stick in the hall:

"You should rouse yourself up a bit, Master Charles!"

"It's past rousing with me, old Cooper."

"It's just this, I'm thinking: there's something on your mind, and you won't tell no one. There's no good keeping it on your stomach. You'll be a deal lighter if you tell it. Come, now, what is it, Master Charlie?"

The Squire looked with his round grey eyes straight into Cooper's eyes. He felt that there was a sort of spell broken. It was like the old rule of the ghost who can't speak till it is spoken to. He looked earnestly into old Cooper's face for some seconds, and sighed deeply.

"It ain't the first good guess you've made in your day, old Cooper, and I'm glad you've spoke. It's bin on my mind, sure enough, ever since I had that fall. Come in here after me, and shut the door."

The Squire pushed open the door of the oak parlour, and looked round on the pictures abstractedly. He had not been there for some time, and, seating himself on the table, he looked again for a while in Cooper's face before he spoke.[28]

"It's not a great deal, Cooper, but it troubles me, and I would not tell it to the parson nor the doctor; for, God knows what they'd say, though there's nothing to signify in it. But you were always true to the family, and I don't mind if I tell you."

"'Tis as safe with Cooper, Master Charles, as if 'twas locked in a chest, and sunk in a well."

"It's only this," said Charles Marston, looking down on the end of his stick, with which he was tracing lines and circles, "all the time I was lying like dead, as you thought, after that fall, I was with the old master." He raised his eyes to Cooper's again as he spoke, and with an awful oath he repeated—"I was with him, Cooper!"

"He was a good man, sir, in his way," repeated old Cooper, returning his gaze with awe." He was a good master to me, and a good father to you, and I hope he's happy. May God rest him!"

"Well," said Squire Charles, "it's only this: the whole of that time I was with him, or he was with me—I don't know which. The upshot is, we were together, and I thought I'd never get out of his hands again, and all the time he was bullying me about some one thing; and if it was to save my life, Tom Cooper, by —— from the time I waked I never could call to mind what it was; and I think I'd give that hand to know; and if you can think of anything it might be—for God's sake! don't be afraid, Tom Cooper, but speak it out, for he threatened me hard, and it was surely him."

Here ensued a silence.

"And what did you think it might be yourself, Master Charles?" said Cooper.

"I han't thought of aught that's likely. I'll never hit on't—*never*. I thought it might happen he knew something about that d—— hump-backed villain, Scroope, that[29] swore before Lawyer Gingham I made away with a paper of settlements—me and father; and, as I hope to be saved, Tom Cooper, there never was a bigger lie! I›d a had the law of him for them identical words, and cast him for more than he›s worth; only Lawyer Gingham never goes into nothing for me since money grew scarce in Gylingden; and I can›t change my lawyer, I owe him such a hatful of money. But he did, he swore he›d hang me yet for it. He said it in them identical words—he›d never rest till he *hanged* me for it, and I think it was, like enough, something about *that*, the old master was troubled; but it's enough to drive a man mad. I *can't* bring it to mind—I can›t remember a word he said, only he threatened awful, and looked—Lord a mercy on us!—frightful bad.»

"There's no need he should. May the Lord a-mercy on him!" said the old butler.

"No, of course; and you're not to tell a soul, Cooper—not a living soul, mind, that I said he looked bad, nor nothing about it."

"God forbid!" said old Cooper, shaking his head. "But I was thinking, sir, it might ha' been about the slight that's bin so long put on him by having no stone over him, and never a scratch o' a chisel to say who he is."

"Ay! Well, I didn't think o' that. Put on your hat, old Cooper, and come down wi' me; for I'll look after that, at any rate."

There is a bye-path leading by a turnstile to the park, and thence to the picturesque old burying-place, which lies in a nook by the roadside, embowered in ancient trees. It was a fine autumnal sunset, and melancholy lights and long shadows spread their peculiar effects over the landscape as "Handsome Charlie" and the old butler made their way slowly toward the place where Handsome Charlie was himself to lie at last.[30]

"Which of the dogs made that howling all last night?" asked the Squire, when they had got on a little way.

"'Twas a strange dog, Master Charlie, in front of the house; ours was all in the yard—a white dog wi' a black head, he looked to be, and he was smelling round them mounting-steps the old master, God be wi' him! set up, the time his knee was bad. When the tyke got up a' top of them, howlin' up at the windows, I'd a liked to shy something at him."

"Hullo! Is that like him?" said the Squire, stopping short, and pointing with his stick at a dirty-white dog, with a large black head, which was scampering round them in a wide circle, half crouching with that air of uncertainty and deprecation which dogs so well know how to assume.

He whistled the dog up. He was a large, half-starved bull-dog.

"That fellow has made a long journey—thin as a whipping-post, and stained all over, and his claws worn to the stumps," said the Squire, musingly. "He isn't a bad dog, Cooper. My poor father liked a good bull-dog, and knew a cur from a good 'un."

The dog was looking up into the Squire's face with the peculiar grim visage of his kind, and the Squire was thinking irreverently how strong a likeness it presented to the character of his father's fierce pug features when he was clutching his horsewhip and swearing at a keeper.

"If I did right I'd shoot him. He'll worry the cattle, and kill our dogs," said the Squire. "Hey, Cooper? I'll tell the keeper to look after him. That fellow could pull down a sheep, and he shan't live on my mutton."

But the dog was not to be shaken off. He looked wistfully after the Squire, and after they had got a little way on, he followed timidly.

It was vain trying to drive him off. The dog ran round[31] them in wide circles, like the infernal dog in «Faust»; only he left no track of thin flame behind him. These manœuvres were executed with a sort of beseeching air, which flattered and touched the object of this odd preference. So he called him up again, patted him, and then and there in a manner adopted him.

The dog now followed their steps dutifully, as if he had belonged to Handsome Charlie all his days. Cooper unlocked the little iron door, and the dog walked in close behind their heels, and followed them as they visited the roofless chapel.

The Marstons were lying under the floor of this little building in rows. There is not a vault. Each has his distinct grave enclosed in a lining of masonry. Each is surmounted by a stone kist, on the upper flag of which is enclosed his epitaph, except that of poor old Squire Toby. Over him was nothing but the grass and the line of masonry which indicate the site of the kist, whenever his family should afford him one like the rest.

"Well, it does look shabby. It's the elder brother's business; but if he won't, I'll see to it myself, and I'll take care, old boy, to cut sharp and deep in it, that the elder son having refused to lend a hand the stone was put there by the younger."

They strolled round this little burial-ground. The sun was now below the horizon, and the red metallic glow from the clouds, still illuminated by the departed sun, mingled luridly with the twilight. When Charlie peeped again into the little chapel, he saw the ugly dog stretched upon Squire Toby's grave, looking at least twice his natural length, and performing such antics as made the young Squire stare. If you have ever seen a cat stretched on the floor, with a bunch of Valerian, straining, writhing, rubbing its jaws in long-drawn caresses, and in the absorption of a sensual[32] ecstasy, you have seen a phenomenon resembling that which Handsome Charlie witnessed on looking in.

The head of the brute looked so large, its body so long and thin, and its joints so ungainly and dislocated, that the Squire, with old Cooper beside him, looked on with a feeling of disgust and astonishment, which, in a moment or two more, brought the Squire's stick down upon him with a couple of heavy thumps. The beast awakened from his ecstasy, sprang to the head of the grave, and there on a sudden, thick and bandy as before, confronted the Squire, who stood at its foot, with a terrible grin, and eyes that glared with the peculiar green of canine fury.

The next moment the dog was crouching abjectly at the Squire's feet.

"Well, he's a rum 'un!" said old Cooper, looking hard at him.

"I like him," said the Squire.

"I don't," said Cooper.

"But he shan't come in here again," said the Squire.

"I shouldn't wonder if he was a witch," said old Cooper, who remembered more tales of witchcraft than are now current in that part of the world.

"He's a good dog," said the Squire, dreamily. "I remember the time I'd a given a handful for him—but I'll never be good for nothing again. Come along."

And he stooped down and patted him. So up jumped the dog and looked up in his face, as if watching for some sign, ever so slight, which he might obey.

Cooper did not like a bone in that dog's skin. He could not imagine what his master saw to admire in him. He kept him all night in the gun-room, and the dog accompanied him in his halting rambles about the place. The fonder his master grew of him, the less did Cooper and the other servants like him.

"He hasn't a point of a good dog about him," Cooper would growl. "I think Master Charlie be blind. And old Captain (an old red parrot, who sat chained to a perch in the oak parlour, and conversed with himself, and nibbled at his claws and bit his perch all day),—old Captain, the only living thing, except one or two of us, and the Squire himself, that remembers the old master, the minute he saw the dog, screeched as if he was struck, shakin' his feathers out quite wild, and drops down, poor old soul, a-hangin' by his foot, in a fit."

But there is no accounting for fancies, and the Squire was one of those dogged persons who persist more obstinately in their whims the more they are opposed. But Charles Marston's health suffered by his lameness. The transition from habitual and violent exercise to such a life as his privation now consigned him to, was never made without a risk to health; and a host of dyspeptic annoyances, the existence of which he had never dreamed of before, now beset him in sad earnest. Among these was the now not unfrequent troubling of his sleep with dreams and nightmares. In these his canine favourite invariably had a part and was generally a central, and sometimes a solitary figure. In these visions the dog seemed to stretch himself up the side of the Squire's bed, and in dilated proportions to sit at his feet, with a horrible likeness to the pug features of old Squire Toby, with his tricks of wagging his head and throwing up his chin; and then he would talk to him about Scroope, and tell him "all wasn't straight," and that he "must make it up wi' Scroope," that he, the old Squire, had "served him an ill turn," that "time was nigh up," and that "fair was fair," and he was "troubled where he was, about Scroope."

Then in his dream this semi-human brute would approach his face to his, crawling and crouching up his[34] body, heavy as lead, till the face of the beast was laid on his, with the same odious caresses and stretchings and writhings which he had seen over the old Squire›s grave. Then Charlie would wake up with a gasp and a howl, and start upright in the bed, bathed in a cold moisture, and fancy he saw something white sliding off the foot of the bed. Sometimes he thought it might be the curtain with white lining that slipped down, or the coverlet disturbed by his uneasy turnings; but he always fancied, at such moments, that he saw something white sliding hastily off the bed; and always when he had been visited by such dreams the dog next morning was more than usually caressing and servile, as if to obliterate, by a more than ordinary welcome, the sentiment of disgust which the horror of the night had left behind it.

The doctor half-satisfied the Squire that there was nothing in these dreams, which, in one shape or another, invariably attended forms of indigestion such as he was suffering from.

For a while, as if to corroborate this theory, the dog ceased altogether to figure in them. But at last there came a vision in which, more unpleasantly than before, he did resume his old place.

In his nightmare the room seemed all but dark; he heard what he knew to be the dog walking from the door round his bed slowly, to the side from which he always had come upon it. A portion of the room was uncarpeted, and he said he distinctly heard the peculiar tread of a dog, in which the faint clatter of the claws is audible. It was a light stealthy step, but at every tread the whole room shook heavily; he felt something place itself at the foot of his bed, and saw a pair of green eyes staring at him in the dark, from which he could not remove his own. Then he heard, as he thought, the old Squire Toby say—"The[35] eleventh hour be passed, Charlie, and ye›ve done nothing—you and I ‹a done Scroope a wrong!» and then came a good deal more, and then—"The time's nigh up, it's going to strike." And with a long low growl, the thing began to creep up upon his feet; the growl continued, and he saw the reflection of the up-turned green eyes upon the bed-clothes, as it began slowly to stretch itself up his body towards his face. With a loud scream, he waked. The light, which of late the Squire was accustomed to have in his bedroom, had accidentally gone out. He was afraid to get up, or even to look about the room for some time; so sure did he feel of seeing the green eyes in the dark fixed on him from some corner. He had hardly recovered from the first agony which nightmare leaves behind it, and was beginning to collect his thoughts, when he heard the clock strike twelve. And he bethought him of the words "the eleventh hour be passed—time's nigh up—it's going to strike!" and he almost feared that he would hear the voice reopening the subject.

Next morning the Squire came down looking ill.

"Do you know a room, old Cooper," said he, "they used to call King Herod's Chamber?"

"Ay, sir; the story of King Herod was on the walls o't when I was a boy."

"There's a closet off it—is there?"

"I can't be sure o' that; but 'tisn't worth your looking at, now; the hangings was rotten, and took off the walls, before you was born; and there's nou't there but some old broken things and lumber. I seed them put there myself by poor Twinks; he was blind of an eye, and footman afterwards. You'll remember Twinks? He died here, about the time o' the great snow. There was a deal o' work to bury him, poor fellow!"

"Get the key, old Cooper; I'll look at the room," said the Squire.

"And what the devil can you want to look at it for?" said Cooper, with the old-world privilege of a rustic butler.

"And what the devil's that to you? But I don't mind if I tell you. I don't want that dog in the gun-room, and I'll put him somewhere else; and I don't care if I put him there."

"A bull-dog in a bedroom! Oons, sir! the folks 'ill say you're clean mad!"

"Well, let them; get you the key, and let us look at the room."

"You'd shoot him if you did right, Master Charlie. You never heard what a noise he kept up all last night in the gun-room, walking to and fro growling like a tiger in a show; and, say what you like, the dog's not worth his feed; he hasn't a point of a dog; he's a bad dog."

"I know a dog better than you—and he's a good dog!" said the Squire, testily.

"If you was a judge of a dog you'd hang that 'un," said Cooper.

"I'm not a-going to hang him, so there's an end. Go you, and get the key; and don't be talking, mind, when you go down. I may change my mind."

Now this freak of visiting King Herod's room had, in truth, a totally different object from that pretended by the Squire. The voice in his nightmare had uttered a particular direction, which haunted him, and would give him no peace until he had tested it. So far from liking that dog to-day, he was beginning to regard it with a horrible suspicion; and if old Cooper had not stirred his obstinate temper by seeming to dictate, I dare say he would have got rid of that inmate effectually before evening.[37]

Up to the third storey, long disused, he and old Cooper mounted. At the end of a dusty gallery, the room lay. The old tapestry, from which the spacious chamber had taken its name, had long given place to modern paper, and this was mildewed, and in some places hanging from the walls. A thick mantle of dust lay over the floor. Some broken chairs and boards, thick with dust, lay, along with other lumber, piled together at one end of the room.

They entered the closet, which was quite empty. The Squire looked round, and you could hardly have said whether he was relieved or disappointed.

"No furniture here," said the Squire, and looked through the dusty window. "Did you say anything to me lately—I don't mean this morning—about this room, or the closet—or anything—I forget—"

"Lor' bless you! Not I. I han't been thinkin' o' this room this forty year."

"Is there any sort of old furniture called a *buffet*—do you remember?" asked the Squire.

"A buffet? why, yes—to be sure—there was a buffet, sure enough, in this closet, now you bring it to my mind," said Cooper. "But it's papered over."

"And what is it?"

"A little cupboard in the wall," answered the old man.

"Ho—I see—and there's such a thing here, is there, under the paper? Show me whereabouts it was."

"Well—I think it was somewhere about here," answered he, rapping his knuckles along the wall opposite the window. "Ay, there it is," he added, as the hollow sound of a wooden door was returned to his knock.

The Squire pulled the loose paper from the wall, and disclosed the doors of a small press, about two feet square, fixed in the wall.[38]

"The very thing for my buckles and pistols, and the rest of my gimcracks," said the Squire. "Come away, we'll leave the dog where he is. Have you the key of that little press?"

No, he had not. The old master had emptied and locked it up, and desired that it should be papered over, and that was the history of it.

Down came the Squire, and took a strong turn-screw from his gun-case; and quietly he reascended to King Herod's room, and, with little trouble, forced the door of the small press in the closet wall. There were in it some letters and cancelled leases, and also a parchment deed which he took to the window and read with much agitation. It was a supplemental deed executed about a fortnight after the others, and previously to his father's marriage, placing Gylingden under strict settlement to the elder son, in what is called "tail male." Handsome Charlie, in his fraternal litigation, had acquired a smattering of technical knowledge, and he perfectly well knew that the effect of this would be not only to transfer the house and lands to his brother Scroope, but to leave him at the mercy of that exasperated brother, who might recover from him personally every guinea he had ever received by way of rent, from the date of his father's death.

It was a dismal, clouded day, with something threatening in its aspect, and the darkness, where he stood, was made deeper by the top of one of the huge old trees overhanging the window.

In a state of awful confusion he attempted to think over his position. He placed the deed in his pocket, and nearly made up his mind to destroy it. A short time ago he would not have hesitated for a moment under such circumstances; but now his health and his nerves were shattered, and he was under a supernatural alarm which[39] the strange discovery of this deed had powerfully confirmed.

In this state of profound agitation he heard a sniffing at the closet-door, and then an impatient scratch and a long low growl. He screwed his courage up, and, not knowing what to expect, threw the door open and saw the dog, not in his dream-shape, but wriggling with joy, and crouching and fawning with eager submission; and then wandering about the closet, the brute growled awfully into the corners of it, and seemed in an unappeasable agitation.

Then the dog returned and fawned and crouched again at his feet.

After the first moment was over, the sensations of abhorrence and fear began to subside, and he almost reproached himself for requiting the affection of this poor friendless brute with the antipathy which he had really done nothing to earn.

The dog pattered after him down the stairs. Oddly enough, the sight of this animal, after the first revulsion, reassured him; it was, in his eyes, so attached, so good-natured, and palpably so mere a dog.

By the hour of evening the Squire had resolved on a middle course; he would not inform his brother of his discovery, nor yet would he destroy the deed. He would never marry. He was past that time. He would leave a letter, explaining the discovery of the deed, addressed to the only surviving trustee—who had probably forgotten everything about it—and having seen out his own tenure, he would provide that all should be set right after his death. Was not that fair? at all events it quite satisfied what he called his conscience, and he thought it a devilish good compromise for his brother; and he went out, towards sunset, to take his usual walk.

Returning in the darkening twilight, the dog, as usual[40] attending him, began to grow frisky and wild, at first scampering round him in great circles, as before, nearly at the top of his speed, his great head between his paws as he raced. Gradually more excited grew the pace and narrower his circuit, louder and fiercer his continuous growl, and the Squire stopped and grasped his stick hard, for the lurid eyes and grin of the brute threatened an attack. Turning round and round as the excited brute encircled him, and striking vainly at him with his stick, he grew at last so tired that he almost despaired of keeping him longer at bay; when on a sudden the dog stopped short and crawled up to his feet wriggling and crouching submissively.

Nothing could be more apologetic and abject; and when the Squire dealt him two heavy thumps with his stick, the dog whimpered only, and writhed and licked his feet. The Squire sat down on a prostrate tree; and his dumb companion, recovering his wonted spirits immediately, began to sniff and nuzzle among the roots. The Squire felt in his breast-pocket for the deed—it was safe; and again he pondered, in this loneliest of spots, on the question whether he should preserve it for restoration after his death to his brother, or destroy it forthwith. He began rather to lean toward the latter solution, when the long low growl of the dog not far off startled him.

He was sitting in a melancholy grove of old trees, that slants gently westward. Exactly the same odd effect of light I have before described—a faint red glow reflected downward from the upper sky, after the sun had set, now gave to the growing darkness a lurid uncertainty. This grove, which lies in a gentle hollow, owing to its circumscribed horizon on all but one side, has a peculiar character of loneliness.

He got up and peeped over a sort of barrier, accidentally[41] formed of the trunks of felled trees laid one over the other, and saw the dog straining up the other side of it, and hideously stretched out, his ugly head looking in consequence twice the natural size. His dream was coming over him again. And now between the trunks the brute›s ungainly head was thrust, and the long neck came straining through, and the body, twining after it like a huge white lizard; and as it came striving and twisting through, it growled and glared as if it would devour him.

As swiftly as his lameness would allow, the Squire hurried from this solitary spot towards the house. What thoughts exactly passed through his mind as he did so, I am sure he could not have told. But when the dog came up with him it seemed appeased, and even in high good-humour, and no longer resembled the brute that haunted his dreams.

That night, near ten o'clock, the Squire, a good deal agitated, sent for the keeper, and told him that he believed the dog was mad, and that he must shoot him. He might shoot the dog in the gun-room, where he was—a grain of shot or two in the wainscot did not matter, and the dog must not have a chance of getting out.

The Squire gave the gamekeeper his double-barrelled gun, loaded with heavy shot. He did not go with him beyond the hall. He placed his hand on the keeper's arm; the keeper said his hand trembled, and that he looked "as white as curds."

"Listen a bit!" said the Squire under his breath.

They heard the dog in a state of high excitement in the room—growling ominously, jumping on the window-stool and down again, and running round the room.

"You'll need to be sharp, mind—don't give him a chance—slip in edgeways, d'ye see? and give him both barrels!"[42]

"Not the first mad dog I've knocked over, sir," said the man, looking very serious as he cocked the gun.

As the keeper opened the door, the dog had sprung into the empty grate. He said he "never see sich a stark, staring devil." The beast made a twist round, as if, he thought, to jump up the chimney—"but that wasn't to be done at no price,"—and he made a yell—not like a dog—like a man caught in a mill-crank, and before he could spring at the keeper, he fired one barrel into him. The dog leaped towards him, and rolled over, receiving the second barrel in his head, as he lay snorting at the keeper's feet!

"I never seed the like; I never heard a screech like that!" said the keeper, recoiling. "It makes a fellow feel queer."

"Quite dead?" asked the Squire.

"Not a stir in him, sir," said the man, pulling him along the floor by the neck.

"Throw him outside the hall-door now," said the Squire;" and mind you pitch him outside the gate to-night—old Cooper says he's a witch," and the pale Squire smiled, "so he shan't lie in Gylingden."

Never was man more relieved than the Squire, and he slept better for a week after this than he had done for many weeks before.

It behoves us all to act promptly on our good resolutions. There is a determined gravitation towards evil, which, if left to itself, will bear down first intentions. If at one moment of superstitious fear, the Squire had made up his mind to a great sacrifice, and resolved in the matter of that deed so strangely recovered, to act honestly by his brother, that resolution very soon gave place to the compromise with fraud, which so conveniently postponed the restitution to the period when further enjoyment on his[43] part was impossible. Then came more tidings of Scroope›s violent and minatory language, with always the same burthen—that he would leave no stone unturned to show that there had existed a deed which Charles had either secreted or destroyed, and that he would never rest till he had hanged him.

This of course was wild talk. At first it had only enraged him; but, with his recent guilty knowledge and suppression, had come fear. His danger was the existence of the deed, and little by little he brought himself to a resolution to destroy it. There were many falterings and recoils before he could bring himself to commit this crime. At length, however, he did it, and got rid of the custody of that which at any time might become the instrument of disgrace and ruin. There was relief in this, but also the new and terrible sense of actual guilt.

He had got pretty well rid of his supernatural qualms. It was a different kind of trouble that agitated him now.

But this night, he imagined, he was awakened by a violent shaking of his bed. He could see, in the very imperfect light, two figures at the foot of it, holding each a bed-post. One of these he half-fancied was his brother Scroope, but the other was the old Squire—of that he was sure—and he fancied that they had shaken him up from his sleep. Squire Toby was talking as Charlie wakened, and he heard him say:

"Put out of our own house by you! It won't hold for long. We'll come in together, friendly, and stay. Fore-warned, wi' yer eyes open, ye did it; and now Scroope'll hang you! We'll hang you together! Look at me, you devil's limb."

And the old Squire tremblingly stretched his face, torn with shot and bloody, and growing every moment more and more into the likeness of the dog, and began to stretch[44] himself out and climb the bed over the foot-board; and he saw the figure at the other side, little more than a black shadow, begin also to scale the bed; and there was instantly a dreadful confusion and uproar in the room, and such a gabbling and laughing; he could not catch the words; but, with a scream, he woke, and found himself standing on the floor. The phantoms and the clamour were gone, but a crash and ringing of fragments was in his ears. The great china bowl, from which for generations the Marstons of Gylingden had been baptized, had fallen from the mantelpiece, and was smashed on the hearth-stone.

"I've bin dreamin' all night about Mr. Scroope, and I wouldn't wonder, old Cooper, if he was dead," said the Squire, when he came down in the morning.

"God forbid! I was adreamed about him, too, sir: I dreamed he was dammin' and sinkin' about a hole was burnt in his coat, and the old master, God be wi' him! said—quite plain—I'd 'a swore 'twas himself—'Cooper, get up, ye d——d land-loupin' thief, and lend a hand to hang him—for he's a daft cur, and no dog o' mine.' 'Twas the dog shot over night, I do suppose, as was runnin' in my old head. I thought old master gied me a punch wi' his knuckles, and says I, wakenin' up, 'At yer service, sir'; and for a while I couldn't get it out o' my head, master was in the room still."

Letters from town soon convinced the Squire that his brother Scroope, so far from being dead, was particularly active; and Charlie's attorney wrote to say, in serious alarm, that he had heard, accidentally, that he intended setting up a case, of a supplementary deed of settlement, of which he had secondary evidence, which would give him Gylingden. And at this menace Handsome Charlie snapped his fingers, and wrote courageously to his at[45]torney; abiding what might follow with, however, a secret foreboding.

Scroope threatened loudly now, and swore after his bitter fashion, and reiterated his old promise of hanging that cheat at last. In the midst of these menaces and preparations, however, a sudden peace proclaimed itself: Scroope died, without time even to make provisions for a posthumous attack upon his brother. It was one of those cases of disease of the heart in which death is as sudden as by a bullet.

Charlie's exultation was undisguised. It was shocking. Not, of course, altogether malignant. For there was the expansion consequent on the removal of a secret fear. There was also the comic piece of luck, that only the day before Scroope had destroyed his old will, which left to a stranger every farthing he possessed, intending in a day or two to execute another to the same person, charged with the express condition of prosecuting the suit against Charlie.

The result was, that all his possessions went unconditionally to his brother Charles as his heir. Here were grounds for abundance of savage elation. But there was also the deep-seated hatred of half a life of mutual and persistent agression and revilings; and Handsome Charlie was capable of nursing a grudge, and enjoying a revenge with his whole heart.

He would gladly have prevented his brother's being buried in the old Gylingden chapel, where he wished to lie; but his lawyers doubted his power, and he was not quite proof against the scandal which would attend his turning back the funeral, which would, he knew, be attended by some of the country gentry and others, with an hereditary regard for the Marstons.

But he warned his servants that not one of them were[46] to attend it; promising, with oaths and curses not to be disregarded, that any one of them who did so, should find the door shut in his face on his return.

I don't think, with the exception of old Cooper, that the servants cared for this prohibition, except as it baulked a curiosity always strong in the solitude of the country. Cooper was very much vexed that the eldest son of the old Squire should be buried in the old family chapel, and no sign of decent respect from Gylingden Hall. He asked his master, whether he would not, at least, have some wine and refreshments in the oak parlour, in case any of the country gentlemen who paid this respect to the old family should come up to the house? But the Squire only swore at him, told him to mind his own business, and ordered him to say, if such a thing happened, that he was out, and no preparations made, and, in fact, to send them away as they came. Cooper expostulated stoutly, and the Squire grew angrier; and after a tempestuous scene, took his hat and stick and walked out, just as the funeral descending the valley from the direction of the "Old Angel Inn" came in sight.

Old Cooper prowled about disconsolately, and counted the carriages as well as he could from the gate. When the funeral was over, and they began to drive away, he returned to the hall, the door of which lay open, and as usual deserted. Before he reached it quite, a mourning coach drove up, and two gentlemen in black cloaks, and with crapes to their hats, got out, and without looking to the right or the left, went up the steps into the house. Cooper followed them slowly. The carriage had, he supposed, gone round to the yard, for, when he reached the door, it was no longer there.

So he followed the two mourners into the house. In the hall he found a fellow-servant, who said he had seen[47] two gentlemen, in black cloaks, pass through the hall, and go up the stairs without removing their hats, or asking leave of anyone. This was very odd, old Cooper thought, and a great liberty; so up-stairs he went to make them out.

But he could not find them then, nor ever. And from that hour the house was troubled.

In a little time there was not one of the servants who had not something to tell. Steps and voices followed them sometimes in the passages, and tittering whispers, always minatory, scared them at corners of the galleries, or from dark recesses; so that they would return panic-stricken to be rebuked by thin Mrs. Beckett, who looked on such stories as worse than idle. But Mrs Beckett herself, a short time after, took a very different view of the matter.

She had herself begun to hear these voices, and with this formidable aggravation, that they came always when she was at her prayers, which she had been punctual in saying all her life, and utterly interrupted them. She was scared at such moments by dropping words and sentences, which grew, as she persisted, into threats and blasphemies.

These voices were not always in the room. They called, as she fancied, through the walls, very thick in that old house, from the neighbouring apartments, sometimes on one side, sometimes on the other; sometimes they seemed to holloa from distant lobbies, and came muffled, but threateningly, through the long panelled passages. As they approached they grew furious, as if several voices were speaking together. Whenever, as I said, this worthy woman applied herself to her devotions, these horrible sentences came hurrying towards the door, and, in panic, she would start from her knees, and all then would subside except the thumping of her heart[48] against her stays, and the dreadful tremors of her nerves.

What these voices said, Mrs. Beckett never could quite remember one minute after they had ceased speaking; one sentence chased another away; gibe and menace and impious denunciation, each hideously articulate, were lost as soon as heard. And this added to the effect of these terrifying mockeries and invectives, that she could not, by any effort, retain their exact import, although their horrible character remained vividly present to her mind.

For a long time the Squire seemed to be the only person in the house absolutely unconscious of these annoyances. Mrs. Beckett had twice made up her mind within the week to leave. A prudent woman, however, who has been comfortable for more than twenty years in a place, thinks oftener than twice before she leaves it. She and old Cooper were the only servants in the house who remembered the good old housekeeping in Squire Toby's day. The others were few, and such as could hardly be accounted regular servants. Meg Dobbs, who acted as housemaid, would not sleep in the house, but walked home, in trepidation, to her father's, at the gate-house, under the escort of her little brother, every night. Old Mrs. Beckett, who was high and mighty with the make-shift servants of fallen Gylingden, let herself down all at once, and made Mrs. Kymes and the kitchenmaid move their beds into her large and faded room, and there, very frankly, shared her nightly terrors with them.

Old Cooper was testy and captious about these stories. He was already uncomfortable enough by reason of the entrance of the two muffled figures into the house, about which there could be no mistake. His own eyes had seen them. He refused to credit the stories of the women, and affected to think that the two mourners might have[49] left the house and driven away, on finding no one to receive them.

Old Cooper was summoned at night to the oak parlour, where the Squire was smoking.

"I say, Cooper," said the Squire, looking pale and angry, "what for ha' you been frightenin' they crazy women wi' your plaguy stories? d—— me, if you see ghosts here it's no place for you, and it's time you should pack. I won't be left without servants. Here has been old Beckett, wi' the cook and the kitchenmaid, as white as pipe-clay, all in a row, to tell me I must have a parson to sleep among them, and preach down the devil! Upon my soul, you're a wise old body, filling their heads wi' maggots! and Meg goes down to the lodge every night, afeared to lie in the house—all your doing, wi' your old wives' stories,—ye withered old Tom o' Bedlam!"

"I'm not to blame, Master Charles. 'Tisn't along o' no stories o' mine, for I'm never done tellin' 'em it's all vanity and vapours. Mrs. Beckett 'ill tell you that, and there's been many a wry word betwixt us on the head o't. Whate'er I may *think*," said old Cooper, significantly, and looking askance, with the sternness of fear in the Squire's face.

The Squire averted his eyes, and muttered angrily to himself, and turned away to knock the ashes out of his pipe on the hob, and then turning suddenly round upon Cooper again, he spoke, with a pale face, but not quite so angrily as before.

"I know you're no fool, old Cooper, when you like. Suppose there was such a thing as a ghost here, don't you see, it ain't to them snipe-headed women it 'id go to tell its story. What ails you, man, that you should think aught about it, but just what *I* think? You had a good headpiece o› yer own once, Cooper, don›t be you clappin›[50] a goosecap over it, as my poor father used to say; d——it, old boy, you mustn›t let ‹em be fools, settin› one another wild wi› their blether, and makin› the folk talk what they shouldn't, about Gylingden and the family. I don't think ye'd like that, old Cooper, I'm sure ye wouldn't. The women has gone out o' the kitchen, make up a bit o' fire, and get your pipe. I'll go to you, when I finish this one, and we'll smoke a bit together, and a glass o' brandy and water."

Down went the old butler, not altogether unused to such condescensions in that disorderly and lonely household; and let not those who can choose their company, be too hard on the Squire who couldn't.

When he had got things tidy, as he said, he sat down in that big old kitchen, with his feet on the fender, the kitchen candle burning in a great brass candlestick, which stood on the deal table at his elbow, with the brandy bottle and tumblers beside it, and Cooper's pipe also in readiness. And these preparations completed, the old butler, who had remembered other generations and better times, fell into rumination, and so, gradually, into a deep sleep.

Old Cooper was half awakened by some one laughing low, near his head. He was dreaming of old times in the Hall, and fancied one of "the young gentlemen" going to play him a trick, and he mumbled something in his sleep, from which he was awakened by a stern deep voice, saying, "You wern't at the funeral; I might take your life, I'll take your ear." At the same moment, the side of his head received a violent push, and he started to his feet. The fire had gone down, and he was chilled. The candle was expiring in the socket, and threw on the white wall long shadows, that danced up and down from the ceiling to the ground, and their black outlines he fancied[51] resembled the two men in cloaks, whom he remembered with a profound horror.

He took the candle, with all the haste he could, getting along the passage, on whose walls the same dance of black shadows was continued, very anxious to reach his room before the light should go out. He was startled half out of his wits by the sudden clang of his master's bell, close over his head, ringing furiously.

"Ha, ha! There it goes—yes, sure enough," said Cooper, reassuring himself with the sound of his own voice, as he hastened on, hearing more and more distinct every moment the same furious ringing. "He's fell asleep, like me; that's it, and his lights is out, I lay you fifty——"

When he turned the handle of the door of the oak parlour, the Squire wildly called, "Who's *there*?" in the tone of a man who expects a robber.

"It's me, old Cooper, all right, Master Charlie, you didn't come to the kitchen after all, sir."

"I'm very bad, Cooper; I don't know how I've been. Did you meet anything?" asked the Squire.

"No," said Cooper.

They stared on one another.

"Come here—stay here! Don't you leave me! Look round the room, and say is all right; and gie us your hand, old Cooper, for I must hold it." The Squire's was damp and cold, and trembled very much. It was not very far from day-break now.

After a time he spoke again: "I'a done many a thing I shouldn't; I'm not fit to go, and wi' God's blessin' I'll look to it—why shouldn't I? I'm as lame as old Billy—I'll never be able to do any good no more, and I'll give over drinking, and marry, as I ought to 'a done long ago—none o' yer fine ladies, but a good homely wench;[52] there›s Farmer Crump›s youngest daughter, a good lass, and discreet. What for shouldn›t I take her? She›d take care o› me, and wouldn›t bring a head full o› romances here, and mantua-makers› trumpery, and I›ll talk with the parson, and I›ll do what›s fair wi› everyone; and mind, I said I›m sorry for many a thing I ‹a done.»

A wild cold dawn had by this time broken. The Squire, Cooper said, looked "awful bad," as he got his hat and stick, and sallied out for a walk, instead of going to his bed, as Cooper besought him, looking so wild and distracted, that it was plain his object was simply to escape from the house. It was twelve o'clock when the Squire walked into the kitchen, where he was sure of finding some of the servants, looking as if ten years had passed over him since yesterday. He pulled a stool by the fire, without speaking a word, and sat down. Cooper had sent to Applebury for the doctor, who had just arrived, but the Squire would not go to him. "If he wants to see me, he may come here," he muttered as often as Cooper urged him. So the doctor did come, charily enough, and found the Squire very much worse than he had expected.

The Squire resisted the order to get to his bed. But the doctor insisted under a threat of death, at which his patient quailed.

"Well, I'll do what you say—only this—you must let old Cooper and Dick Keeper stay wi' me. I mustn't be left alone, and they must keep awake o' nights; and stay a while, do *you*. When I get round a bit, I'll go and live in a town. It's dull livin' here, now that I can't do nou't, as I used, and I'll live a better life, mind ye; ye heard me say that, and I don't care who laughs, and I'll talk wi' the parson. I like 'em to laugh, hang 'em, it's a sign I'm doin' right, at last."[53]

The doctor sent a couple of nurses from the County Hospital, not choosing to trust his patient to the management he had selected, and he went down himself to Gylingden to meet them in the evening. Old Cooper was ordered to occupy the dressing-room, and sit up at night, which satisfied the Squire, who was in a strangely excited state, very low, and threatened, the doctor said, with fever.

The clergyman came, an old, gentle, "book-learned" man, and talked and prayed with him late that evening. After he had gone the Squire called the nurses to his bedside, and said:

"There's a fellow sometimes comes; you'll never mind him. He looks in at the door and beckons,—a thin, hump-backed chap in mourning, wi' black gloves on; ye'll know him by his lean face, as brown as the wainscot: don't ye mind his smilin'. You don't go out to him, nor ask him in; he won't say nout; and if he grows anger'd and looks awry at ye, don't ye be afeared, for he can't hurt ye, and he'll grow tired waitin', and go away; and for God's sake mind ye don't ask him in, nor go out after him!"

The nurses put their heads together when this was over, and held afterwards a whispering conference with old Cooper. "Law bless ye!— no, there's no madman in the house," he protested; "not a soul but what ye saw,—it's just a trifle o' the fever in his head—no more."

The Squire grew worse as the night wore on. He was heavy and delirious, talking of all sorts of things—of wine, and dogs, and lawyers; and then he began to talk, as it were, to his brother Scroope. As he did so, Mrs. Oliver, the nurse, who was sitting up alone with him, heard, as she thought, a hand softly laid on the door-handle outside, and a stealthy attempt to turn it. "Lord[54] bless us! who›s there?» she cried, and her heart jumped into her mouth, as she thought of the hump-backed man in black, who was to put in his head smiling and beckoning—»Mr. Cooper! sir! are you there?» she cried. «Come here, Mr. Cooper, please—do, sir, quick!»

Old Cooper, called up from his doze by the fire, stumbled in from the dressing-room, and Mrs. Oliver seized him tightly as he emerged.

"The man with the hump has been atryin' the door, Mr. Cooper, as sure as I am here." The Squire was moaning and mumbling in his fever, understanding nothing, as she spoke. "No, no! Mrs. Oliver, ma'am, it's impossible, for there's no sich man in the house: what is Master Charlie sayin'?"

"He's saying *Scroope* every minute, whatever he means by that, and—and—hisht!—listen—there›s the handle again,» and, with a loud scream, she added—»Look at his head and neck in at the door!» and in her tremour she strained old Cooper in an agonizing embrace.

The candle was flaring, and there was a wavering shadow at the door that looked like the head of a man with a long neck, and a longish sharp nose, peeping in and drawing back.

"Don't be a d—— fool, ma'am!" cried Cooper, very white, and shaking her with all his might. "It's only the candle, I tell you—nothing in life but that. Don't you see?" and he raised the light; "and I'm sure there was no one at the door, and I'll try, if you let me go."

The other nurse was asleep on a sofa, and Mrs. Oliver called her up in a panic, for company, as old Cooper opened the door. There was no one near it, but at the angle of the gallery was a shadow resembling that which he had seen in the room. He raised the candle a little, and it seemed to beckon with a long hand as the head[55] drew back. «Shadow from the candle!» exclaimed Cooper aloud, resolved not to yield to Mrs. Oliver›s panic; and, candle in hand, he walked to the corner. There was nothing. He could not forbear peeping down the long gallery from this point, and as he moved the light, he saw precisely the same sort of shadow, a little further down, and as he advanced the same withdrawal, and beckon. "Gammon!" said he; "it is nout but the candle." And on he went, growing half angry and half frightened at the persistency with which this ugly shadow—a literal shadow he was sure it was—presented itself. As he drew near the point where it now appeared, it seemed to collect itself, and nearly dissolve in the central panel of an old carved cabinet which he was now approaching.

In the centre panel of this is a sort of boss carved into a wolf's head. The light fell oddly upon this, and the fugitive shadow seemed to be breaking up, and re-arranging itself as oddly. The eye-ball gleamed with a point of reflected light, which glittered also upon the grinning mouth, and he saw the long, sharp nose of Scroope Marston, and his fierce eye looking at him, he thought, with a steadfast meaning.

Old Cooper stood gazing upon this sight, unable to move, till he saw the face, and the figure that belonged to it, begin gradually to emerge from the wood. At the same time he heard voices approaching rapidly up a side gallery, and Cooper, with a loud "Lord a-mercy on us!" turned and ran back again, pursued by a sound that seemed to shake the old house like a mighty gust of wind.

Into his master's room burst old Cooper, half wild with fear, and clapped the door and turned the key in a twinkling, looking as if he had been pursued by murderers.

"Did you hear it?" whispered Cooper, now standing[56] near the dressing-room door. They all listened, but not a sound from without disturbed the utter stillness of night. «God bless us! I doubt it›s my old head that›s gone crazy!» exclaimed Cooper.

He would tell them nothing but that he was himself "an old fool," to be frightened by their talk, and that "the rattle of a window, or the dropping o' a pin" was enough to scare him now; and so he helped himself through that night with brandy, and sat up talking by his master's fire.

The Squire recovered slowly from his brain fever, but not perfectly. A very little thing, the doctor said, would suffice to upset him. He was not yet sufficiently strong to remove for change of scene and air, which were necessary for his complete restoration.

Cooper slept in the dressing-room, and was now his only nightly attendant. The ways of the invalid were odd: he liked, half sitting up in his bed, to smoke his churchwarden o' nights, and made old Cooper smoke, for company, at the fireside. As the Squire and his humble friend indulged in it, smoking is a taciturn pleasure, and it was not until the Master of Gylingden had finished his third pipe that he essayed conversation, and when he did, the subject was not such as Cooper would have chosen.

"I say, old Cooper, look in my face, and don't be afeared to speak out," said the Squire, looking at him with a steady, cunning smile; "you know all this time, as well as I do, who's in the house. You needn't deny— hey?—Scroope and my father?"

"Don't you be talking like that, Charlie," said old Cooper, rather sternly and frightened, after a long silence; still looking in his face, which did not change.

"What's the good o' shammin', Cooper? Scroope's took the hearin' o' yer right ear—you know he did. He's[57] looking angry. He›s nigh took my life wi› this fever. But he›s not done wi› me yet, and he looks awful wicked. Ye saw him—ye know ye did.»

Cooper was awfully frightened, and the odd smile on the Squire's lips frightened him still more. He dropped his pipe, and stood gazing in silence at his master, and feeling as if he were in a dream.

"If ye think so, ye should not be smiling like that," said Cooper, grimly.

"I'm tired, Cooper, and it's as well to smile as t'other thing; so I'll even smile while I can. You know what they mean to do wi' me. That's all I wanted to say. Now, lad, go on wi' yer pipe—I'm goin' asleep."

So the Squire turned over in his bed, and lay down serenely, with his head on the pillow. Old Cooper looked at him, and glanced at the door, and then half-filled his tumbler with brandy, and drank it off, and felt better, and got to his bed in the dressing-room.

In the dead of night he was suddenly awakened by the Squire, who was standing, in his dressing-gown and slippers, by his bed.

"I've brought you a bit o' a present. I got the rents o' Hazelden yesterday, and ye'll keep that for yourself—it's a fifty—and give t' other to Nelly Carwell, to-morrow; I'll sleep the sounder; and I saw Scroope since; he's not such a bad 'un after all, old fellow! He's got a crape over his face—for I told him I couldn't bear it; and I'd do many a thing for him now. I never could stand shilly-shally. Good-night, old Cooper!"

And the Squire laid his trembling hand kindly on the old man's shoulder, and returned to his own room. "I don't half like how he is. Doctor don't come half often enough. I don't like that queer smile o' his, and his hand was as cold as death. I hope in God his brain's not a-turnin'!"[58]

With these reflections, he turned to the pleasanter subject of his present, and at last fell asleep.

In the morning, when he went into the Squire's room, the Squire had left his bed. "Never mind; he'll come back, like a bad shillin'," thought old Cooper, preparing the room as usual. But he did not return. Then began an uneasiness, succeeded by a panic, when it began to be plain that the Squire was not in the house. What had become of him? None of his clothes, but his dressing-gown and slippers, were missing. Had he left the house, in his present sickly state, in that garb? and, if so, could he be in his right senses; and was there a chance of his surviving a cold, damp night, so passed, in the open air?

Tom Edwards was up to the house, and told them, that, walking a mile or so that morning, at four o'clock—there being no moon—along with Farmer Nokes, who was driving his cart to market, in the dark, three men walked, in front of the horse, not twenty yards before them, all the way from near Gylingden Lodge to the burial-ground, the gate of which was opened for them from within, and the three men entered, and the gate was shut. Tom Edwards thought they were gone in to make preparation for a funeral of some member of the Marston family. But the occurrence seemed to Cooper, who knew there was no such thing, horribly ominous.

He now commenced a careful search, and at last bethought him of the lonely upper storey, and King Herod's chamber. He saw nothing changed there, but the closet door was shut, and, dark as was the morning, something, like a large white knot sticking out over the door, caught his eye.

The door resisted his efforts to open it for a time; some great weight forced it down against the floor; at length, however, it did yield a little, and a heavy crash,[59] shaking the whole floor, and sending an echo flying through all the silent corridors, with a sound like receding laughter, half stunned him.

When he pushed open the door, his master was lying dead upon the floor. His cravat was drawn halter-wise tight round his throat, and had done its work well. The body was cold, and had been long dead.

In due course the coroner held his inquest, and the jury pronounced, "that the deceased, Charles Marston, had died by his own hand, in a state of temporary insanity." But old Cooper had his own opinion about the Squire's death, though his lips were sealed, and he never spoke about it. He went and lived for the residue of his days in York, where there are still people who remember him, a taciturn and surly old man, who attended church regularly, and also drank a little, and was known to have saved some money.

3
DICKON THE DEVIL

Contributed to the Christmas Number of *London Society* (1872): signed.

About thirty years ago I was selected by two rich old maids to visit a property in that part of Lancashire which lies near the famous forest of Pendle, with which Mr. Ainsworth's "Lancashire Witches" has made us so pleasantly familiar. My business was to make partition of a small property, including a house and demesne, to which they had a long time before succeeded as co-heiresses.

The last forty miles of my journey I was obliged to post, chiefly by cross-roads, little known, and less frequented, and presenting scenery often extremely interesting and pretty. The picturesqueness of the landscape was enhanced by the season, the beginning of September, at which I was travelling.

I had never been in this part of the world before; I am told it is now a great deal less wild, and, consequently, less beautiful.

At the inn where I had stopped for a relay of horses and some dinner— for it was then past five o'clock—I found the host, a hale old fellow of five-and-sixty, as he told me, a man of easy and garrulous benevolence, willing to[61] accommodate his guests with any amount of talk, which the slightest tap sufficed to set flowing, on any subject you pleased.

I was curious to learn something about Barwyke, which was the name of the demesne and house I was going to. As there was no inn within some miles of it, I had written to the steward to put me up there, the best way he could, for a night.

The host of the "Three Nuns," which was the sign under which he entertained wayfarers, had not a great deal to tell. It was twenty years, or more, since old Squire Bowes died, and no one had lived in the Hall ever since, except the gardener and his wife.

"Tom Wyndsour will be as old a man as myself; but he's a bit taller, and not so much in flesh, quite," said the fat innkeeper.

"But there were stories about the house," I repeated, "that they said, prevented tenants from coming into it?"

"Old wives' tales; many years ago, that will be, sir; I forget 'em; I forget 'em all. Oh yes, there always will be, when a house is left so; foolish folk will always be talkin'; but I hadn't heard a word about it this twenty year."

It was vain trying to pump him; the old landlord of the "Three Nuns," for some reason, did not choose to tell tales of Barwyke Hall, if he really did, as I suspected, remember them.

I paid my reckoning, and resumed my journey, well pleased with the good cheer of that old-world inn, but a little disappointed.

We had been driving for more than an hour, when we began to cross a wild common; and I knew that, this passed, a quarter of an hour would bring me to the door of Barwyke Hall.[62]

The peat and furze were pretty soon left behind; we were again in the wooded scenery that I enjoyed so much, so entirely natural and pretty, and so little disturbed by traffic of any kind. I was looking from the chaise-window, and soon detected the object of which, for some time, my eye had been in search. Barwyke Hall was a large, quaint house, of that cage-work fashion known as "black-and-white," in which the bars and angles of an oak framework contrast, black as ebony, with the white plaster that overspreads the masonry built into its interstices. This steep-roofed Elizabethan house stood in the midst of park-like grounds of no great extent, but rendered imposing by the noble stature of the old trees that now cast their lengthening shadows eastward over the sward, from the declining sun.

The park-wall was grey with age, and in many places laden with ivy. In deep grey shadow, that contrasted with the dim fires of evening reflected on the foliage above it, in a gentle hollow, stretched a lake that looked cold and black, and seemed, as it were, to skulk from observation with a guilty knowledge.

I had forgot that there was a lake at Barwyke; but the moment this caught my eye, like the cold polish of a snake in the shadow, my instinct seemed to recognise something dangerous, and I knew that the lake was connected, I could not remember how, with the story I had heard of this place in my boyhood.

I drove up a grass-grown avenue, under the boughs of these noble trees, whose foliage, dyed in autumnal red and yellow, returned the beams of the western sun gorgeously.

We drew up at the door. I got out, and had a good look at the front of the house; it was a large and melancholy mansion, with signs of long neglect upon it; great[63] wooden shutters, in the old fashion, were barred, outside, across the windows; grass, and even nettles, were growing thick on the courtyard, and a thin moss streaked the timber beams; the plaster was discoloured by time and weather, and bore great russet and yellow stains. The gloom was increased by several grand old trees that crowded close about the house.

I mounted the steps, and looked round; the dark lake lay near me now, a little to the left. It was not large; it may have covered some ten or twelve acres; but it added to the melancholy of the scene. Near the centre of it was a small island, with two old ash trees, leaning toward each other, their pensive images reflected in the stirless water. The only cheery influence in this scene of antiquity, solitude, and neglect was that the house and landscape were warmed with the ruddy western beams. I knocked, and my summons resounded hollow and ungenial in my ear; and the bell, from far away, returned a deep-mouthed and surly ring, as if it resented being roused from a score years' slumber.

A light-limbed, jolly-looking old fellow, in a barracan jacket and gaiters, with a smile of welcome, and a very sharp, red nose, that seemed to promise good cheer, opened the door with a promptitude that indicated a hospitable expectation of my arrival.

There was but little light in the hall, and that little lost itself in darkness in the background. It was very spacious and lofty, with a gallery running round it, which, when the door was open, was visible at two or three points. Almost in the dark my new acquaintance led me across this wide hall into the room destined for my reception. It was spacious, and wainscoted up to the ceiling. The furniture of this capacious chamber was old-fashioned and clumsy. There were curtains still to the windows,[64] and a piece of Turkey carpet lay upon the floor; those windows were two in number, looking out, through the trunks of the trees close to the house, upon the lake. It needed all the fire, and all the pleasant associations of my entertainer›s red nose, to light up this melancholy chamber. A door at its farther end admitted to the room that was prepared for my sleeping apartment. It was wainscoted, like the other. It had a four-post bed, with heavy tapestry curtains, and in other respects was furnished in the same old-world and ponderous style as the other room. Its window, like those of that apartment, looked out upon the lake.

Sombre and sad as these rooms were, they were yet scrupulously clean. I had nothing to complain of; but the effect was rather dispiriting. Having given some directions about supper—a pleasant incident to look forward to—and made a rapid toilet, I called on my friend with the gaiters and red nose (Tom Wyndsour) whose occupation was that of a "bailiff," or under-steward, of the property, to accompany me, as we had still an hour or so of sun and twilight, in a walk over the grounds.

It was a sweet autumn evening, and my guide, a hardy old fellow, strode at a pace that tasked me to keep up with.

Among clumps of trees at the northern boundary of the demesne we lighted upon the little antique parish church. I was looking down upon it, from an eminence, and the park-wall interposed; but a little way down was a stile affording access to the road, and by this we approached the iron gate of the churchyard. I saw the church door open; the sexton was replacing his pick, shovel and spade, with which he had just been digging a grave in the churchyard, in their little repository under the stone stair of the tower. He was a polite, shrewd little hunchback,[65] who was very happy to show me over the church. Among the monuments was one that interested me; it was erected to commemorate the very Squire Bowes from whom my two old maids had inherited the house and estate of Barwyke. It spoke of him in terms of grandiloquent eulogy, and informed the Christian reader that he had died, in the bosom of the Church of England, at the age of seventy-one.

I read this inscription by the parting beams of the setting sun, which disappeared behind the horizon just as we passed out from under the porch.

"Twenty years since the Squire died," said I, reflecting as I loitered still in the churchyard.

"Ay, sir; 'twill be twenty year the ninth o' last month."

"And a very good old gentleman?"

"Good-natured enough, and an easy gentleman he was, sir; I don't think while he lived he ever hurt a fly," acquiesced Tom Wyndsour. "It ain't always easy sayin' what's in 'em though, and what they may take or turn to afterwards; and some o' them sort, I think, goes mad."

"You don't think he was out of his mind?" I asked.

"He? La! no; not he, sir; a bit lazy, mayhap, like other old fellows; but a knew devilish well what he was about."

Tom Wyndsour's account was a little enigmatical; but, like old Squire Bowes I was "a bit lazy" that evening, and asked no more questions about him.

We got over the stile upon the narrow road that skirts the churchyard. It is overhung by elms more than a hundred years old, and in the twilight, which now prevailed, was growing very dark. As side-by-side we walked along this road, hemmed in by two loose stone-like[66] walls, something running towards us in a zig-zag line passed us at a wild pace, with a sound like a frightened laugh or a shudder, and I saw, as it passed, that it was a human figure. I may confess now, that I was a little startled. The dress of this figure was, in part, white: I know I mistook it at first for a white horse coming down the road at a gallop. Tom Wyndsour turned about and looked after the retreating figure.

"He'll be on his travels to-night," he said, in a low tone. "Easy served with a bed, *that* lad be; six foot o› dry peat or heath, or a nook in a dry ditch. That lad hasn›t slept once in a house this twenty year, and never will while grass grows.»

"Is he mad?" I asked.

"Something that way, sir; he's an idiot, an awpy; we call him 'Dickon the devil,' because the devil's almost the only word that's ever in his mouth."

It struck me that this idiot was in some way connected with the story of old Squire Bowes.

"Queer things are told of him, I dare say?" I suggested.

"More or less, sir; more or less. Queer stories, some."

"Twenty years since he slept in a house? That's about the time the Squire died," I continued.

"So it will be, sir; and not very long after."

"You must tell me all about that, Tom, to-night, when I can hear it comfortably, after supper."

Tom did not seem to like my invitation; and looking straight before him as we trudged on, he said,

"You see, sir, the house has been quiet, and nout's been troubling folk inside the walls or out, all round the woods of Barwyke, this ten year, or more; and my old woman, down there, is clear against talking about such[67] matters, and thinks it best—and so do I—to let sleepin› dogs be.»

He dropped his voice towards the close of the sentence, and nodded significantly.

We soon reached a point where he unlocked a wicket in the park wall, by which we entered the grounds of Barwyke once more.

The twilight deepening over the landscape, the huge and solemn trees, and the distant outline of the haunted house, exercised a sombre influence on me, which, together with the fatigue of a day of travel, and the brisk walk we had had, disinclined me to interrupt the silence in which my companion now indulged.

A certain air of comparative comfort, on our arrival, in great measure dissipated the gloom that was stealing over me. Although it was by no means a cold night, I was very glad to see some wood blazing in the grate; and a pair of candles aiding the light of the fire, made the room look cheerful. A small table, with a very white cloth, and preparations for supper, was also a very agreeable object.

I should have liked very well, under these influences, to have listened to Tom Wyndsour's story; but after supper I grew too sleepy to attempt to lead him to the subject; and after yawning for a time, I found there was no use in contending against my drowsiness, so I betook myself to my bedroom, and by ten o'clock was fast asleep.

What interruption I experienced that night I shall tell you presently. It was not much, but it was very odd.

By next night I had completed my work at Barwyke. From early morning till then I was so incessantly occupied and hard-worked, that I had no time to think over the singular occurrence to which I have just referred. Behold me, however, at length once more seated at my little[68] supper-table, having ended a comfortable meal. It had been a sultry day, and I had thrown one of the large windows up as high as it would go. I was sitting near it, with my brandy and water at my elbow, looking out into the dark. There was no moon, and the trees that are grouped about the house make the darkness round it supernaturally profound on such nights.

"Tom," said I, so soon as the jug of hot punch I had supplied him with began to exercise its genial and communicative influence; "you must tell me who beside your wife and you and myself slept in the house last night."

Tom, sitting near the door, set down his tumbler, and looked at me askance, while you might count seven, without speaking a word.

"Who else slept in the house?" he repeated, very deliberately. "Not a living soul, sir"; and he looked hard at me, still evidently expecting something more.

"That *is* very odd,» I said returning his stare, and feeling really a little odd. «You are sure *you* were not in my room last night?»

"Not till I came to call you, sir, this morning; *I* can make oath of that.»

"Well," said I, "there was some one there, *I* can make oath of that. I was so tired I could not make up my mind to get up; but I was waked by a sound that I thought was some one flinging down the two tin boxes in which my papers were locked up violently on the floor. I heard a slow step on the ground, and there was light in the room, although I remembered having put out my candle. I thought it must have been you, who had come in for my clothes, and upset the boxes by accident. Whoever it was, he went out and the light with him. I was about to settle again, when, the curtain being a[69] little open at the foot of the bed, I saw a light on the wall opposite; such as a candle from outside would cast if the door were very cautiously opening. I started up in the bed, drew the side curtain, and saw that the door *was* opening, and admitting light from outside. It is close, you know, to the head of the bed. A hand was holding on the edge of the door and pushing it open; not a bit like yours; a very singular hand. Let me look at yours.»

He extended it for my inspection.

"Oh no; there's nothing wrong with your hand. This was differently shaped; fatter; and the middle finger was stunted, and shorter than the rest, looking as if it had once been broken, and the nail was crooked like a claw. I called out 'Who's there?' and the light and the hand were withdrawn, and I saw and heard no more of my visitor."

"So sure as you're a living man, that was him!" exclaimed Tom Wyndsour, his very nose growing pale, and his eyes almost starting out of his head.

"Who?" I asked.

"Old Squire Bowes; 'twas *his* hand you saw; the Lord a› mercy on us!» answered Tom. «The broken finger, and the nail bent like a hoop. Well for you, sir, he didn›t come back when you called, that time. You came here about them Miss Dymock›s business, and he never meant they should have a foot o› ground in Barwyke; and he was making a will to give it away quite different, when death took him short. He never was uncivil to no one; but he couldn›t abide them ladies. My mind misgave me when I heard ‹twas about their business you were coming; and now you see how it is; he›ll be at his old tricks again!»

With some pressure and a little more punch, I induced[70] Tom Wyndsour to explain his mysterious allusions by recounting the occurrences which followed the old Squire›s death.

"Squire Bowes of Barwyke died without making a will, as you know," said Tom. "And all the folk round were sorry; that is to say, sir, as sorry as folk will be for an old man that has seen a long tale of years, and has no right to grumble that death has knocked an hour too soon at his door. The Squire was well liked; he was never in a passion, or said a hard word; and he would not hurt a fly; and that made what happened after his decease the more surprising.

"The first thing these ladies did, when they got the property was to buy stock for the park.

"It was not wise, in any case, to graze the land on their own account. But they little knew all they had to contend with.

"Before long something went wrong with the cattle; first one, and then another, took sick and died, and so on, till the loss began to grow heavy. Then, queer stories, little by little, began to be told. It was said, first by one, then by another, that Squire Bowes was seen, about evening time, walking, just as he used to do when he was alive, among the old trees, leaning on his stick; and, sometimes when he came up with the cattle, he would stop and lay his hand kindly like on the back of one of them; and that one was sure to fall sick next day, and die soon after.

"No one ever met him in the park, or in the woods, or ever saw him, except a good distance off. But they knew his gait and his figure well, and the clothes he used to wear; and they could tell the beast he laid his hand on by its colour—white, dun, or black; and that beast was sure to sicken and die. The neighbours grew shy of[71] taking the path over the park; and no one liked to walk in the woods, or come inside the bounds of Barwyke; and the cattle went on sickening and dying as before.

"At that time there was one Thomas Pyke; he had been a groom to the old Squire; and he was in care of the place, and was the only one that used to sleep in the house.

"Tom was vexed, hearing these stories; which he did not believe the half on 'em; and more especial as he could not get man or boy to herd the cattle; all being afeared. So he wrote to Matlock in Derbyshire, for his brother, Richard Pyke, a clever lad, and one that knew nout o' the story of the old Squire walking.

"Dick came; and the cattle was better; folk said they could still see the old Squire, sometimes, walking, as before, in openings of the wood, with his stick in his hand; but he was shy of coming nigh the cattle, whatever his reason might be, since Dickon Pyke came; and he used to stand a long bit off, looking at them, with no more stir in him than a trunk o' one of the old trees, for an hour at a time, till the shape melted away, little by little, like the smoke of a fire that burns out.

"Tom Pyke and his brother Dickon, being the only living souls in the house, lay in the big bed in the servants' room, the house being fast barred and locked, one night in November.

"Tom was lying next the wall, and he told me, as wide awake as ever he was at noonday. His brother Dickon lay outside, and was sound asleep.

"Well, as Tom lay thinking, with his eyes turned toward the door, it opens slowly, and who should come in but old Squire Bowes, his face lookin' as dead as he was in his coffin.

"Tom's very breath left his body; he could not take[72] his eyes off him; and he felt the hair rising up on his head.

"The Squire came to the side of the bed, and put his arms under Dickon, and lifted the boy—in a dead sleep all the time—and carried him out so, at the door.

"Such was the appearance, to Tom Pyke's eyes, and he was ready to swear to it, anywhere.

"When this happened, the light, wherever it came from, all on a sudden went out, and Tom could not see his own hand before him.

"More dead than alive, he lay till daylight.

"Sure enough his brother Dickon was gone. No sign of him could he discover about the house; and with some trouble he got a couple of the neighbours to help him to search the woods and grounds. Not a sign of him anywhere.

"At last one of them thought of the island in the lake; the little boat was moored to the old post at the water's edge. In they got, though with small hope of finding him there. Find him, nevertheless, they did, sitting under the big ash tree, quite out of his wits; and to all their questions he answered nothing but one cry—'Bowes, the devil! See him; see him; Bowes, the devil!' An idiot they found him; and so he will be till God sets all things right. No one could ever get him to sleep under roof-tree more. He wanders from house to house while daylight lasts; and no one cares to lock the harmless creature in the workhouse. And folk would rather not meet him after nightfall, for they think where he is there may be worse things near."

A silence followed Tom's story. He and I were alone in that large room; I was sitting near the open window, looking into the dark night air. I fancied I saw something white move across it; and I heard a sound like low talking[73] that swelled into a discordant shriek—»Hoo-oo-oo! Bowes, the devil! Over your shoulder. Hoo-oo-oo! ha! ha! ha!» I started up, and saw, by the light of the candle with which Tom strode to the window, the wild eyes and blighted face of the idiot, as, with a sudden change of mood, he drew off, whispering and tittering to himself, and holding up his long fingers, and looking at the tips like a «hand of glory.»

Tom pulled down the window. The story and its epilogue were over. I confess I was rather glad when I heard the sound of the horses' hoofs on the courtyard, a few minutes later; and still gladder when, having bidden Tom a kind farewell, I had left the neglected house of Barwyke a mile behind me.

4
THE CHILD THAT WENT WITH THE FAIRIES

Anonymous in *All the Year Round* (1869-70). Readers of «Carmilla» in *In a Glass Darkly* will recognize the negro woman in the coach.

Eastward of the old city of Limerick, about ten Irish miles under the range of mountains known as the Slieveelim hills, famous as having afforded Sarsfield a shelter among their rocks and hollows, when he crossed them in his gallant descent upon the cannon and ammunition of King William, on its way to the beleaguering army, there runs a very old and narrow road. It connects the Limerick road to Tipperary with the old road from Limerick to Dublin, and runs by bog and pasture, hill and hollow, straw-thatched village, and roofless castle, not far from twenty miles.

Skirting the heathy mountains of which I have spoken, at one part it becomes singularly lonely. For more than three Irish miles it traverses a deserted country. A wide, black bog, level as a lake, skirted with copse, spreads at the left, as you journey northward, and the long and irregular line of mountain rises at the right, clothed in heath, broken with lines of grey rock that resemble the bold and irregular outlines of fortifications, and riven with[75] many a gully, expanding here and there into rocky and wooded glens, which open as they approach the road.

A scanty pasturage, on which browsed a few scattered sheep or kine, skirts this solitary road for some miles, and under shelter of a hillock, and of two or three great ash-trees, stood, not many years ago, the little thatched cabin of a widow named Mary Ryan.

Poor was this widow in a land of poverty. The thatch had acquired the grey tint and sunken outlines, that show how the alternations of rain and sun have told upon that perishable shelter.

But whatever other dangers threatened, there was one well provided against by the care of other times. Round the cabin stood half a dozen mountain ashes, as the rowans, inimical to witches, are there called. On the worn planks of the door were nailed two horse-shoes, and over the lintel and spreading along the thatch, grew, luxuriant, patches of that ancient cure for many maladies, and prophylactic against the machinations of the evil one, the house-leek. Descending into the doorway, in the *chiaroscuro* of the interior, when your eye grew sufficiently accustomed to that dim light, you might discover, hanging at the head of the widow›s wooden-roofed bed, her beads and a phial of holy water.

Here certainly were defences and bulwarks against the intrusion of that unearthly and evil power, of whose vicinity this solitary family were constantly reminded by the outline of Lisnavoura, that lonely hill-haunt of the "Good people," as the fairies are called euphemistically, whose strangely dome-like summit rose not half a mile away, looking like an outwork of the long line of mountain that sweeps by it.

It was at the fall of the leaf, and an autumnal sunset threw the lengthening shadow of haunted Lisnavoura,[76] close in front of the solitary little cabin, over the undulating slopes and sides of Slieveelim. The birds were singing among the branches in the thinning leaves of the melancholy ash-trees that grew at the roadside in front of the door. The widow›s three younger children were playing on the road, and their voices mingled with the evening song of the birds. Their elder sister, Nell, was «within in the house,» as their phrase is, seeing after the boiling of the potatoes for supper.

Their mother had gone down to the bog, to carry up a hamper of turf on her back. It is, or was at least, a charitable custom—and if not disused, long may it continue—for the wealthier people when cutting their turf and stacking it in the bog, to make a smaller stack for the behoof of the poor, who were welcome to take from it so long as it lasted, and thus the potato pot was kept boiling, and the hearth warm that would have been cold enough but for that good-natured bounty, through wintry months.

Moll Ryan trudged up the steep "bohereen" whose banks were overgrown with thorn and brambles, and stooping under her burden, re-entered her door, where her dark-haired daughter Nell met her with a welcome, and relieved her of her hamper.

Moll Ryan looked round with a sigh of relief, and drying her forehead, uttered the Munster ejaculation:

"Eiah, wisha! It's tired I am with it, God bless it. And where's the craythurs, Nell?"

"Playin' out on the road, mother; didn't ye see them and you comin' up?"

"No; there was no one before me on the road," she said, uneasily; "not a soul, Nell; and why didn't ye keep an eye on them?"

"Well, they're in the haggard, playin' there, or round by the back o' the house. Will I call them in?"[77]

"Do so, good girl, in the name o' God. The hens is comin' home, see, and the sun was just down over Knockdoulah, an' I comin' up."

So out ran tall, dark-haired Nell, and standing on the road, looked up and down it; but not a sign of her two little brothers, Con and Bill, or her little sister, Peg, could she see. She called them; but no answer came from the little haggard, fenced with straggling bushes. She listened, but the sound of their voices was missing. Over the stile, and behind the house she ran—but there all was silent and deserted.

She looked down toward the bog, as far as she could see; but they did not appear. Again she listened—but in vain. At first she had felt angry, but now a different feeling overcame her, and she grew pale. With an undefined boding she looked toward the heathy boss of Lisnavoura, now darkening into the deepest purple against the flaming sky of sunset.

Again she listened with a sinking heart, and heard nothing but the farewell twitter and whistle of the birds in the bushes around. How many stories had she listened to by the winter hearth, of children stolen by the fairies, at nightfall, in lonely places! With this fear she knew her mother was haunted.

No one in the country round gathered her little flock about her so early as this frightened widow, and no door "in the seven parishes" was barred so early.

Sufficiently fearful, as all young people in that part of the world are of such dreaded and subtle agents, Nell was even more than usually afraid of them, for her terrors were infected and redoubled by her mother's. She was looking towards Lisnavoura in a trance of fear, and crossed herself again and again, and whispered prayer after prayer. She was interrupted by her mother's voice[78] on the road calling her loudly. She answered, and ran round to the front of the cabin, where she found her standing.

"And where in the world's the craythurs—did ye see sight o' them anywhere?" cried Mrs. Ryan, as the girl came over the stile.

"Arrah! mother, 'tis only what they're run down the road a bit. We'll see them this minute coming back. It's like goats they are, climbin' here and runnin' there; an' if I had them here, in my hand, maybe I wouldn't give them a hiding all round."

"May the Lord forgive you, Nell! the childhers gone. They're took, and not a soul near us, and Father Tom three miles away! And what'll I do, or who's to help us this night? Oh, wirristhru, wirristhru! The craythurs is gone!"

"Whisht, mother, be aisy; don't ye see them comin' up."

And then she shouted in menacing accents, waving her arm, and beckoning the children, who were seen approaching on the road, which some little way off made a slight dip, which had concealed them. They were approaching from the westward, and from the direction of the dreaded hill of Lisnavoura.

But there were only two of the children, and one of them, the little girl, was crying. Their mother and sister hurried forward to meet them, more alarmed than ever.

"Where is Billy—where is he?" cried the mother, nearly breathless, so soon as she was within hearing.

"He's gone—they took him away; but they said he'll come back again," answered little Con, with the dark brown hair.

"He's gone away with the grand ladies," blubbered the little girl.[79]

"What ladies—where? Oh, Leum, asthora! My darlin', are you gone away at last? Where is he? Who took him? What ladies are you talkin' about? What way did he go?" she cried in distraction.

"I couldn't see where he went, mother; 'twas like as if he was going to Lisnavoura."

With a wild exclamation the distracted woman ran on towards the hill alone, clapping her hands, and crying aloud the name of her lost child.

Scared and horrified, Nell, not daring to follow, gazed after her, and burst into tears; and the other children raised high their lamentations in shrill rivalry.

Twilight was deepening. It was long past the time when they were usually barred securely within their habitation. Nell led the younger children into the cabin, and made them sit down by the turf fire, while she stood in the open door, watching in great fear for the return of her mother.

After a long while they did see their mother return. She came in and sat down by the fire, and cried as if her heart would break.

"Will I bar the doore, mother?" asked Nell.

"Ay, do—didn't I lose enough, this night, without lavin' the doore open, for more o' yez to go; but first take an' sprinkle a dust o' the holy waters over ye, acuishla, and bring it here till I throw a taste iv it over myself and the craythurs; an' I wondher, Nell, you'd forget to do the like yourself, lettin' the craythurs out so near nightfall. Come here and sit on my knees, asthora, come to me, mavourneen, and hould me fast, in the name o' God, and I'll hould you fast that none can take yez from me, and tell me all about it, and what it was—the Lord between us and harm—an' how it happened, and who was in it."

And the door being barred, the two children, sometimes speaking together, often interrupting one another, often[80] interrupted by their mother, managed to tell this strange story, which I had better relate connectedly and in my own language.

The Widow Ryan's three children were playing, as I have said, upon the narrow old road in front of her door. Little Bill or Leum, about five years old, with golden hair and large blue eyes, was a very pretty boy, with all the clear tints of healthy childhood, and that gaze of earnest simplicity which belongs not to town children of the same age. His little sister Peg, about a year elder, and his brother Con, a little more than a year elder than she, made up the little group.

Under the great old ash-trees, whose last leaves were falling at their feet, in the light of an October sunset, they were playing with the hilarity and eagerness of rustic children, clamouring together, and their faces were turned toward the west and storied hill of Lisnavoura.

Suddenly a startling voice with a screech called to them from behind, ordering them to get out of the way, and turning, they saw a sight, such as they never beheld before. It was a carriage drawn by four horses that were pawing and snorting, in impatience, as if just pulled up. The children were almost under their feet, and scrambled to the side of the road next their own door.

This carriage and all its appointments were old-fashioned and gorgeous, and presented to the children, who had never seen anything finer than a turf car, and once, an old chaise that passed that way from Killaloe, a spectacle perfectly dazzling.

Here was antique splendour. The harness and trappings were scarlet, and blazing with gold. The horses were huge, and snow white, with great manes, that as they tossed and shook them in the air, seemed to stream and float sometimes longer and sometimes shorter, like so much smoke[81] their tails were long, and tied up in bows of broad scarlet and gold ribbon. The coach itself was glowing with colours, gilded and emblazoned. There were footmen in gay liveries, and three-cocked hats, like the coachman›s; but he had a great wig, like a judge›s, and their hair was frizzed out and powdered, and a long thick «pigtail,» with a bow to it, hung down the back of each.

All these servants were diminutive, and ludicrously out of proportion with the enormous horses of the equipage, and had sharp, sallow features, and small, restless fiery eyes, and faces of cunning and malice that chilled the children. The little coachman was scowling and showing his white fangs under his cocked hat, and his little blazing beads of eyes were quivering with fury in their sockets as he whirled his whip round and round over their heads, till the lash of it looked like a streak of fire in the evening sun, and sounded like the cry of a legion of "fillapoueeks" in the air.

"Stop the princess on the highway!" cried the coachman, in a piercing treble.

"Stop the princess on the highway!" piped each footman in turn, scowling over his shoulder down on the children, and grinding his keen teeth.

The children were so frightened they could only gape and turn white in their panic. But a very sweet voice from the open window of the carriage reassured them, and arrested the attack of the lackeys.

A beautiful and "very grand-looking" lady was smiling from it on them, and they all felt pleased in the strange light of that smile.

"The boy with the golden hair, I think," said the lady, bending her large and wonderfully clear eyes on little Leum.

The upper sides of the carriage were chiefly of glass, so[82] that the children could see another woman inside, whom they did not like so well.

This was a black woman, with a wonderfully long neck, hung round with many strings of large variously-coloured beads, and on her head was a sort of turban of silk striped with all the colours of the rainbow, and fixed in it was a golden star.

This black woman had a face as thin almost as a death's-head, with high cheek-bones, and great goggle eyes, the whites of which, as well as her wide range of teeth, showed in brilliant contrast with her skin, as she looked over the beautiful lady's shoulder, and whispered something in her ear.

"Yes; the boy with the golden hair, I think," repeated the lady.

And her voice sounded sweet as a silver bell in the children's ears, and her smile beguiled them like the light of an enchanted lamp, as she leaned from the window with a look of ineffable fondness on the golden-haired boy, with the large blue eyes; insomuch that little Billy, looking up, smiled in return with a wondering fondness, and when she stooped down, and stretched her jewelled arms towards him, he stretched his little hands up, and how they touched the other children did not know; but, saying, "Come and give me a kiss, my darling," she raised him, and he seemed to ascend in her small fingers as lightly as a feather, and she held him in her lap and covered him with kisses.

Nothing daunted, the other children would have been only too happy to change places with their favoured little brother. There was only one thing that was unpleasant, and a little frightened them, and that was the black woman, who stood and stretched forward, in the carriage as before. She gathered a rich silk and gold handkerchief that was in her fingers up to her lips, and seemed to thrust ever so[83] much of it, fold after fold, into her capacious mouth, as they thought to smother her laughter, with which she seemed convulsed, for she was shaking and quivering, as it seemed, with suppressed merriment; but her eyes, which remained uncovered, looked angrier than they had ever seen eyes look before.

But the lady was so beautiful they looked on her instead, and she continued to caress and kiss the little boy on her knee; and smiling at the other children she held up a large russet apple in her fingers, and the carriage began to move slowly on, and with a nod inviting them to take the fruit, she dropped it on the road from the window; it rolled some way beside the wheels, they following, and then she dropped another, and then another, and so on. And the same thing happened to all; for just as either of the children who ran beside had caught the rolling apple, somehow it slipt into a hole or ran into a ditch, and looking up they saw the lady drop another from the window, and so the chase was taken up and continued till they got, hardly knowing how far they had gone, to the old cross-road that leads to Owney. It seemed that there the horses' hoofs and carriage wheels rolled up a wonderful dust, which being caught in one of those eddies that whirl the dust up into a column, on the calmest day, enveloped the children for a moment, and passed whirling on towards Lisnavoura, the carriage, as they fancied, driving in the centre of it; but suddenly it subsided, the straws and leaves floated to the ground, the dust dissipated itself, but the white horses and the lackeys, the gilded carriage, the lady and their little golden-haired brother were gone.

At the same moment suddenly the upper rim of the clear setting sun disappeared behind the hill of Knockdoulah, and it was twilight. Each child felt the transition[84] like a shock—and the sight of the rounded summit of Lisnavoura, now closely overhanging them, struck them with a new fear.

They screamed their brother's name after him, but their cries were lost in the vacant air. At the same time they thought they heard a hollow voice say, close to them, "Go home."

Looking round and seeing no one, they were scared, and hand in hand— the little girl crying wildly, and the boy white as ashes, from fear, they trotted homeward, at their best speed, to tell, as we have seen, their strange story.

Molly Ryan never more saw her darling. But something of the lost little boy was seen by his former play-mates.

Sometimes when their mother was away earning a trifle at hay-making, and Nelly washing the potatoes for their dinner, or "beatling" clothes in the little stream that flows in the hollow close by, they saw the pretty face of little Billy peeping in archly at the door, and smiling silently at them, and as they ran to embrace him, with cries of delight, he drew back, still smiling archly, and when they got out into the open day, he was gone, and they could see no trace of him anywhere.

This happened often, with slight variations in the circumstances of the visit. Sometimes he would peep for a longer time, sometimes for a shorter time, sometimes his little hand would come in, and, with bended finger, beckon them to follow; but always he was smiling with the same arch look and wary silence—and always he was gone when they reached the door. Gradually these visits grew less and less frequent, and in about eight months they ceased altogether, and little Billy, irretrievably lost, took rank in their memories with the dead.[85]

One wintry morning, nearly a year and a half after his disappearance, their mother having set out for Limerick soon after cock-crow, to sell some fowls at the market, the little girl, lying by the side of her elder sister, who was fast asleep, just at the grey of the morning heard the latch lifted softly, and saw little Billy enter and close the door gently after him. There was light enough to see that he was barefoot and ragged, and looked pale and famished. He went straight to the fire, and cowered over the turf embers, and rubbed his hands slowly, and seemed to shiver as he gathered the smouldering turf together.

The little girl clutched her sister in terror and whispered, "Waken, Nelly, waken; here's Billy come back!"

Nelly slept soundly on, but the little boy, whose hands were extended close over the coals, turned and looked toward the bed, it seemed to her, in fear, and she saw the glare of the embers reflected on his thin cheek as he turned toward her. He rose and went, on tiptoe, quickly to the door, in silence, and let himself out as softly as he had come in.

After that, the little boy was never seen any more by any one of his kindred.

"Fairy doctors," as the dealers in the preternatural, who in such cases were called in, are termed, did all that in them lay—but in vain. Father Tom came down, and tried what holier rites could do, but equally without result. So little Billy was dead to mother, brother, and sisters; but no grave received him. Others whom affection cherished, lay in holy ground, in the old churchyard of Abington, with headstone to mark the spot over which the survivor might kneel and say a kind prayer for the peace of the departed soul. But there was no landmark to show where little Billy was hidden from their loving eyes, unless it was in the old hill of Lisnavoura, that cast its[86] long shadow at sunset before the cabin-door; or that, white and filmy in the moonlight, in later years, would occupy his brother›s gaze as he returned from fair or market, and draw from him a sigh and a prayer for the little brother he had lost so long ago, and was never to see again.

5
THE WHITE CAT OF DRUMGUNNIOL

Anonymous in *All the Year Round* (1869-70).

There is a famous story of a white cat, with which we all become acquainted in the nursery. I am going to tell a story of a white cat very different from the amiable and enchanted princess who took that disguise for a season. The white cat of which I speak was a more sinister animal.

The traveller from Limerick toward Dublin, after passing the hills of Killaloe upon the left, as Keeper Mountain rises high in view, finds himself gradually hemmed in, up the right, by a range of lower hills. An undulating plain that dips gradually to a lower level than that of the road interposes, and some scattered hedgerows relieve its somewhat wild and melancholy character.

One of the few human habitations that send up their films of turf-smoke from that lonely plain, is the loosely-thatched, earth-built dwelling of a "strong farmer," as the more prosperous of the tenant-farming classes are termed in Munster. It stands in a clump of trees near the edge of a wandering stream, about half-way between the mountains and the Dublin road, and had been for generations tenanted by people named Donovan.

In a distant place, desirous of studying some Irish records which had fallen into my hands, and inquiring for[88] a teacher capable of instructing me in the Irish language, a Mr. Donovan, dreamy, harmless, and learned, was recommended to me for the purpose.

I found that he had been educated as a Sizar in Trinity College, Dublin. He now supported himself by teaching, and the special direction of my studies, I suppose, flattered his national partialities, for he unbosomed himself of much of his long-reserved thoughts, and recollections about his country and his early days. It was he who told me this story, and I mean to repeat it, as nearly as I can, in his own words.

I have myself seen the old farm-house, with its orchard of huge mossgrown apple trees. I have looked round on the peculiar landscape; the roofless, ivied tower, that two hundred years before had afforded a refuge from raid and rapparee, and which still occupies its old place in the angle of the haggard; the bush-grown "liss," that scarcely a hundred and fifty steps away records the labours of a bygone race; the dark and towering outline of old Keeper in the background; and the lonely range of furze and heath-clad hills that form a nearer barrier, with many a line of grey rock and clump of dwarf oak or birch. The pervading sense of loneliness made it a scene not unsuited for a wild and unearthly story. And I could quite fancy how, seen in the grey of a wintry morning, shrouded far and wide in snow, or in the melancholy glory of an autumnal sunset, or in the chill splendour of a moonlight night, it might have helped to tone a dreamy mind like honest Dan Donovan's to superstition and a proneness to the illusions of fancy. It is certain, however, that I never anywhere met with a more simple-minded creature, or one on whose good faith I could more entirely rely.

When I was a boy, said he, living at home at Drumgunniol, I used to take my Goldsmith's *Roman History* in[89] my hand and go down to my favourite seat, the flat stone, sheltered by a hawthorn tree beside the little lough, a large and deep pool, such as I have heard called a tarn in England. It lay in the gentle hollow of a field that is overhung toward the north by the old orchard, and being a deserted place was favourable to my studious quietude.

One day reading here, as usual, I wearied at last, and began to look about me, thinking of the heroic scenes I had just been reading of. I was as wide awake as I am at this moment, and I saw a woman appear at the corner of the orchard and walk down the slope. She wore a long, light grey dress, so long that it seemed to sweep the grass behind her, and so singular was her appearance in a part of the world where female attire is so inflexibly fixed by custom, that I could not take my eyes off her. Her course lay diagonally from corner to corner of the field, which was a large one, and she pursued it without swerving.

When she came near I could see that her feet were bare, and that she seemed to be looking steadfastly upon some remote object for guidance. Her route would have crossed me—had the tarn not interposed—about ten or twelve yards below the point at which I was sitting. But instead of arresting her course at the margin of the lough, as I had expected, she went on without seeming conscious of its existence, and I saw her, as plainly as I see you, sir, walk across the surface of the water, and pass, without seeming to see me, at about the distance I had calculated.

I was ready to faint from sheer terror. I was only thirteen years old then, and I remember every particular as if it had happened this hour.

The figure passed through the gap at the far corner of the field, and there I lost sight of it. I had hardly strength to walk home, and was so nervous, and ultimately so ill, that for three weeks I was confined to the house, and could[90] not bear to be alone for a moment. I never entered that field again, such was the horror with which from that moment every object in it was clothed. Even at this distance of time I should not like to pass through it.

This apparition I connected with a mysterious event; and, also, with a singular liability, that has for nearly eight years distinguished, or rather afflicted, our family. It is no fancy. Everybody in that part of the country knows all about it. Everybody connected what I had seen with it.

I will tell it all to you as well as I can.

When I was about fourteen years old—that is about a year after the sight I had seen in the lough field—we were one night expecting my father home from the fair of Killaloe. My mother sat up to welcome him home, and I with her, for I liked nothing better than such a vigil. My brothers and sisters, and the farm servants, except the men who were driving home the cattle from the fair, were asleep in their beds. My mother and I were sitting in the chimney corner chatting together, and watching my father's supper, which was kept hot over the fire. We knew that he would return before the men who were driving home the cattle, for he was riding, and told us that he would only wait to see them fairly on the road, and then push homeward.

At length we heard his voice and the knocking of his loaded whip at the door, and my mother let him in. I don't think I ever saw my father drunk, which is more than most men of my age, from the same part of the country, could say of theirs. But he could drink his glass of whisky as well as another, and he usually came home from fair or market a little merry and mellow, and with a jolly flush in his cheeks.

To-night he looked sunken, pale and sad. He entered with the saddle and bridle in his hand, and he dropped[91] them against the wall, near the door, and put his arms round his wife›s neck, and kissed her kindly.

"Welcome home, Meehal," said she, kissing him heartily.

"God bless you, mavourneen," he answered.

And hugging her again, he turned to me, who was plucking him by the hand, jealous of his notice. I was little, and light of my age, and he lifted me up in his arms, and kissed me, and my arms being about his neck, he said to my mother:

"Draw the bolt, acuishla."

She did so, and setting me down very dejectedly, he walked to the fire and sat down on a stool, and stretched his feet toward the glowing turf, leaning with his hands on his knees.

"Rouse up, Mick, darlin'," said my mother, who was growing anxious, "and tell me how did the cattle sell, and did everything go lucky at the fair, or is there anything wrong with the landlord, or what in the world is it that ails you, Mick, jewel?"

"Nothin', Molly. The cows sould well, thank God, and there's nothin' fell out between me an' the landlord, an' everything's the same way. There's no fault to find anywhere."

"Well, then, Mickey, since so it is, turn round to your hot supper, and ate it, and tell us is there anything new."

"I got my supper, Molly, on the way, and I can't ate a bit," he answered.

"Got your supper on the way, an' you knowin' 'twas waiting for you at home, an' your wife sittin' up an' all!" cried my mother, reproachfully.

"You're takin' a wrong meanin' out of what I say," said my father. "There's something happened that leaves me that I can't ate a mouthful, and I'll not be dark with[92] you, Molly, for, maybe, it ain›t very long I have to be here, an› I›ll tell you what it was. It›s what I›ve seen, the white cat.»

"The Lord between us and harm!" exclaimed my mother, in a moment as pale and as chap-fallen as my father; and then, trying to rally, with a laugh, she said: "Ha! 'tis only funnin' me you are. Sure a white rabbit was snared a Sunday last, in Grady's wood; an' Teigue seen a big white rat in the haggard yesterday."

"'Twas neither rat nor rabbit was in it. Don't ye think but I'd know a rat or a rabbit from a big white cat, with green eyes as big as halfpennies, and its back riz up like a bridge, trottin' on and across me, and ready, if I dar' stop, to rub its sides against my shins, and maybe to make a jump and seize my throat, if that it's a cat, at all, an' not something worse?"

As he ended his description in a low tone, looking straight at the fire, my father drew his big hand across his forehead once or twice, his face being damp and shining with the moisture of fear, and he sighed, or rather groaned, heavily.

My mother had relapsed into panic, and was praying again in her fear. I, too, was terribly frightened, and on the point of crying, for I knew all about the white cat.

Clapping my father on the shoulder, by way of encouragement, my mother leaned over him, kissing him, and at last began to cry. He was wringing her hands in his, and seemed in great trouble.

"There was nothin' came into the house with me?" he asked, in a very low tone, turning to me.

"There was nothin', father," I said, "but the saddle and bridle that was in your hand."

"Nothin' white kem in at the doore wid me," he repeated.[93]

"Nothin' at all," I answered.

"So best," said my father, and making the sign of the cross, he began mumbling to himself, and I knew he was saying his prayers.

Waiting for a while, to give him time for this exercise, my mother asked him where he first saw it.

"When I was riding up the bohereen,"—the Irish term meaning a little road, such as leads up to a farm-house—"I bethought myself that the men was on the road with the cattle, and no one to look to the horse barrin' myself, so I thought I might as well leave him in the crooked field below, an' I tuck him there, he bein' cool, and not a hair turned, for I rode him aisy all the way. It was when I turned, after lettin' him go—the saddle and bridle bein' in my hand—that I saw it, pushin' out o' the long grass at the side o' the path, an' it walked across it, in front of me, an' then back again, before me, the same way, an' sometimes at one side, an' then at the other, lookin' at me wid them shinin' eyes; and I consayted I heard it growlin' as it kep' beside me—as close as ever you see—till I kem up to the doore, here, an' knocked an' called, as ye heerd me."

Now, what was it, in so simple an incident, that agitated my father, my mother, myself, and finally, every member of this rustic household, with a terrible foreboding? It was this that we, one and all, believed that my father had received, in thus encountering the white cat, a warning of his approaching death.

The omen had never failed hitherto. It did not fail now. In a week after my father took the fever that was going, and before a month he was dead.

My honest friend, Dan Donovan, paused here; I could perceive that he was praying, for his lips were busy, and I concluded that it was for the repose of that departed soul.[94]

In a little while he resumed.

It is eighty years now since that omen first attached to my family. Eighty years? Ay, is it. Ninety is nearer the mark. And I have spoken to many old people, in those earlier times, who had a distinct recollection of everything connected with it.

It happened in this way.

My grand-uncle, Connor Donovan, had the old farm of Drumgunniol in his day. He was richer than ever my father was, or my father's father either, for he took a short lease of Balraghan, and made money of it. But money won't soften a hard heart, and I'm afraid my grand-uncle was a cruel man—a profligate man he was, surely, and that is mostly a cruel man at heart. He drank his share, too, and cursed and swore, when he was vexed, more than was good for his soul, I'm afraid.

At that time there was a beautiful girl of the Colemans, up in the mountains, not far from Capper Cullen. I'm told that there are no Colemans there now at all, and that family has passed away. The famine years made great changes.

Ellen Coleman was her name. The Colemans were not rich. But, being such a beauty, she might have made a good match. Worse than she did for herself, poor thing, she could not.

Con Donovan—my grand-uncle, God forgive him!—sometimes in his rambles saw her at fairs or patterns, and he fell in love with her, as who might not?

He used her ill. He promised her marriage, and persuaded her to come away with him; and, after all, he broke his word. It was just the old story. He tired of her, and he wanted to push himself in the world; and he married a girl of the Collopys, that had a great fortune—twenty-four cows, seventy sheep, and a hundred and twenty goats.[95]

He married this Mary Collopy, and grew richer than before; and Ellen Coleman died broken-hearted. But that did not trouble the strong farmer much.

He would have liked to have children, but he had none, and this was the only cross he had to bear, for everything else went much as he wished.

One night he was returning from the fair of Nenagh. A shallow stream at that time crossed the road—they have thrown a bridge over it, I am told, some time since—and its channel was often dry in summer weather. When it was so, as it passes close by the old farm-house of Drumgunniol, without a great deal of winding, it makes a sort of road, which people then used as a short cut to reach the house by. Into this dry channel, as there was plenty of light from the moon, my grand-uncle turned his horse, and when he had reached the two ash-trees at the meering of the farm he turned his horse short into the river-field, intending to ride through the gap at the other end, under the oak-tree, and so he would have been within a few hundred yards of his door.

As he approached the "gap" he saw, or thought he saw, with a slow motion, gliding along the ground toward the same point, and now and then with a soft bound, a white object, which he described as being no bigger than his hat, but what it was he could not see, as it moved along the hedge and disappeared at the point to which he was himself tending.

When he reached the gap the horse stopped short. He urged and coaxed it in vain. He got down to lead it through, but it recoiled, snorted, and fell into a wild trembling fit. He mounted it again. But its terror continued, and it obstinately resisted his caresses and his whip. It was bright moonlight, and my grand-uncle was chafed by the horse's resistance, and, seeing nothing to account[96] for it, and being so near home, what little patience he possessed forsook him, and, plying his whip and spur in earnest, he broke into oaths and curses.

All on a sudden the horse sprang through, and Con Donovan, as he passed under the broad branch of the oak, saw clearly a woman standing on the bank beside him, her arm extended, with the hand of which, as he flew by, she struck him a blow upon the shoulders. It threw him forward upon the neck of the horse, which, in wild terror, reached the door at a gallop, and stood there quivering and steaming all over.

Less alive than dead, my grand-uncle got in. He told his story, at least, so much as he chose. His wife did not quite know what to think. But that something very bad had happened she could not doubt. He was very faint and ill, and begged that the priest should be sent for forthwith. When they were getting him to his bed they saw distinctly the marks of five fingerpoints on the flesh of his shoulder, where the spectral blow had fallen. These singular marks—which they said resembled in tint the hue of a body struck by lightning—remained imprinted on his flesh, and were buried with him.

When he had recovered sufficiently to talk with the people about him—speaking, like a man at his last hour, from a burdened heart, and troubled conscience—he repeated his story, but said he did not see, or, at all events, know, the face of the figure that stood in the gap. No one believed him. He told more about it to the priest than to others. He certainly had a secret to tell. He might as well have divulged it frankly, for the neighbours all knew well enough that it was the face of dead Ellen Coleman that he had seen.

From that moment my grand-uncle never raised his head. He was a scared, silent, broken-spirited man. It[97] was early summer then, and at the fall of the leaf in the same year he died.

Of course there was a wake, such as beseemed a strong farmer so rich as he. For some reason the arrangements of this ceremonial were a little different from the usual routine.

The usual practice is to place the body in the great room, or kitchen, as it is called, of the house. In this particular case there was, as I told you, for some reason, an unusual arrangement. The body was placed in a small room that opened upon the greater one. The door of this, during the wake, stood open. There were candles about the bed, and pipes and tobacco on the table, and stools for such guests as chose to enter, the door standing open for their reception.

The body, having been laid out, was left alone, in this smaller room, during the preparations for the wake. After nightfall one of the women, approaching the bed to get a chair which she had left near it, rushed from the room with a scream, and, having recovered her speech at the further end of the "kitchen," and surrounded by a gaping audience, she said, at last:

"*May* I never sin, if his face bain›t riz up again the back o› the bed, and he starin› down to the doore, wid eyes as big as pewter plates, that id be shinin› in the moon!»

"Arra, woman! Is it cracked you are?" said one of the farm boys as they are termed, being men of any age you please.

"Agh, Molly, don't be talkin', woman! 'Tis what ye consayted it, goin' into the dark room, out o' the light. Why didn't ye take a candle in your fingers, ye aumadhaun?" said one of her female companions.

"Candle, or no candle; I seen it," insisted Molly.[98] «An› what›s more, I could a›most tak› my oath I seen his arum, too, stretchin› out o› the bed along the flure, three times as long as it should be, to take hould o› me be the fut.»

"Nansinse, ye fool, what id he want o' yer fut?" exclaimed one scornfully.

"Gi' me the candle, some o' yez—in the name o' God," said old Sal Doolan, that was straight and lean, and a woman that could pray like a priest almost.

"Give her a candle," agreed all.

But whatever they might say, there wasn't one among them that did not look pale and stern enough as they followed Mrs. Doolan, who was praying as fast as her lips could patter, and leading the van with a tallow candle, held like a taper, in her fingers.

The door was half open, as the panic-stricken girl had left it; and holding the candle on high the better to examine the room, she made a step or so into it.

If my grand-uncle's hand had been stretched along the floor, in the unnatural way described, he had drawn it back again under the sheet that covered him. And tall Mrs. Doolan was in no danger of tripping over his arm as she entered. But she had not gone more than a step or two with her candle aloft, when, with a drowning face, she suddenly stopped short, staring at the bed which was now fully in view.

"Lord, bless us, Mrs. Doolan, ma'am, come back," said the woman next her, who had fast hold of her dress, or her 'coat,' as they call it, and drawing her backwards with a frightened pluck, while a general recoil among her followers betokened the alarm which her hesitation had inspired.

"Whisht, will yez?" said the leader, peremptorily, "I can't hear my own ears wid the noise ye're makin',[99] an› which iv yez let the cat in here, an› whose cat is it?» she asked, peering suspiciously at a white cat that was sitting on the breast of the corpse.

"Put it away, will yez?" she resumed, with horror at the profanation. "Many a corpse as I sthretched and crossed in the bed, the likes o' that I never seen yet. The man o' the house, wid a brute baste like that mounted on him, like a phooka, Lord forgi' me for namin' the like in this room.

Dhrive it away, some o' yez! out o' that, this minute, I tell ye."

Each repeated the order, but no one seemed inclined to execute it. They were crossing themselves, and whispering their conjectures and misgivings as to the nature of the beast, which was no cat of that house, nor one that they had ever seen before. On a sudden, the white cat placed itself on the pillow over the head of the body, and having from that place glared for a time at them over the features of the corpse, it crept softly along the body towards them, growling low and fiercely as it drew near.

Out of the room they bounced, in dreadful confusion, shutting the door fast after them, and not for a good while did the hardiest venture to peep in again.

The white cat was sitting in its old place, on the dead man's breast, but this time it crept quietly down the side of the bed, and disappeared under it, the sheet which was spread like a coverlet, and hung down nearly to the floor, concealing it from view.

Praying, crossing themselves, and not forgetting a sprinkling of holy water, they peeped, and finally searched, poking spades, "wattles," pitchforks and such implements under the bed. But the cat was not to be found, and they concluded that it had made its escape among their feet as they stood near the threshold. So they secured the door carefully, with hasp and padlock.[100] But when the door was opened next morning they found the white cat sitting, as if it had never been disturbed, upon the breast of the dead man.

Again occurred very nearly the same scene with a like result, only that some said they saw the cat afterwards lurking under a big box in a corner of the outer-room, where my grand-uncle kept his leases and papers, and his prayer-book and beads.

Mrs. Doolan heard it growling at her heels wherever she went; and although she could not see it, she could hear it spring on the back of her chair when she sat down, and growl in her ear, so that she would bounce up with a scream and a prayer, fancying that it was on the point of taking her by the throat.

And the priest's boy, looking round the corner, under the branches of the old orchard, saw a white cat sitting under the little window of the room where my grand-uncle was laid out and looking up at the four small panes of glass as a cat will watch a bird.

The end of it was that the cat was found on the corpse again, when the room was visited, and do what they might, whenever the body was left alone, the cat was found again in the same ill-omened contiguity with the dead man. And this continued, to the scandal and fear of the neighbourhood, until the door was opened finally for the wake.

My grand-uncle being dead, and, with all due solemnities, buried, I have done with him. But not quite yet with the white cat. No banshee ever yet was more inalienably attached to a family than this ominous apparition is to mine. But there is this difference. The banshee seems to be animated with an affectionate sympathy with the bereaved family to whom it is hereditarily attached, whereas this thing has about it a suspicion of malice. It is the messenger simply of death. And its taking the[101] shape of a cat—the coldest, and they say, the most vindictive of brutes—is indicative of the spirit of its visit.

When my grandfather's death was near, although he seemed quite well at the time, it appeared not exactly, but very nearly in the same way in which I told you it showed itself to my father.

The day before my Uncle Teigue was killed by the bursting of his gun, it appeared to him in the evening, at twilight, by the lough, in the field where I saw the woman who walked across the water, as I told you. My uncle was washing the barrel of his gun in the lough. The grass is short there, and there is no cover near it. He did not know how it approached; but the first he saw of it, the white cat was walking close round his feet, in the twilight, with an angry twist of its tail, and a green glare in its eyes, and do what he would, it continued walking round and round him, in larger or smaller circles, till he reached the orchard, and there he lost it.

My poor Aunt Peg—she married one of the O'Brians, near Oolah—came to Drumgunniol to go to the funeral of a cousin who died about a mile away. She died herself, poor woman, only a month after.

Coming from the wake, at two or three o'clock in the morning, as she got over the style into the farm of Drumgunniol, she saw the white cat at her side, and it kept close beside her, she ready to faint all the time, till she reached the door of the house, where it made a spring up into the white-thorn tree that grows close by, and so it parted from her. And my little brother Jim saw it also, just three weeks before he died. Every member of our family who dies, or takes his death-sickness, at Drumgunniol, is sure to see the white cat, and no one of us who sees it need hope for long life after.

6

AN ACCOUNT OF SOME STRANGE DISTURBANCES IN AUNGIER STREET

Anonymous in the *Dublin University Magazine* (1853). It is an anticipation of «Mr. Justice Harbottle,» who may be found in *In a Glass Darkly*.

It is not worth telling, this story of mine—at least, not worth writing. Told, indeed, as I have sometimes been called upon to tell it, to a circle of intelligent and eager faces, lighted up by a good after-dinner fire on a winter's evening, with a cold wind rising and wailing outside, and all snug and cosy within, it has gone off—though I say it, who should not—indifferent well. But it is a venture to do as you would have me. Pen, ink, and paper are cold vehicles for the marvellous, and a "reader" decidedly a more critical animal than a "listener". If, however, you can induce your friends to read it after nightfall, and when the fireside talk has run for a while on thrilling tales of shapeless terror; in short, if you will secure me the *mollia tempora fandi*, I will go to my work, and say my say, with better heart. Well, then, these conditions presupposed, I shall waste no more words, but tell you simply how it all happened.

My cousin (Tom Ludlow) and I studied medicine together. I think he would have succeeded, had he stuck[103] to the profession; but he preferred the Church, poor fellow, and died early, a sacrifice to contagion, contracted in the noble discharge of his duties. For my present purpose, I say enough of his character when I mention that he was of a sedate but frank and cheerful nature; very exact in his observance of truth, and not by any means like myself—of an excitable or nervous temperament.

My Uncle Ludlow—Tom's father—while we were attending lectures, purchased three or four old houses in Aungier Street, one of which was unoccupied. *He* resided in the country, and Tom proposed that we should take up our abode in the untenanted house, so long as it should continue unlet; a move which would accomplish the double end of settling us nearer alike to our lecture-rooms and to our amusements, and of relieving us from the weekly charge of rent for our lodgings.

Our furniture was very scant—our whole equipage remarkably modest and primitive; and, in short, our arrangements pretty nearly as simple as those of a bivouac. Our new plan was, therefore, executed almost as soon as conceived. The front drawing-room was our sitting-room. I had the bedroom over it, and Tom the back bedroom on the same floor, which nothing could have induced me to occupy.

The house, to begin with, was a very old one. It had been, I believe, newly fronted about fifty years before; but with this exception, it had nothing modern about it. The agent who bought it and looked into the titles for my uncle, told me that it was sold, along with much other forfeited property, at Chichester House, I think, in 1702; and had belonged to Sir Thomas Hacket, who was Lord Mayor of Dublin in James II.'s time. How old it was *then*, I can't say; but, at all events, it had seen years and changes enough to have contracted all that mysterious[104] and saddened air, at once exciting and depressing, which belongs to most old mansions.

There had been very little done in the way of modernising details; and, perhaps, it was better so; for there was something queer and bygone in the very walls and ceilings—in the shape of doors and windows—in the odd diagonal site of the chimney-pieces—in the beams and ponderous cornices—not to mention the singular solidity of all the woodwork, from the bannisters to the window-frames, which hopelessly defied disguise, and would have emphatically proclaimed their antiquity through any conceivable amount of modern finery and varnish.

An effort had, indeed, been made, to the extent of papering the drawing-rooms; but somehow, the paper looked raw and out of keeping; and the old woman, who kept a little dirt-pie of a shop in the lane, and whose daughter—a girl of two and fifty—was our solitary handmaid, coming in at sunrise, and chastely receding again as soon as she had made all ready for tea in our state apartment;—this woman, I say, remembered it, when old Judge Horrocks (who, having earned the reputation of a particularly "hanging judge," ended by hanging himself, as the coroner's jury found, under an impulse of "temporary insanity," with a child's skipping-rope, over the massive old bannisters) resided there, entertaining good company, with fine venison and rare old port. In those halcyon days, the drawing-rooms were hung with gilded leather, and, I dare say, cut a good figure, for they were really spacious rooms.

The bedrooms were wainscoted, but the front one was not gloomy; and in it the cosiness of antiquity quite overcame its sombre associations. But the back bedroom, with its two queerly-placed melancholy windows, staring vacantly at the foot of the bed, and with the[105] shadowy recess to be found in most old houses in Dublin, like a large ghostly closet, which, from congeniality of temperament, had amalgamated with the bed-chamber, and dissolved the partition. At night-time, this «alcove»—as our «maid» was wont to call it—had, in my eyes, a specially sinister and suggestive character. Tom›s distant and solitary candle glimmered vainly into its darkness. *There* it was always overlooking him—always itself impenetrable. But this was only part of the effect. The whole room was, I can›t tell how, repulsive to me. There was, I suppose, in its proportions and features, a latent discord—a certain mysterious and indescribable relation, which jarred indistinctly upon some secret sense of the fitting and the safe, and raised indefinable suspicions and apprehensions of the imagination. On the whole, as I began by saying, nothing could have induced me to pass a night alone in it.

I had never pretended to conceal from poor Tom my superstitious weakness; and he, on the other hand, most unaffectedly ridiculed my tremors. The sceptic was, however, destined to receive a lesson, as you shall hear.

We had not been very long in occupation of our respective dormitories, when I began to complain of uneasy nights and disturbed sleep. I was, I suppose, the more impatient under this annoyance, as I was usually a sound sleeper, and by no means prone to nightmares. It was now, however, my destiny, instead of enjoying my customary repose, every night to "sup full of horrors". After a preliminary course of disagreeable and frightful dreams, my troubles took a definite form, and the same vision, without an appreciable variation in a single detail, visited me at least (on an average) every second night in the week.[106]

Now, this dream, nightmare, or infernal illusion—which you please—of which I was the miserable sport, was on this wise:—

I saw, or thought I saw, with the most abominable distinctness, although at the time in profound darkness, every article of furniture and accidental arrangement of the chamber in which I lay. This, as you know, is incidental to ordinary nightmare. Well, while in this clairvoyant condition, which seemed but the lighting up of the theatre in which was to be exhibited the monotonous tableau of horror, which made my nights insupportable, my attention invariably became, I know not why, fixed upon the windows opposite the foot of my bed; and, uniformly with the same effect, a sense of dreadful anticipation always took slow but sure possession of me. I became somehow conscious of a sort of horrid but undefined preparation going forward in some unknown quarter, and by some unknown agency, for my torment; and, after an interval, which always seemed to me of the same length, a picture suddenly flew up to the window, where it remained fixed, as if by an electrical attraction, and my discipline of horror then commenced, to last perhaps for hours. The picture thus mysteriously glued to the window-panes, was the portrait of an old man, in a crimson flowered silk dressing-gown, the folds of which I could now describe, with a countenance embodying a strange mixture of intellect, sensuality, and power, but withal sinister and full of malignant omen. His nose was hooked, like the beak of a vulture; his eyes large, grey, and prominent, and lighted up with a more than mortal cruelty and coldness. These features were surmounted by a crimson velvet cap, the hair that peeped from under which was white with age, while the eyebrows retained their original blackness. Well I remember every line, hue, and[107] shadow of that stony countenance, and well I may! The gaze of this hellish visage was fixed upon me, and mine returned it with the inexplicable fascination of nightmare, for what appeared to me to be hours of agony. At last—

"The cock he crew, away then flew"

the fiend who had enslaved me through the awful watches of the night; and, harassed and nervous, I rose to the duties of the day.

I had—I can't say exactly why, but it may have been from the exquisite anguish and profound impressions of unearthly horror, with which this strange phantasmagoria was associated—an insurmountable antipathy to describing the exact nature of my nightly troubles to my friend and comrade. Generally, however, I told him that I was haunted by abominable dreams; and, true to the imputed materialism of medicine, we put our heads together to dispel my horrors, not by exorcism, but by a tonic.

I will do this tonic justice, and frankly admit that the accursed portrait began to intermit its visits under its influence. What of that? Was this singular apparition—as full of character as of terror—therefore the creature of my fancy, or the invention of my poor stomach? Was it, in short, *subjective* (to borrow the technical slang of the day) and not the palpable aggression and intrusion of an external agent? That, good friend, as we will both admit, by no means follows. The evil spirit, who enthralled my senses in the shape of that portrait, may have been just as near me, just as energetic, just as malignant, though I saw him not. What means the whole moral code of revealed religion regarding the due keeping of our own bodies, soberness, temperance, etc.? here is an obvious connexion between the material and the invisible;[108] the healthy tone of the system, and its unimpaired energy may, for aught we can tell, guard us against influences which would otherwise render life itself terrific. The mesmerist and the electro-biologist will fail upon an average with nine patients out of ten—so may the evil spirit. Special conditions of the corporeal system are indispensable to the production of certain spiritual phenomena. The operation succeeds sometimes—sometimes fails—that is all.

I found afterwards that my would-be sceptical companion had his troubles too. But of these I knew nothing yet. One night, for a wonder, I was sleeping soundly, when I was roused by a step on the lobby outside my room, followed by the loud clang of what turned out to be a large brass candlestick, flung with all his force by poor Tom Ludlow over the banisters, and rattling with a rebound down the second flight of stairs; and almost concurrently with this, Tom burst open my door, and bounced into my room backwards, in a state of extraordinary agitation.

I had jumped out of bed and clutched him by the arm before I had any distinct idea of my own whereabouts. There we were—in our shirts— standing before the open door—staring through the great old banister opposite, at the lobby window, through which the sickly light of a clouded moon was gleaming.

"What's the matter, Tom? What's the matter with you? What the devil's the matter with you, Tom?" I demanded shaking him with nervous impatience.

He took a long breath before he answered me, and then it was not very coherently.

"It's nothing, nothing at all—did I speak?—what did I say?—where's the candle, Richard? It's dark; I—I had a candle!"[109]

"Yes, dark enough," I said; "but what's the matter?—what *is* it?—why don›t you speak, Tom?—have you lost your wits?—what is the matter?»

"The matter?—oh, it is all over. It must have been a dream—nothing at all but a dream—don't you think so? It could not be anything more than a dream."

"Of *course*," said I, feeling uncommonly nervous, "it *was* a dream.»

"I thought," he said, "there was a man in my room, and—and I jumped out of bed; and—and—where's the candle?"

"In your room, most likely," I said, "shall I go and bring it?"

"No; stay here—don't go; it's no matter—don't, I tell you; it was all a dream. Bolt the door, Dick; I'll stay here with you—I feel nervous. So, Dick, like a good fellow, light your candle and open the window—I am in a *shocking state*."

I did as he asked me, and robing himself like Granuaile in one of my blankets, he seated himself close beside my bed.

Every body knows how contagious is fear of all sorts, but more especially that particular kind of fear under which poor Tom was at that moment labouring. I would not have heard, nor I believe would he have recapitulated, just at that moment, for half the world, the details of the hideous vision which had so unmanned him.

"Don't mind telling me anything about your nonsensical dream, Tom," said I, affecting contempt, really in a panic; "let us talk about something else; but it is quite plain that this dirty old house disagrees with us both, and hang me if I stay here any longer, to be pestered with indigestion and—and—bad nights, so we may as well look out for lodgings—don't you think so?—at once."[110]

Tom agreed, and, after an interval, said—

"I have been thinking, Richard, that it is a long time since I saw my father, and I have made up my mind to go down to-morrow and return in a day or two, and you can take rooms for us in the meantime."

I fancied that this resolution, obviously the result of the vision which had so profoundly scared him, would probably vanish next morning with the damps and shadows of night. But I was mistaken. Off went Tom at peep of day to the country, having agreed that so soon as I had secured suitable lodgings, I was to recall him by letter from his visit to my Uncle Ludlow.

Now, anxious as I was to change my quarters, it so happened, owing to a series of petty procrastinations and accidents, that nearly a week elapsed before my bargain was made and my letter of recall on the wing to Tom; and, in the meantime, a trifling adventure or two had occurred to your humble servant, which, absurd as they now appear, diminished by distance, did certainly at the time serve to whet my appetite for change considerably.

A night or two after the departure of my comrade, I was sitting by my bedroom fire, the door locked, and the ingredients of a tumbler of hot whisky-punch upon the crazy spider-table; for, as the best mode of keeping the

"Black spirits and white,Blue spirits and grey,"

with which I was environed, at bay, I had adopted the practice recommended by the wisdom of my ancestors, and "kept my spirits up by pouring spirits down." I had thrown aside my volume of Anatomy, and was treating myself by way of a tonic, preparatory to my punch and bed, to half-a-dozen pages of the *Spectator*, when I heard a step on the flight of stairs descending from the attics.[111] It was two o›clock, and the streets were as silent as a churchyard—the sounds were, therefore, perfectly distinct. There was a slow, heavy tread, characterised by the emphasis and deliberation of age, descending by the narrow staircase from above; and, what made the sound more singular, it was plain that the feet which produced it were perfectly bare, measuring the descent with something between a pound and a flop, very ugly to hear.

I knew quite well that my attendant had gone away many hours before, and that nobody but myself had any business in the house. It was quite plain also that the person who was coming down stairs had no intention whatever of concealing his movements; but, on the contrary, appeared disposed to make even more noise, and proceed more deliberately, than was at all necessary. When the step reached the foot of the stairs outside my room, it seemed to stop; and I expected every moment to see my door open spontaneously, and give admission to the original of my detested portrait. I was, however, relieved in a few seconds by hearing the descent renewed, just in the same manner, upon the staircase leading down to the drawing-rooms, and thence, after another pause, down the next flight, and so on to the hall, whence I heard no more.

Now, by the time the sound had ceased, I was wound up, as they say, to a very unpleasant pitch of excitement. I listened, but there was not a stir. I screwed up my courage to a decisive experiment—opened my door, and in a stentorian voice bawled over the banisters, "Who's there?" There was no answer but the ringing of my own voice through the empty old house,—no renewal of the movement; nothing, in short, to give my unpleasant sensations a definite direction. There is, I think, something most disagreeably disenchanting in the sound of[112] one›s own voice under such circumstances, exerted in solitude, and in vain. It redoubled my sense of isolation, and my misgivings increased on perceiving that the door, which I certainly thought I had left open, was closed behind me; in a vague alarm, lest my retreat should be cut off, I got again into my room as quickly as I could, where I remained in a state of imaginary blockade, and very uncomfortable indeed, till morning.

Next night brought no return of my bare-footed fellow-lodger; but the night following, being in my bed, and in the dark—somewhere, I suppose, about the same hour as before, I distinctly heard the old fellow again descending from the garrets.

This time I had had my punch, and the *morale* of the garrison was consequently excellent. I jumped out of bed, clutched the poker as I passed the expiring fire, and in a moment was upon the lobby. The sound had ceased by this time—the dark and chill were discouraging; and, guess my horror, when I saw, or thought I saw, a black monster, whether in the shape of a man or a bear I could not say, standing, with its back to the wall, on the lobby, facing me, with a pair of great greenish eyes shining dimly out. Now, I must be frank, and confess that the cupboard which displayed our plates and cups stood just there, though at the moment I did not recollect it. At the same time I must honestly say, that making every allowance for an excited imagination, I never could satisfy myself that I was made the dupe of my own fancy in this matter; for this apparition, after one or two shiftings of shape, as if in the act of incipient transformation, began, as it seemed on second thoughts, to advance upon me in its original form. From an instinct of terror rather than of courage, I hurled the poker, with all my force, at its head; and to the music of a horrid crash made my way[113] into my room, and double-locked the door. Then, in a minute more, I heard the horrid bare feet walk down the stairs, till the sound ceased in the hall, as on the former occasion.

If the apparition of the night before was an ocular delusion of my fancy sporting with the dark outlines of our cupboard, and if its horrid eyes were nothing but a pair of inverted teacups, I had, at all events, the satisfaction of having launched the poker with admirable effect, and in true "fancy" phrase, "knocked its two daylights into one," as the commingled fragments of my tea-service testified. I did my best to gather comfort and courage from these evidences; but it would not do. And then what could I say of those horrid bare feet, and the regular tramp, tramp, tramp, which measured the distance of the entire staircase through the solitude of my haunted dwelling, and at an hour when no good influence was stirring? Confound it!—the whole affair was abominable. I was out of spirits, and dreaded the approach of night.

It came, ushered ominously in with a thunder-storm and dull torrents of depressing rain. Earlier than usual the streets grew silent; and by twelve o'clock nothing but the comfortless pattering of the rain was to be heard.

I made myself as snug as I could. I lighted *two* candles instead of one. I forswore bed, and held myself in readiness for a sally, candle in hand; for, *coute qui coute*, I was resolved to *see* the being, if visible at all, who troubled the nightly stillness of my mansion. I was fidgetty and nervous and, tried in vain to interest myself with my books. I walked up and down my room, whistling in turn martial and hilarious music, and listening ever and anon for the dreaded noise. I sate down and stared at the square label on the solemn and reserved-looking[114] black bottle, until «FLANAGAN & CO.'S BEST OLD MALT WHISKY" grew into a sort of subdued accompaniment to all the fantastic and horrible speculations which chased one another through my brain.

Silence, meanwhile, grew more silent, and darkness darker. I listened in vain for the rumble of a vehicle, or the dull clamour of a distant row. There was nothing but the sound of a rising wind, which had succeeded the thunder-storm that had travelled over the Dublin mountains quite out of hearing. In the middle of this great city I began to feel myself alone with nature, and Heaven knows what beside. My courage was ebbing. Punch, however, which makes beasts of so many, made a man of me again—just in time to hear with tolerable nerve and firmness the lumpy, flabby, naked feet deliberately descending the stairs again.

I took a candle, not without a tremour. As I crossed the floor I tried to extemporise a prayer, but stopped short to listen, and never finished it. The steps continued. I confess I hesitated for some seconds at the door before I took heart of grace and opened it. When I peeped out the lobby was perfectly empty—there was no monster standing on the staircase; and as the detested sound ceased, I was reassured enough to venture forward nearly to the banisters. Horror of horrors! within a stair or two beneath the spot where I stood the unearthly tread smote the floor. My eye caught something in motion; it was about the size of Goliah's foot—it was grey, heavy, and flapped with a dead weight from one step to another. As I am alive, it was the most monstrous grey rat I ever beheld or imagined.

Shakespeare says—"Some men there are cannot abide a gaping pig, and some that are mad if they behold a cat." I went well-nigh out of my wits when I beheld this *rat*;[115] for, laugh at me as you may, it fixed upon me, I thought, a perfectly human expression of malice; and, as it shuffled about and looked up into my face almost from between my feet, I saw, I could swear it—I felt it then, and know it now, the infernal gaze and the accursed countenance of my old friend in the portrait, transfused into the visage of the bloated vermin before me.

I bounced into my room again with a feeling of loathing and horror I cannot describe, and locked and bolted my door as if a lion had been at the other side. D——n him or *it*; curse the portrait and its original! I felt in my soul that the rat—yes, the *rat*, the RAT I had just seen, was that evil being in masquerade, and rambling through the house upon some infernal night lark.

Next morning I was early trudging through the miry streets; and, among other transactions, posted a peremptory note recalling Tom. On my return, however, I found a note from my absent "chum," announcing his intended return next day. I was doubly rejoiced at this, because I had succeeded in getting rooms; and because the change of scene and return of my comrade were rendered specially pleasant by the last night's half ridiculous half horrible adventure.

I slept extemporaneously in my new quarters in Digges' Street that night, and next morning returned for breakfast to the haunted mansion, where I was certain Tom would call immediately on his arrival.

I was quite right—he came; and almost his first question referred to the primary object of our change of residence.

"Thank God," he said with genuine fervour, on hearing that all was arranged. "On *your* account I am delighted. As to myself, I assure you that no earthly consideration could have induced me ever again to pass a night in this disastrous old house.»[116]

"Confound the house!" I ejaculated, with a genuine mixture of fear and detestation, "we have not had a pleasant hour since we came to live here"; and so I went on, and related incidentally my adventure with the plethoric old rat.

"Well, if that were *all*," said my cousin, affecting to make light of the matter, "I don't think I should have minded it very much."

"Ay, but its eye—its countenance, my dear Tom," urged I; "if you had seen *that*, you would have felt it might be *anything* but what it seemed.»

"I inclined to think the best conjurer in such a case would be an able-bodied cat," he said, with a provoking chuckle.

"But let us hear your own adventure," I said tartly.

At this challenge he looked uneasily round him. I had poked up a very unpleasant recollection.

"You shall hear it, Dick; I'll tell it to you," he said. "Begad, sir, I should feel quite queer, though, telling it *here*, though we are too strong a body for ghosts to meddle with just now."

Though he spoke this like a joke, I think it was serious calculation. Our Hebe was in a corner of the room, packing our cracked delf tea and dinner-services in a basket. She soon suspended operations, and with mouth and eyes wide open became an absorbed listener. Tom's experiences were told nearly in these words:—

"I saw it three times, Dick—three distinct times; and I am perfectly certain it meant me some infernal harm. I was, I say, in danger—in *extreme* danger; for, if nothing else had happened, my reason would most certainly have failed me, unless I had escaped so soon. Thank God. I *did* escape.

"The first night of this hateful disturbance, I was[117] lying in the attitude of sleep, in that lumbering old bed. I hate to think of it. I was really wide awake, though I had put out my candle, and was lying as quietly as if I had been asleep; and although accidentally restless, my thoughts were running in a cheerful and agreeable channel.

"I think it must have been two o'clock at least when I thought I heard a sound in that—that odious dark recess at the far end of the bedroom. It was as if someone was drawing a piece of cord slowly along the floor, lifting it up, and dropping it softly down again in coils. I sate up once or twice in my bed, but could see nothing, so I concluded it must be mice in the wainscot. I felt no emotion graver than curiosity, and after a few minutes ceased to observe it.

"While lying in this state, strange to say; without at first a suspicion of anything supernatural, on a sudden I saw an old man, rather stout and square, in a sort of roan-red dressing-gown, and with a black cap on his head, moving stiffly and slowly in a diagonal direction, from the recess, across the floor of the bedroom, passing my bed at the foot, and entering the lumber-closet at the left. He had something under his arm; his head hung a little at one side; and, merciful God! when I saw his face."

Tom stopped for a while, and then said—

"That awful countenance, which living or dying I never can forget, disclosed what he was. Without turning to the right or left, he passed beside me, and entered the closet by the bed's head.

"While this fearful and indescribable type of death and guilt was passing, I felt that I had no more power to speak or stir than if I had been myself a corpse. For hours after it had disappeared, I was too terrified and weak to move. As soon as daylight came, I took courage, and[118] examined the room, and especially the course which the frightful intruder had seemed to take, but there was not a vestige to indicate anybody›s having passed there; no sign of any disturbing agency visible among the lumber that strewed the floor of the closet.

"I now began to recover a little. I was fagged and exhausted, and at last, overpowered by a feverish sleep. I came down late; and finding you out of spirits, on account of your dreams about the portrait, whose *original* I am now certain disclosed himself to me, I did not care to talk about the infernal vision. In fact, I was trying to persuade myself that the whole thing was an illusion, and I did not like to revive in their intensity the hated impressions of the past night—or, to risk the constancy of my scepticism, by recounting the tale of my sufferings.

"It required some nerve, I can tell you, to go to my haunted chamber next night, and lie down quietly in the same bed," continued Tom. "I did so with a degree of trepidation, which, I am not ashamed to say, a very little matter would have sufficed to stimulate to downright panic. This night, however, passed off quietly enough, as also the next; and so too did two or three more. I grew more confident, and began to fancy that I believed in the theories of spectral illusions, with which I had at first vainly tried to impose upon my convictions.

"The apparition had been, indeed, altogether anomalous. It had crossed the room without any recognition of my presence: I had not disturbed *it*, and *it* had no mission to *me*. What, then, was the imaginable use of its crossing the room in a visible shape at all? Of course it might have *been* in the closet instead of *going* there, as easily as it introduced itself into the recess without entering the chamber in a shape discernible by the senses.[119] Besides, how the deuce *had* I seen it? It was a dark night; I had no candle; there was no fire; and yet I saw it as distinctly, in colouring and outline, as ever I beheld human form! A cataleptic dream would explain it all; and I was determined that a dream it should be.

"One of the most remarkable phenomena connected with the practice of mendacity is the vast number of deliberate lies we tell ourselves, whom, of all persons, we can least expect to deceive. In all this, I need hardly tell you, Dick, I was simply lying to myself, and did not believe one word of the wretched humbug. Yet I went on, as men will do, like persevering charlatans and impostors, who tire people into credulity by the mere force of reiteration; so I hoped to win myself over at last to a comfortable scepticism about the ghost.

"He had not appeared a second time—that certainly was a comfort; and what, after all, did I care for him, and his queer old toggery and strange looks? Not a fig! I was nothing the worse for having seen him, and a good story the better. So I tumbled into bed, put out my candle, and, cheered by a loud drunken quarrel in the back lane, went fast asleep.

"From this deep slumber I awoke with a start. I knew I had had a horrible dream; but what it was I could not remember. My heart was thumping furiously; I felt bewildered and feverish; I sate up in the bed and looked about the room. A broad flood of moonlight came in through the curtainless window; everything was as I had last seen it; and though the domestic squabble in the back lane was, unhappily for me, allayed, I yet could hear a pleasant fellow singing, on his way home, the then popular comic ditty called, 'Murphy Delany.' Taking advantage of this diversion I lay down again, with my face towards the fireplace, and closing my eyes, did my[120] best to think of nothing else but the song, which was every moment growing fainter in the distance:—

' 'Twas Murphy Delany, so funny and frisky,Stept into a shebeen shop to get his skin full;He reeled out again pretty well lined with whiskey,As fresh as a shamrock, as blind as a bull.'

"The singer, whose condition I dare say resembled that of his hero, was soon too far off to regale my ears any more; and as his music died away, I myself sank into a doze, neither sound nor refreshing. Somehow the song had got into my head, and I went meandering on through the adventures of my respectable fellow-countryman, who, on emerging from the 'shebeen shop,' fell into a river, from which he was fished up to be 'sat upon' by a coroner's jury, who having learned from a 'horse-doctor' that he was 'dead as a door-nail, so there was an end,' returned their verdict accordingly, just as he returned to his senses, when an angry altercation and a pitched battle between the body and the coroner winds up the lay with due spirit and pleasantry.

"Through this ballad I continued with a weary monotony to plod, down to the very last line, and then *da capo*, and so on, in my uncomfortable half-sleep, for how long, I can't conjecture. I found myself at last, however, muttering, '*dead* as a door-nail, so there was an end›; and something like another voice within me, seemed to say, very faintly, but sharply, ‹dead! dead! *dead*! and may the Lord have mercy on your soul!' and instantaneously I was wide awake, and staring right before me from the pillow.

"Now—will you believe it, Dick?—I saw the same accursed figure standing full front, and gazing at me with its stony and fiendish countenance, not two yards from the bedside."[121]

Tom stopped here, and wiped the perspiration from his face. I felt very queer. The girl was as pale as Tom; and, assembled as we were in the very scene of these adventures, we were all, I dare say, equally grateful for the clear daylight and the resuming bustle out of doors.

"For about three seconds only I saw it plainly; then it grew indistinct; but, for a long time, there was something like a column of dark vapour where it had been standing, between me and the wall; and I felt sure that he was still there. After a good while, this appearance went too. I took my clothes down-stairs to the hall, and dressed there, with the door half open; then went out into the street, and walked about the town till morning, when I came back, in a miserable state of nervousness and exhaustion. I was such a fool, Dick, as to be ashamed to tell you how I came to be so upset. I thought you would laugh at me; especially as I had always talked philosophy, and treated *your* ghosts with contempt. I concluded you would give me no quarter; and so kept my tale of horror to myself.

"Now, Dick, you will hardly believe me, when I assure you, that for many nights after this last experience, I did not go to my room at all. I used to sit up for a while in the drawing-room after you had gone up to your bed; and then steal down softly to the hall-door, let myself out, and sit in the 'Robin Hood' tavern until the last guest went off; and then I got through the night like a sentry, pacing the streets till morning.

"For more than a week I never slept in bed. I sometimes had a snooze on a form in the 'Robin Hood,' and sometimes a nap in a chair during the day; but regular sleep I had absolutely none.

"I was quite resolved that we should get into another house; but I could not bring myself to tell you the reason,[122] and I somehow put it off from day to day, although my life was, during every hour of this procrastination, rendered as miserable as that of a felon with the constables on his track. I was growing absolutely ill from this wretched mode of life.

"One afternoon I determined to enjoy an hour's sleep upon your bed. I hated mine; so that I had never, except in a stealthy visit every day to unmake it, lest Martha should discover the secret of my nightly absence, entered the ill-omened chamber.

"As ill-luck would have it, you had locked your bedroom, and taken away the key. I went into my own to unsettle the bed-clothes, as usual, and give the bed the appearance of having been slept in. Now, a variety of circumstances concurred to bring about the dreadful scene through which I was that night to pass. In the first place, I was literally overpowered with fatigue, and longing for sleep; in the next place, the effect of this extreme exhaustion upon my nerves resembled that of a narcotic, and rendered me less susceptible than, perhaps I should in any other condition have been, of the exciting fears which had become habitual to me. Then again, a little bit of the window was open, a pleasant freshness pervaded the room, and, to crown all, the cheerful sun of day was making the room quite pleasant. What was to prevent my enjoying an hour's nap *here*? The whole air was resonant with the cheerful hum of life, and the broad matter-of-fact light of day filled every corner of the room.

"I yielded—stifling my qualms—to the almost over-powering temptation; and merely throwing off my coat, and loosening my cravat, I lay down, limiting myself to *half*-an-hour's doze in the unwonted enjoyment of a feather bed, a coverlet, and a bolster.

"It was horribly insidious; and the demon, no doubt,[123] marked my infatuated preparations. Dolt that I was, I fancied, with mind and body worn out for want of sleep, and an arrear of a full week's rest to my credit, that such measure as *half*-an-hour's sleep, in such a situation, was possible. My sleep was death-like, long, and dreamless.

"Without a start or fearful sensation of any kind, I waked gently, but completely. It was, as you have good reason to remember, long past midnight—I believe, about two o'clock. When sleep has been deep and long enough to satisfy nature thoroughly, one often wakens in this way, suddenly, tranquilly, and completely.

"There was a figure seated in that lumbering, old sofa-chair, near the fireplace. Its back was rather towards me, but I could not be mistaken; it turned slowly round, and, merciful heavens! there was the stony face, with its infernal lineaments of malignity and despair, gloating on me. There was now no doubt as to its consciousness of my presence, and the hellish malice with which it was animated, for it arose, and drew close to the bedside. There was a rope about its neck, and the other end, coiled up, it held stiffly in its hand.

"My good angel nerved me for this horrible crisis. I remained for some seconds transfixed by the gaze of this tremendous phantom. He came close to the bed, and appeared on the point of mounting upon it. The next instant I was upon the floor at the far side, and in a moment more was, I don't know how, upon the lobby.

"But the spell was not yet broken; the valley of the shadow of death was not yet traversed. The abhorred phantom was before me there; it was standing near the banisters, stooping a little, and with one end of the rope round its own neck, was poising a noose at the other, as if to throw over mine; and while engaged in this baleful pantomime, it wore a smile so sensual, so unspeakably[124] dreadful, that my senses were nearly overpowered, I saw and remember nothing more, until I found myself in your room.

"I had a wonderful escape, Dick—there is no disputing *that*—an escape for which, while I live, I shall bless the mercy of heaven. No one can conceive or imagine what it is for flesh and blood to stand in the presence of such a thing, but one who has had the terrific experience. Dick, Dick, a shadow has passed over me—a chill has crossed my blood and marrow, and I will never be the same again—never, Dick—never!"

Our handmaid, a mature girl of two-and-fifty, as I have said, stayed her hand, as Tom's story proceeded, and by little and little drew near to us, with open mouth, and her brows contracted over her little, beady black eyes, till stealing a glance over her shoulder now and then, she established herself close behind us. During the relation, she had made various earnest comments, in an undertone; but these and her ejaculations, for the sake of brevity and simplicity, I have omitted in my narration.

"It's often I heard tell of it," she now said, "but I never believed it rightly till now—though, indeed, why should not I? Does not my mother, down there in the lane, know quare stories, God bless us, beyant telling about it? But you ought not to have slept in the back bedroom. She was loath to let me be going in and out of that room even in the day time, let alone for any Christian to spend the night in it; for sure she says it was his own bedroom."

"*Whose* own bedroom?» we asked, in a breath.

"Why, *his*—the ould Judge's—Judge Horrock's, to be sure, God rest his sowl"; and she looked fearfully round.

"Amen!" I muttered. "But did he die there?"

"Die there! No, not quite *there*," she said. "Shure,[125] was not it over the bannisters he hung himself, the ould sinner, God be merciful to us all? and was not it in the alcove they found the handles of the skipping-rope cut off, and the knife where he was settling the cord, God bless us, to hang himself with? It was his housekeeper›s daughter owned the rope, my mother often told me, and the child never throve after, and used to be starting up out of her sleep, and screeching in the night time, wid dhrames and frights that cum an her; and they said how it was the speerit of the ould Judge that was tormentin› her; and she used to be roaring and yelling out to hould back the big ould fellow with the crooked neck; and then she›d screech ‹Oh, the master! the master! he›s stampin› at me, and beckoning to me! Mother, darling, don›t let me go!› And so the poor crathure died at last, and the docthers said it was wather on the brain, for it was all they could say.»

"How long ago was all this?" I asked.

"Oh, then, how would I know?" she answered. "But it must be a wondherful long time ago, for the housekeeper was an ould woman, with a pipe in her mouth, and not a tooth left, and better nor eighty years ould when my mother was first married; and they said she was a rale buxom, fine-dressed woman when the ould Judge come to his end; an', indeed, my mother's not far from eighty years ould herself this day; and what made it worse for the unnatural ould villain, God rest his soul, to frighten the little girl out of the world the way he did, was what was mostly thought and believed by every one. My mother says how the poor little crathure was his own child; for he was by all accounts an ould villain every way, an' the hangin'est judge that ever was known in Ireland's ground."

"From what you said about the danger of sleeping in[126] that bedroom,» said I, «I suppose there were stories about the ghost having appeared there to others.»

"Well, there *was* things said—quare things, surely,» she answered, as it seemed, with some reluctance. «And why would not there? Sure was it not up in that same room he slept for more than twenty years? and was it not in the *alcove* he got the rope ready that done his own business at last, the way he done many a betther man›s in his lifetime?—and was not the body lying in the same bed after death, and put in the coffin there, too, and carried out to his grave from it in Pether›s churchyard, after the coroner was done? But there was quare stories—my mother has them all—about how one Nicholas Spaight got into trouble on the head of it.»

"And what did they say of this Nicholas Spaight?" I asked.

"Oh, for that matther, it's soon told," she answered.

And she certainly did relate a very strange story, which so piqued my curiosity, that I took occasion to visit the ancient lady, her mother, from whom I learned many very curious particulars. Indeed, I am tempted to tell the tale, but my fingers are weary, and I must defer it. But if you wish to hear it another time, I shall do my best.[1]

When we had heard the strange tale I have *not* told you, we put one or two further questions to her about the alleged spectral visitations, to which the house had, ever since the death of the wicked old Judge, been subjected.

"No one ever had luck in it," she told us. "There was always cross accidents, sudden deaths, and short times in it. The first that tuck it was a family—I forget their name—but at any rate there was two young ladies and their papa. He was about sixty, and a stout healthy [127]gentleman as you'd wish to see at that age. Well, he slept in that unlucky back bedroom; and, God between us an' harm! sure enough he was found dead one morning, half out of the bed, with his head as black as a sloe, and swelled like a puddin', hanging down near the floor. It was a fit, they said. He was as dead as a mackerel, and so *he* could not say what it was; but the ould people was all sure that it was nothing at all but the ould Judge, God bless us! that frightened him out of his senses and his life together.

"Some time after there was a rich old maiden lady took the house. I don't know which room *she* slept in, but she lived alone; and at any rate, one morning, the servants going down early to their work, found her sitting on the passage-stairs, shivering and talkin› to herself, quite mad; and never a word more could any of *them* or her friends get from her ever afterwards but, ‹Don›t ask me to go, for I promised to wait for him.› They never made out from her who it was she meant by *him*, but of course those that knew all about the ould house were at no loss for the meaning of all that happened to her.

"Then afterwards, when the house was let out in lodgings, there was Micky Byrne that took the same room, with his wife and three little children; and sure I heard Mrs. Byrne myself telling how the children used to be lifted up in the bed at night, she could not see by what mains; and how they were starting and screeching every hour, just all as one as the housekeeper's little girl that died, till at last one night poor Micky had a dhrop in him, the way he used now and again; and what do you think in the middle of the night he thought he heard a noise on the stairs, and being in liquor, nothing less id do him but out he must go himself to see what was wrong. Well, after that, all she ever heard of him was himself sayin',[128] ‹Oh, God!› and a tumble that shook the very house; and there, sure enough, he was lying on the lower stairs under the lobby, with his neck smashed double undher him, where he was flung over the banisters.»

Then the handmaiden added—

"I'll go down to the lane, and send up Joe Gavvey to pack up the rest of the taythings, and bring all the things across to your new lodgings."

And so we all sallied out together, each of us breathing more freely, I have no doubt, as we crossed that ill-omened threshold for the last time.

Now, I may add thus much, in compliance with the immemorial usage of the realm of fiction, which sees the hero not only through his adventures, but fairly out of the world. You must have perceived that what the flesh, blood, and bone hero of romance proper is to the regular compounder of fiction, this old house of brick, wood, and mortar is to the humble recorder of this true tale. I, therefore, relate, as in duty bound, the catastrophe which ultimately befell it, which was simply this—that about two years subsequently to my story it was taken by a quack doctor, who called himself Baron Duhlstoerf, and filled the parlour windows with bottles of indescribable horrors preserved in brandy, and the newspapers with the usual grandiloquent and mendacious advertisements. This gentleman among his virtues did not reckon sobriety, and one night, being overcome with much wine, he set fire to his bed curtains, partially burned himself, and totally consumed the house. It was afterwards rebuilt, and for a time an undertaker established himself in the premises.

I have now told you my own and Tom's adventures, together with some valuable collateral particulars; and having acquitted myself of my engagement, I wish you a very good night, and pleasant dreams.

7
GHOST STORIES OF CHAPELIZOD

Anonymous in the *Dublin University Magazine* (1851). We see Le Fanu beginning to be attracted by the old village, a suburb of Dublin, which he made the scene of what is perhaps his best novel, *The House by the Churchyard* (1862-3).

Take my word for it, there is no such thing as an ancient village, especially if it has seen better days, unillustrated by its legends of terror. You might as well expect to find a decayed cheese without mites, or an old house without rats, as an antique and dilapidated town without an authentic population of goblins. Now, although this class of inhabitants are in nowise amenable to the police authorities, yet, as their demeanour directly affects the comforts of her Majesty's subjects, I cannot but regard it as a grave omission that the public have hitherto been left without any statistical returns of their numbers, activity, etc., etc. And I am persuaded that a Commission to inquire into and report upon the numerical strength, habits, haunts, etc., etc., of supernatural agents resident in Ireland, would be a great deal more innocent and entertaining than half the Commissions for which the country pays, and at least as instructive. This I say, more from a sense of duty, and to deliver my mind of a[130] grave truth, than with any hope of seeing the suggestion adopted. But, I am sure, my readers will deplore with me that the comprehensive powers of belief, and apparently illimitable leisure, possessed by parliamentary commissions of inquiry, should never have been applied to the subject I have named, and that the collection of that species of information should be confided to the gratuitous and desultory labours of individuals, who, like myself, have other occupations to attend to. This, however, by the way.

Among the village outposts of Dublin, Chapelizod once held a considerable, if not a foremost rank. Without mentioning its connexion with the history of the great Kilmainham Preceptory of the Knights of St. John, it will be enough to remind the reader of its ancient and celebrated Castle, not one vestige of which now remains, and of the fact that it was for, we believe, some centuries, the summer residence of the Viceroys of Ireland. The circumstance of its being up, we believe, to the period at which that corps was disbanded, the head-quarters of the Royal Irish Artillery, gave it also a consequence of an humbler, but not less substantial kind. With these advantages in its favour, it is not wonderful that the town exhibited at one time an air of substantial and semi-aristocratic prosperity unknown to Irish villages in modern times.

A broad street, with a well-paved foot-path, and houses as lofty as were at that time to be found in the fashionable streets of Dublin; a goodly stone-fronted barrack; an ancient church, vaulted beneath, and with a tower clothed from its summit to its base with the richest ivy; an humble Roman Catholic chapel; a steep bridge spanning the Liffey, and a great old mill at the near end of it, were the principal features of the town. These, or at[131] least most of them, remain still, but the greater part in a very changed and forlorn condition. Some of them indeed are superseded, though not obliterated by modern erections, such as the bridge, the chapel, and the church in part; the rest forsaken by the order who originally raised them, and delivered up to poverty, and in some cases to absolute decay.

The village lies in the lap of the rich and wooded valley of the Liffey, and is overlooked by the high grounds of the beautiful Phoenix Park on the one side, and by the ridge of the Palmerstown hills on the other. Its situation, therefore, is eminently picturesque; and factory-fronts and chimneys notwithstanding, it has, I think, even in its decay, a sort of melancholy picturesqueness of its own. Be that as it may, I mean to relate two or three stories of that sort which may be read with very good effect by a blazing fire on a shrewd winter's night, and are all directly connected with the altered and somewhat melancholy little town I have named. The first I shall relate concerns

THE VILLAGE BULLY.

About thirty years ago there lived in the town of Chapelizod an ill-conditioned fellow of herculean strength, well known throughout the neighbourhood by the title of Bully Larkin. In addition to his remarkable physical superiority, this fellow had acquired a degree of skill as a pugilist which alone would have made him formidable. As it was, he was the autocrat of the village, and carried not the sceptre in vain. Conscious of his superiority, and perfectly secure of impunity, he lorded it over his fellows in a spirit of cowardly and brutal insolence, which made him hated even more profoundly than he was feared.

Upon more than one occasion he had deliberately forced quarrels upon men whom he had singled out for the exhibition of his savage prowess; and in every encounter his over-matched antagonist had received an amount of "punishment" which edified and appalled the spectators, and in some instances left ineffaceable scars and lasting injuries after it.

Bully Larkin's pluck had never been fairly tried. For, owing to his prodigious superiority in weight, strength, and skill, his victories had always been certain and easy; and in proportion to the facility with which he uniformly smashed an antagonist, his pugnacity and insolence were inflamed. He thus became an odious nuisance in the neighbourhood, and the terror of every mother who had a son, and of every wife who had a husband who possessed a spirit to resent insult, or the smallest confidence in his own pugilistic capabilities.

Now it happened that there was a young fellow named Ned Moran—better known by the soubriquet of "Long Ned," from his slender, lathy proportions—at that time living in the town. He was, in truth, a mere lad, nineteen years of age, and fully twelve years younger than the stalwart bully. This, however, as the reader will see, secured for him no exemption from the dastardly provocations of the ill-conditioned pugilist. Long Ned, in an evil hour, had thrown eyes of affection upon a certain buxom damsel, who, notwithstanding Bully Larkin's amorous rivalry, inclined to reciprocate them.

I need not say how easily the spark of jealousy, once kindled, is blown into a flame, and how naturally, in a coarse and ungoverned nature, it explodes in acts of violence and outrage.

"The bully" watched his opportunity, and contrived to provoke Ned Moran, while drinking in a public-house[133] with a party of friends, into an altercation, in the course of which he failed not to put such insults upon his rival as manhood could not tolerate. Long Ned, though a simple, good-natured sort of fellow, was by no means deficient in spirit, and retorted in a tone of defiance which edified the more timid, and gave his opponent the opportunity he secretly coveted.

Bully Larkin challenged the heroic youth, whose pretty face he had privately consigned to the mangling and bloody discipline he was himself so capable of administering. The quarrel, which he had himself contrived to get up, to a certain degree covered the ill blood and malignant premeditation which inspired his proceedings, and Long Ned, being full of generous ire and whiskey punch, accepted the gauge of battle on the instant. The whole party, accompanied by a mob of idle men and boys, and in short by all who could snatch a moment from the calls of business, proceeded in slow procession through the old gate into the Phoenix Park, and mounting the hill overlooking the town, selected near its summit a level spot on which to decide the quarrel.

The combatants stripped, and a child might have seen in the contrast presented by the slight, lank form and limbs of the lad, and the muscular and massive build of his veteran antagonist, how desperate was the chance of Poor Ned Moran.

"Seconds" and "bottle-holders"—selected of course for their love of the game—were appointed, and "the fight" commenced.

I will not shock my readers with a description of the cool-blooded butchery that followed. The result of the combat was what anybody might have predicted. At the eleventh round, poor Ned refused to "give in"; the brawny pugilist, unhurt, in good wind, and pale with[134] concentrated and as yet unslaked revenge, had the gratification of seeing his opponent seated upon his second›s knee, unable to hold up his head, his left arm disabled; his face a bloody, swollen, and shapeless mass; his breast scarred and bloody, and his whole body panting and quivering with rage and exhaustion.

"Give in Ned, my boy," cried more than one of the bystanders.

"Never, never," shrieked he, with a voice hoarse and choking.

Time being "up," his second placed him on his feet again. Blinded with his own blood, panting and staggering, he presented but a helpless mark for the blows of his stalwart opponent. It was plain that a touch would have been sufficient to throw him to the earth. But Larkin had no notion of letting him off so easily. He closed with him without striking a blow (the effect of which, prematurely dealt, would have been to bring him at once to the ground, and so put an end to the combat), and getting his battered and almost senseless head under his arm, fast in that peculiar "fix" known to the fancy pleasantly by the name of "chancery," he held him firmly, while with monotonous and brutal strokes he beat his fist, as it seemed, almost into his face. A cry of "shame" broke from the crowd, for it was plain that the beaten man was now insensible, and supported only by the herculean arm of the bully. The round and the fight ended by his hurling him upon the ground, falling upon him at the same time with his knee upon his chest.

The bully rose, wiping the perspiration from his white face with his blood-stained hands, but Ned lay stretched and motionless upon the grass. It was impossible to get him upon his legs for another round. So he was carried down, just as he was, to the pond which then lay close[135] to the old Park gate, and his head and body were washed beside it. Contrary to the belief of all he was not dead. He was carried home, and after some months to a certain extent recovered. But he never held up his head again, and before the year was over he had died of consumption. Nobody could doubt how the disease had been induced, but there was no actual proof to connect the cause and effect, and the ruffian Larkin escaped the vengeance of the law. A strange retribution, however, awaited him.

After the death of Long Ned, he became less quarrelsome than before, but more sullen and reserved. Some said "he took it to heart," and others, that his conscience was not at ease about it. Be this as it may, however, his health did not suffer by reason of his presumed agitations, nor was his worldly prosperity marred by the blasting curses with which poor Moran's enraged mother pursued him; on the contrary, he had rather risen in the world, and obtained regular and well-remunerated employment from the Chief Secretary's gardener, at the other side of the Park. He still lived in Chapelizod, whither, on the close of his day's work, he used to return across the Fifteen Acres.

It was about three years after the catastrophe we have mentioned, and late in the autumn, when, one night, contrary to his habit, he did not appear at the house where he lodged, neither had he been seen anywhere, during the evening, in the village. His hours of return had been so very regular, that his absence excited considerable surprise, though, of course, no actual alarm; and, at the usual hour, the house was closed for the night, and the absent lodger consigned to the mercy of the elements, and the care of his presiding star. Early in the morning, however, he was found lying in a state of utter helplessness upon the slope immediately overlooking the Chapelizod[136] gate. He had been smitten with a paralytic stroke: his right side was dead; and it was many weeks before he had recovered his speech sufficiently to make himself at all understood.

He then made the following relation:—He had been detained, it appeared, later than usual, and darkness had closed before he commenced his homeward walk across the Park. It was a moonlit night, but masses of ragged clouds were slowly drifting across the heavens. He had not encountered a human figure, and no sounds but the softened rush of the wind sweeping through bushes and hollows met his ear. These wild and monotonous sounds, and the utter solitude which surrounded him, did not, however, excite any of those uneasy sensations which are ascribed to superstition, although he said he did feel depressed, or, in his own phraseology, "lonesome." Just as he crossed the brow of the hill which shelters the town of Chapelizod, the moon shone out for some moments with unclouded lustre, and his eye, which happened to wander by the shadowy enclosures which lay at the foot of the slope, was arrested by the sight of a human figure climbing, with all the haste of one pursued, over the churchyard wall, and running up the steep ascent directly towards him. Stories of "resurrectionists" crossed his recollection, as he observed this suspicious-looking figure. But he began, momentarily, to be aware with a sort of fearful instinct which he could not explain, that the running figure was directing his steps, with a sinister purpose, towards himself.

The form was that of a man with a loose coat about him, which, as he ran, he disengaged, and as well as Larkin could see, for the moon was again wading in clouds, threw from him. The figure thus advanced until within some two score yards of him, it arrested its[137] speed, and approached with a loose, swaggering gait. The moon again shone out bright and clear, and, gracious God! what was the spectacle before him? He saw as distinctly as if he had been presented there in the flesh, Ned Moran, himself, stripped naked from the waist upward, as if for pugilistic combat, and drawing towards him in silence. Larkin would have shouted, prayed, cursed, fled across the Park, but he was absolutely powerless; the apparition stopped within a few steps, and leered on him with a ghastly mimicry of the defiant stare with which pugilists strive to cow one another before combat. For a time, which he could not so much as conjecture, he was held in the fascination of that unearthly gaze, and at last the thing, whatever it was, on a sudden swaggered close up to him with extended palms. With an impulse of horror, Larkin put out his hand to keep the figure off, and their palms touched—at least, so he believed—for a thrill of unspeakable agony, running through his arm, pervaded his entire frame, and he fell senseless to the earth.

Though Larkin lived for many years after, his punishment was terrible. He was incurably maimed; and being unable to work, he was forced, for existence, to beg alms of those who had once feared and flattered him. He suffered, too, increasingly, under his own horrible interpretation of the preternatural encounter which was the beginning of all his miseries. It was vain to endeavour to shake his faith in the reality of the apparition, and equally vain, as some compassionately did, to try to persuade him that the greeting with which his vision closed was intended, while inflicting a temporary trial, to signify a compensating reconciliation.

"No, no," he used to say, "all won't do. I know the meaning of it well enough; it is a challenge to meet[138] him in the other world—in Hell, where I am going—that›s what it means, and nothing else.»

And so, miserable and refusing comfort, he lived on for some years, and then died, and was buried in the same narrow churchyard which contains the remains of his victim.

I need hardly say, how absolute was the faith of the honest inhabitants, at the time when I heard the story, in the reality of the preternatural summons which, through the portals of terror, sickness, and misery, had summoned Bully Larkin to his long, last home, and that, too, upon the very ground on which he had signalised the guiltiest triumph of his violent and vindictive career.

I recollect another story of the preternatural sort, which made no small sensation, some five-and-thirty years ago, among the good gossips of the town; and, with your leave, courteous reader, I shall relate it.

THE SEXTON'S ADVENTURE.

Those who remember Chapelizod a quarter of a century ago, or more, may possibly recollect the parish sexton. Bob Martin was held much in awe by truant boys who sauntered into the churchyard on Sundays, to read the tomb-stones, or play leap frog over them, or climb the ivy in search of bats or sparrows' nests, or peep into the mysterious aperture under the eastern window, which opened a dim perspective of descending steps losing themselves among profounder darkness, where lidless coffins gaped horribly among tattered velvet, bones, and dust, which time and mortality had strewn there. Of such horribly curious, and otherwise enterprising juveniles, Bob was, of course, the special scourge and terror. But terrible as was the official aspect of the sexton, and re[139]pugnant as his lank form, clothed in rusty, sable vesture, his small, frosty visage, suspicious grey eyes, and rusty, brown scratch-wig, might appear to all notions of genial frailty; it was yet true, that Bob Martin's severe morality sometimes nodded, and that Bacchus did not always solicit him in vain.

Bob had a curious mind, a memory well stored with "merry tales," and tales of terror. His profession familiarised him with graves and goblins, and his tastes with weddings, wassail, and sly frolics of all sorts. And as his personal recollections ran back nearly three score years into the perspective of the village history, his fund of local anecdote was copious, accurate, and edifying.

As his ecclesiastical revenues were by no means considerable, he was not unfrequently obliged, for the indulgence of his tastes, to arts which were, at the best, undignified.

He frequently invited himself when his entertainers had forgotten to do so; he dropped in accidentally upon small drinking parties of his acquaintance in public houses, and entertained them with stories, queer or terrible, from his inexhaustible reservoir, never scrupling to accept an acknowledgment in the shape of hot whiskey-punch, or whatever else was going.

There was at that time a certain atrabilious publican, called Philip Slaney, established in a shop nearly opposite the old turnpike. This man was not, when left to himself, immoderately given to drinking; but being naturally of a saturnine complexion, and his spirits constantly requiring a fillip, he acquired a prodigious liking for Bob Martin's company. The sexton's society, in fact, gradually became the solace of his existence, and he seemed to lose his constitutional melancholy in the fascination of his sly jokes and marvellous stories.[140]

This intimacy did not redound to the prosperity or reputation of the convivial allies. Bob Martin drank a good deal more punch than was good for his health, or consistent with the character of an ecclesiastical functionary. Philip Slaney, too, was drawn into similar indulgences, for it was hard to resist the genial seductions of his gifted companion; and as he was obliged to pay for both, his purse was believed to have suffered even more than his head and liver.

Be this as it may, Bob Martin had the credit of having made a drunkard of "black Phil Slaney"—for by this cognomen was he distinguished; and Phil Slaney had also the reputation of having made the sexton, if possible, a "bigger bliggard" than ever. Under these circumstances, the accounts of the concern opposite the turnpike became somewhat entangled; and it came to pass one drowsy summer morning, the weather being at once sultry and cloudy, that Phil Slaney went into a small back parlour, where he kept his books, and which commanded, through its dirty window-panes, a full view of a dead wall, and having bolted the door, he took a loaded pistol, and clapping the muzzle in his mouth, blew the upper part of his skull through the ceiling.

This horrid catastrophe shocked Bob Martin extremely; and partly on this account, and partly because having been, on several late occasions, found at night in a state of abstraction, bordering on insensibility, upon the high road, he had been threatened with dismissal; and, as some said, partly also because of the difficulty of finding anybody to "treat" him as poor Phil Slaney used to do, he for a time forswore alcohol in all its combinations, and became an eminent example of temperance and sobriety.

Bob observed his good resolutions, greatly to the[141] comfort of his wife, and the edification of the neighbourhood, with tolerable punctuality. He was seldom tipsy, and never drunk, and was greeted by the better part of society with all the honours of the prodigal son.

Now it happened, about a year after the grisly event we have mentioned, that the curate having received, by the post, due notice of a funeral to be consummated in the churchyard of Chapelizod, with certain instructions respecting the site of the grave, despatched a summons for Bob Martin, with a view to communicate to that functionary these official details.

It was a lowering autumn night: piles of lurid thunder-clouds, slowly rising from the earth, had loaded the sky with a solemn and boding canopy of storm. The growl of the distant thunder was heard afar off upon the dull, still air, and all nature seemed, as it were, hushed and cowering under the oppressive influence of the approaching tempest.

It was past nine o'clock when Bob, putting on his official coat of seedy black, prepared to attend his professional superior.

"Bobby, darlin'," said his wife, before she delivered the hat she held in her hand to his keeping, "sure you won't, Bobby, darlin'—you won't—you know what."

"I *don't* know what,» he retorted, smartly, grasping at his hat.

"You won't be throwing up the little finger, Bobby, acushla?" she said, evading his grasp.

"Arrah, why would I, woman? there, give me my hat, will you?"

"But won't you promise me, Bobby darlin'—won't you, alanna?"

"Ay, ay, to be sure I will—why not?—there, give me my hat, and let me go."[142]

"Ay, but you're not promisin', Bobby, mavourneen; you're not promisin' all the time."

"Well, divil carry me if I drink a drop till I come back again," said the sexton, angrily; "will that do you? And *now* will you give me my hat?»

"Here it is, darlin'," she said, "and God send you safe back."

And with this parting blessing she closed the door upon his retreating figure, for it was now quite dark, and resumed her knitting till his return, very much relieved; for she thought he had of late been oftener tipsy than was consistent with his thorough reformation, and feared the allurements of the half dozen "publics" which he had at that time to pass on his way to the other end of the town.

They were still open, and exhaled a delicious reek of whiskey, as Bob glided wistfully by them; but he stuck his hands in his pockets and looked the other way, whistling resolutely, and filling his mind with the image of the curate and anticipations of his coming fee. Thus he steered his morality safely through these rocks of offence, and reached the curate's lodging in safety.

He had, however, an unexpected sick call to attend, and was not at home, so that Bob Martin had to sit in the hall and amuse himself with the devil's tattoo until his return. This, unfortunately, was very long delayed, and it must have been fully twelve o'clock when Bob Martin set out upon his homeward way. By this time the storm had gathered to a pitchy darkness, the bellowing thunder was heard among the rocks and hollows of the Dublin mountains, and the pale, blue lightning shone upon the staring fronts of the houses.

By this time, too, every door was closed; but as Bob trudged homeward, his eye mechanically sought the public-house which had once belonged to Phil Slaney.[143] A faint light was making its way through the shutters and the glass panes over the doorway, which made a sort of dull, foggy halo about the front of the house.

As Bob's eyes had become accustomed to the obscurity by this time, the light in question was quite sufficient to enable him to see a man in a sort of loose riding-coat seated upon a bench which, at that time, was fixed under the window of the house. He wore his hat very much over his eyes, and was smoking a long pipe. The outline of a glass and a quart bottle were also dimly traceable beside him; and a large horse saddled, but faintly discernible, was patiently awaiting his master's leisure.

There was something odd, no doubt, in the appearance of a traveller refreshing himself at such an hour in the open street; but the sexton accounted for it easily by supposing that, on the closing of the house for the night, he had taken what remained of his refection to the place where he was now discussing it al fresco.

At another time Bob might have saluted the stranger as he passed with a friendly "good night"; but, somehow, he was out of humour and in no genial mood, and was about passing without any courtesy of the sort, when the stranger, without taking the pipe from his mouth, raised the bottle, and with it beckoned him familiarly, while, with a sort of lurch of the head and shoulders, and at the same time shifting his seat to the end of the bench, he pantomimically invited him to share his seat and his cheer. There was a divine fragrance of whiskey about the spot, and Bob half relented; but he remembered his promise just as he began to waver, and said:

"No, I thank you, sir, I can't stop to-night."

The stranger beckoned with vehement welcome, and pointed to the vacant space on the seat beside him.

"I thank you for your polite offer," said Bob, "but[144] it›s what I›m too late as it is, and haven›t time to spare, so I wish you a good night.»

The traveller jingled the glass against the neck of the bottle, as if to intimate that he might at least swallow a dram without losing time. Bob was mentally quite of the same opinion; but, though his mouth watered, he remembered his promise, and shaking his head with incorruptible resolution, walked on.

The stranger, pipe in mouth, rose from his bench, the bottle in one hand, and the glass in the other, and followed at the Sexton's heels, his dusky horse keeping close in his wake.

There was something suspicious and unaccountable in this importunity.

Bob quickened his pace, but the stranger followed close. The sexton began to feel queer, and turned about. His pursuer was behind, and still inviting him with impatient gestures to taste his liquor.

"I told you before," said Bob, who was both angry and frightened, "that I would not taste it, and that's enough. I don't want to have anything to say to you or your bottle; and in God's name," he added, more vehemently, observing that he was approaching still closer, "fall back and don't be tormenting me this way."

These words, as it seemed, incensed the stranger, for he shook the bottle with violent menace at Bob Martin; but, notwithstanding this gesture of defiance, he suffered the distance between them to increase. Bob, however, beheld him dogging him still in the distance, for his pipe shed a wonderful red glow, which duskily illuminated his entire figure like the lurid atmosphere of a meteor.

"I wish the devil had his own, my boy," muttered the excited sexton, "and I know well enough where you'd be."

The next time he looked over his shoulder, to his dismay he observed the importunate stranger as close as ever upon his track.

"Confound you," cried the man of skulls and shovels, almost beside himself with rage and horror, "what is it you want of me?"

The stranger appeared more confident, and kept wagging his head and extending both glass and bottle toward him as he drew near, and Bob Martin heard the horse snorting as it followed in the dark.

"Keep it to yourself, whatever it is, for there is neither grace nor luck about you," cried Bob Martin, freezing with terror; "leave me alone, will you."

And he fumbled in vain among the seething confusion of his ideas for a prayer or an exorcism. He quickened his pace almost to a run; he was now close to his own door, under the impending bank by the river side.

"Let me in, let me in, for God's sake; Molly, open the door," he cried, as he ran to the threshold, and leant his back against the plank. His pursuer confronted him upon the road; the pipe was no longer in his mouth, but the dusky red glow still lingered round him. He uttered some inarticulate cavernous sounds, which were wolfish and indescribable, while he seemed employed in pouring out a glass from the bottle.

The sexton kicked with all his force against the door, and cried at the same time with a despairing voice.

"In the name of God Almighty, once for all, leave me alone."

His pursuer furiously flung the contents of the bottle at Bob Martin; but instead of fluid it issued out in a scream of flame, which expanded and whirled round them, and for a moment they were both enveloped in a faint blaze; at the same instant a sudden gust whisked off[146] the stranger›s hat, and the sexton beheld that his skull was roofless. For an instant he beheld the gaping aperture, black and shattered, and then he fell senseless into his own doorway, which his affrighted wife had just unbarred.

I need hardly give my reader the key to this most intelligible and authentic narrative. The traveller was acknowledged by all to have been the spectre of the suicide, called up by the Evil One to tempt the convivial sexton into a violation of his promise, sealed, as it was, by an imprecation. Had he succeeded, no doubt the dusky steed, which Bob had seen saddled in attendance, was destined to have carried back a double burden to the place from whence he came.

As an attestation of the reality of this visitation, the old thorn tree which overhung the doorway was found in the morning to have been blasted with the infernal fires which had issued from the bottle, just as if a thunder-bolt had scorched it.

The moral of the above tale is upon the surface, apparent, and, so to speak, *self-acting*—a circumstance which happily obviates the necessity of our discussing it together. Taking our leave, therefore, of honest Bob Martin, who now sleeps soundly in the same solemn dormitory where, in his day, he made so many beds for others, I come to a legend of the

Royal Irish Artillery, whose head-quarters were for so long a time in the town of Chapelizod. I don't mean to say that I cannot tell a great many more stories, equally authentic and marvellous, touching this old town; but as I may possibly have to perform a like office for other localities, and as Anthony Poplar [2] is known, [147]like Atropos, to carry a shears, wherewith to snip across all "yarns" which exceed reasonable bounds, I consider it, on the whole, safer to despatch the traditions of Chapelizod with one tale more.

Let me, however, first give it a name; for an author can no more despatch a tale without a title, than an apothecary can deliver his physic without a label. We shall, therefore, call it—

THE SPECTRE LOVERS.

There lived some fifteen years since in a small and ruinous house, little better than a hovel, an old woman who was reported to have considerably exceeded her eightieth year, and who rejoiced in the name of Alice, or popularly, Ally Moran. Her society was not much courted, for she was neither rich, nor, as the reader may suppose, beautiful. In addition to a lean cur and a cat she had one human companion, her grandson, Peter Brien, whom, with laudable good-nature, she had supported from the period of his orphanage down to that of my story, which finds him in his twentieth year. Peter was a good-natured slob of a fellow, much more addicted to wrestling, dancing, and love-making, than to hard work, and fonder of whiskey punch than good advice. His grandmother had a high opinion of his accomplishments, which indeed was but natural, and also of his genius, for Peter had of late years begun to apply his mind to politics; and as it was plain that he had a mortal hatred of honest labour, his grandmother predicted, like a true fortune-teller, that he was born to marry an heiress, and Peter himself (who had no mind to forego his freedom even on such terms) that he was destined to find a pot of gold. Upon one point both agreed, that being unfitted[148] by the peculiar bias of his genius for work, he was to acquire the immense fortune to which his merits entitled him by means of a pure run of good luck. This solution of Peter's future had the double effect of reconciling both himself and his grandmother to his idle courses, and also of maintaining that even flow of hilarious spirits which made him everywhere welcome, and which was in truth the natural result of his consciousness of approaching affluence.

It happened one night that Peter had enjoyed himself to a very late hour with two or three choice spirits near Palmerstown. They had talked politics and love, sung songs, and told stories, and, above all, had swallowed, in the chastened disguise of punch, at least a pint of good whiskey, every man.

It was considerably past one o'clock when Peter bid his companions good-bye, with a sigh and a hiccough, and lighting his pipe set forth on his solitary homeward way.

The bridge of Chapelizod was pretty nearly the midway point of his night march, and from one cause or another his progress was rather slow, and it was past two o'clock by the time he found himself leaning over its old battlements, and looking up the river, over whose winding current and wooded banks the soft moonlight was falling.

The cold breeze that blew lightly down the stream was grateful to him. It cooled his throbbing head, and he drank it in at his hot lips. The scene, too, had, without his being well sensible of it, a secret fascination. The village was sunk in the profoundest slumber, not a mortal stirring, not a sound afloat, a soft haze covered it all, and the fairy moonlight hovered over the entire landscape.

In a state between rumination and rapture, Peter continued to lean over the battlements of the old bridge, and as he did so he saw, or fancied he saw, emerging one[149] after another along the river bank in the little gardens and enclosures in the rear of the street of Chapelizod, the queerest little white-washed huts and cabins he had ever seen there before. They had not been there that evening when he passed the bridge on the way to his merry tryst. But the most remarkable thing about it was the odd way in which these quaint little cabins showed themselves. First he saw one or two of them just with the corner of his eye, and when he looked full at them, strange to say, they faded away and disappeared. Then another and another came in view, but all in the same coy way, just appearing and gone again before he could well fix his gaze upon them; in a little while, however, they began to bear a fuller gaze, and he found, as it seemed to himself, that he was able by an effort of attention to fix the vision for a longer and a longer time, and when they waxed faint and nearly vanished, he had the power of recalling them into light and substance, until at last their vacillating indistinctness became less and less, and they assumed a permanent place in the moonlit landscape.

"Be the hokey," said Peter, lost in amazement, and dropping his pipe into the river unconsciously, "them is the quarist bits iv mud cabins I ever seen, growing up like musharoons in the dew of an evening, and poppin' up here and down again there, and up again in another place, like so many white rabbits in a warren; and there they stand at last as firm and fast as if they were there from the Deluge; bedad it's enough to make a man a'most believe in the fairies."

This latter was a large concession from Peter, who was a bit of a free-thinker, and spoke contemptuously in his ordinary conversation of that class of agencies.

Having treated himself to a long last stare at these mysterious fabrics,

Peter prepared to pursue his homeward[150] way; having crossed the bridge and passed the mill, he arrived at the corner of the main-street of the little town, and casting a careless look up the Dublin road, his eye was arrested by a most unexpected spectacle.

This was no other than a column of foot-soldiers, marching with perfect regularity towards the village, and headed by an officer on horseback. They were at the far side of the turnpike, which was closed; but much to his perplexity he perceived that they marched on through it without appearing to sustain the least check from that barrier.

On they came at a slow march; and what was most singular in the matter was, that they were drawing several cannons along with them; some held ropes, others spoked the wheels, and others again marched in front of the guns and behind them, with muskets shouldered, giving a stately character of parade and regularity to this, as it seemed to Peter, most unmilitary procedure.

It was owing either to some temporary defect in Peter's vision, or to some illusion attendant upon mist and moonlight, or perhaps to some other cause, that the whole procession had a certain waving and vapoury character which perplexed and tasked his eyes not a little. It was like the pictured pageant of a phantasmagoria reflected upon smoke. It was as if every breath disturbed it; sometimes it was blurred, sometimes obliterated; now here, now there. Sometimes, while the upper part was quite distinct, the legs of the column would nearly fade away or vanish outright, and then again they would come out into clear relief, marching on with measured tread, while the cocked hats and shoulders grew, as it were, transparent, and all but disappeared.

Notwithstanding these strange optical fluctuations,[151] however, the column continued steadily to advance. Peter crossed the street from the corner near the old bridge, running on tiptoe, and with his body stooped to avoid observation, and took up a position upon the raised foot-path in the shadow of the houses, where, as the soldiers kept the middle of the road, he calculated that he might, himself undetected, see them distinctly enough as they passed.

"What the div——, what on airth," he muttered, checking the irreligious ejaculation with which he was about to start, for certain queer misgivings were hovering about his heart, notwithstanding the factitious courage of the whiskey bottle. "What on airth is the manin' of all this? is it the French that's landed at last to give us a hand and help us in airnest to this blessed repale? If it is not them, I simply ask who the div——, I mane who on airth are they, for such sogers as them I never seen before in my born days?"

By this time the foremost of them were quite near, and truth to say they were the queerest soldiers he had ever seen in the course of his life. They wore long gaiters and leather breeches, three-cornered hats, bound with silver lace, long blue coats, with scarlet facings and linings, which latter were shewn by a fastening which held together the two opposite corners of the skirt behind; and in front the breasts were in like manner connected at a single point, where and below which they sloped back, disclosing a long-flapped waistcoat of snowy whiteness; they had very large, long cross-belts, and wore enormous pouches of white leather hung extraordinarily low, and on each of which a little silver star was glittering. But what struck him as most grotesque and outlandish in their costume was their extraordinary display of shirt-frill in front, and of ruffle about their[152] wrists, and the strange manner in which their hair was frizzled out and powdered under their hats, and clubbed up into great rolls behind. But one of the party was mounted. He rode a tall white horse, with high action and arching neck; he had a snow-white feather in his three-cornered hat, and his coat was shimmering all over with a profusion of silver lace. From these circumstances Peter concluded that he must be the commander of the detachment, and examined him as he passed attentively. He was a slight, tall man, whose legs did not half fill his leather breeches, and he appeared to be at the wrong side of sixty. He had a shrunken, weather-beaten, mulberry-coloured face, carried a large black patch over one eye, and turned neither to the right nor to the left, but rode on at the head of his men, with a grim, military inflexibility.

The countenances of these soldiers, officers as well as men, seemed all full of trouble, and, so to speak, scared and wild. He watched in vain for a single contented or comely face. They had, one and all, a melancholy and hang-dog look; and as they passed by, Peter fancied that the air grew cold and thrilling.

He had seated himself upon a stone bench, from which, staring with all his might, he gazed upon the grotesque and noiseless procession as it filed by him. Noiseless it was; he could neither hear the jingle of accoutrements, the tread of feet, nor the rumble of the wheels; and when the old colonel turned his horse a little, and made as though he were giving the word of command, and a trumpeter, with a swollen blue nose and white feather fringe round his hat, who was walking beside him, turned about and put his bugle to his lips, still Peter heard nothing, although it was plain the sound had reached the soldiers, for they instantly changed their front to three abreast.[153]

"Botheration!" muttered Peter, "is it deaf I'm growing?"

But that could not be, for he heard the sighing of the breeze and the rush of the neighbouring Liffey plain enough.

"Well," said he, in the same cautious key, "by the piper, this bangs

Banagher fairly! It's either the Frinch army that's in it, come to take the town iv Chapelizod by surprise, an' makin' no noise for feard iv wakenin' the inhabitants; or else it's—it's—what it's—somethin' else. But, tundher-an-ouns, what's gone wid Fitzpatrick's shop across the way?"

The brown, dingy stone building at the opposite side of the street looked newer and cleaner than he had been used to see it; the front door of it stood open, and a sentry, in the same grotesque uniform, with shouldered musket, was pacing noiselessly to and fro before it. At the angle of this building, in like manner, a wide gate (of which Peter had no recollection whatever) stood open, before which, also, a similar sentry was gliding, and into this gateway the whole column gradually passed, and Peter finally lost sight of it.

"I'm not asleep; I'm not dhramin'," said he, rubbing his eyes, and stamping slightly on the pavement, to assure himself that he was wide awake. "It is a quare business, whatever it is; an' it's not alone that, but everything about the town looks strange to me. There's Tresham's house new painted, bedad, an' them flowers in the windies! An' Delany's house, too, that had not a whole pane of glass in it this morning, and scarce a slate on the roof of it! It is not possible it's what it's dhrunk I am. Sure there's the big tree, and not a leaf of it changed since I passed, and the stars overhead, all right. I don't think it is in my eyes it is."[154]

And so looking about him, and every moment finding or fancying new food for wonder, he walked along the pavement, intending, without further delay, to make his way home.

But his adventures for the night were not concluded. He had nearly reached the angle of the short lane that leads up to the church, when for the first time he perceived that an officer, in the uniform he had just seen, was walking before, only a few yards in advance of him.

The officer was walking along at an easy, swinging gait, and carried his sword under his arm, and was looking down on the pavement with an air of reverie.

In the very fact that he seemed unconscious of Peter's presence, and disposed to keep his reflections to himself, there was something reassuring. Besides, the reader must please to remember that our hero had a *quantum sufficit* of good punch before his adventure commenced, and was thus fortified against those qualms and terrors under which, in a more reasonable state of mind, he might not impossibly have sunk.

The idea of the French invasion revived in full power in Peter's fuddled imagination, as he pursued the nonchalant swagger of the officer.

"Be the powers iv Moll Kelly, I'll ax him what it is," said Peter, with a sudden accession of rashness. "He may tell me or not, as he plases, but he can't be offinded, anyhow."

With this reflection having inspired himself, Peter cleared his voice and began—

"Captain!" said he, "I ax your pardon, captain, an' maybe you'd be so condescindin' to my ignorance as to tell me, if it's plasin' to yer honour, whether your honour is not a Frinchman, if it's plasin' to you."

This he asked, not thinking that, had it been as he[155] suspected, not one word of his question in all probability would have been intelligible to the person he addressed. He was, however, understood, for the officer answered him in English, at the same time slackening his pace and moving a little to the side of the pathway, as if to invite his interrogator to take his place beside him.

"No; I am an Irishman," he answered.

"I humbly thank your honour," said Peter, drawing nearer—for the affability and the nativity of the officer encouraged him—"but maybe your honour is in the *sarvice* of the King of France?»

"I serve the same King as you do," he answered, with a sorrowful significance which Peter did not comprehend at the time; and, interrogating in turn, he asked, "But what calls you forth at this hour of the day?"

"The *day*, your honour!—the night, you mane."

"It was always our way to turn night into day, and we keep to it still," remarked the soldier. "But, no matter, come up here to my house; I have a job for you, if you wish to earn some money easily. I live here."

As he said this, he beckoned authoritatively to Peter, who followed almost mechanically at his heels, and they turned up a little lane near the old Roman Catholic chapel, at the end of which stood, in Peter's time, the ruins of a tall, stone-built house.

Like everything else in the town, it had suffered a metamorphosis. The stained and ragged walls were now erect, perfect, and covered with pebble-dash; window-panes glittered coldly in every window; the green hall-door had a bright brass knocker on it. Peter did not know whether to believe his previous or his present impressions; seeing is believing, and Peter could not dispute the reality of the scene. All the records of his memory seemed but the images of a tipsy dream. In a[156] trance of astonishment and perplexity, therefore, he submitted himself to the chances of his adventure.

The door opened, the officer beckoned with a melancholy air of authority to Peter, and entered. Our hero followed him into a sort of hall, which was very dark, but he was guided by the steps of the soldier, and, in silence, they ascended the stairs. The moonlight, which shone in at the lobbies, showed an old, dark wainscoting, and a heavy, oak banister. They passed by closed doors at different landing-places, but all was dark and silent as, indeed, became that late hour of the night.

Now they ascended to the topmost floor. The captain paused for a minute at the nearest door, and, with a heavy groan, pushing it open, entered the room. Peter remained at the threshold. A slight female form in a sort of loose, white robe, and with a great deal of dark hair hanging loosely about her, was standing in the middle of the floor, with her back towards them.

The soldier stopped short before he reached her, and said, in a voice of great anguish, "Still the same, sweet bird—sweet bird! still the same." Whereupon, she turned suddenly, and threw her arms about the neck of the officer, with a gesture of fondness and despair, and her frame was agitated as if by a burst of sobs. He held her close to his breast in silence; and honest Peter felt a strange terror creep over him, as he witnessed these mysterious sorrows and endearments.

"To-night, to-night—and then ten years more—ten long years—another ten years."

The officer and the lady seemed to speak these words together; her voice mingled with his in a musical and fearful wail, like a distant summer wind, in the dead hour of night, wandering through ruins. Then he heard the officer say, alone, in a voice of anguish[157]—

"Upon me be it all, for ever, sweet birdie, upon me."

And again they seemed to mourn together in the same soft and desolate wail, like sounds of grief heard from a great distance.

Peter was thrilled with horror, but he was also under a strange fascination; and an intense and dreadful curiosity held him fast.

The moon was shining obliquely into the room, and through the window Peter saw the familiar slopes of the Park, sleeping mistily under its shimmer. He could also see the furniture of the room with tolerable distinctness—the old balloon-backed chairs, a four-post bed in a sort of recess, and a rack against the wall, from which hung some military clothes and accoutrements; and the sight of all these homely objects reassured him somewhat, and he could not help feeling unspeakably curious to see the face of the girl whose long hair was streaming over the officer's epaulet.

Peter, accordingly, coughed, at first slightly, and afterward more loudly, to recall her from her reverie of grief; and, apparently, he succeeded; for she turned round, as did her companion, and both, standing hand in hand, gazed upon him fixedly. He thought he had never seen such large, strange eyes in all his life; and their gaze seemed to chill the very air around him, and arrest the pulses of his heart. An eternity of misery and remorse was in the shadowy faces that looked upon him.

If Peter had taken less whisky by a single thimbleful, it is probable that he would have lost heart altogether before these figures, which seemed every moment to assume a more marked and fearful, though hardly definable, contrast to ordinary human shapes.

"What is it you want with me?" he stammered.

"To bring my lost treasure to the churchyard,"[158] replied the lady, in a silvery voice of more than mortal desolation.

The word "treasure" revived the resolution of Peter, although a cold sweat was covering him, and his hair was bristling with horror; he believed, however, that he was on the brink of fortune, if he could but command nerve to brave the interview to its close.

"And where," he gasped, "is it hid—where will I find it?"

They both pointed to the sill of the window, through which the moon was shining at the far end of the room, and the soldier said—

"Under that stone."

Peter drew a long breath, and wiped the cold dew from his face, preparatory to passing to the window, where he expected to secure the reward of his protracted terrors. But looking steadfastly at the window, he saw the faint image of a new-born child sitting upon the sill in the moonlight, with its little arms stretched toward him, and a smile so heavenly as he never beheld before.

At sight of this, strange to say, his heart entirely failed him, he looked on the figures that stood near, and beheld them gazing on the infantine form with a smile so guilty and distorted, that he felt as if he were entering alive among the scenery of hell, and shuddering, he cried in an irrepressible agony of horror—

"I'll have nothing to say with you, and nothing to do with you; I don't know what yez are or what yez want iv me, but let me go this minute, every one of yez, in the name of God."

With these words there came a strange rumbling and sighing about Peter's ears; he lost sight of everything, and felt that peculiar and not unpleasant sensation of falling softly, that sometimes supervenes in sleep, ending[159] in a dull shock. After that he had neither dream nor consciousness till he wakened, chill and stiff, stretched between two piles of old rubbish, among the black and roofless walls of the ruined house.

We need hardly mention that the village had put on its wonted air of neglect and decay, or that Peter looked around him in vain for traces of those novelties which had so puzzled and distracted him upon the previous night.

"Ay, ay," said his grandmother, removing her pipe, as he ended his description of the view from the bridge, "sure enough I remember myself, when I was a slip of a girl, these little white cabins among the gardens by the river side. The artillery sogers that was married, or had not room in the barracks, used to be in them, but they're all gone long ago."

"The Lord be merciful to us!" she resumed, when he had described the military procession, "it's often I seen the regiment marchin' into the town, jist as you saw it last night, acushla. Oh, voch, but it makes my heart sore to think iv them days; they were pleasant times, sure enough; but is not it terrible, avick, to think it's what it was the ghost of the rigiment you seen? The Lord betune us an' harm, for it was nothing else, as sure as I'm sittin' here."

When he mentioned the peculiar physiognomy and figure of the old officer who rode at the head of the regiment—

"*That*," said the old crone, dogmatically, "was ould Colonel Grimshaw, the Lord presarve us! he's buried in the churchyard iv Chapelizod, and well I remember him, when I was a young thing, an' a cross ould floggin' fellow he was wid the men, an' a devil's boy among the girls—rest his soul!"

"Amen!" said Peter; "it's often I read his tombstone myself; but he's a long time dead."[160]

"Sure, I tell you he died when I was no more nor a slip iv a girl—the Lord betune us and harm!"

"I'm afeard it is what I'm not long for this world myself, afther seeing such a sight as that," said Peter, fearfully.

"Nonsinse, avourneen," retorted his grandmother, indignantly, though she had herself misgivings on the subject; "sure there was Phil Doolan, the ferryman, that seen black Ann Scanlan in his own boat, and what harm ever kem of it?"

Peter proceeded with his narrative, but when he came to the description of the house, in which his adventure had had so sinister a conclusion, the old woman was at fault.

"I know the house and the ould walls well, an' I can remember the time there was a roof on it, and the doors an' windows in it, but it had a bad name about being haunted, but by who, or for what, I forget intirely."

"Did you ever hear was there goold or silver there?" he inquired.

"No, no, aviek, don't be thinking about the likes; take a fool's advice, and never go next or near them ugly black walls again the longest day you have to live; an' I'd take my davy, it's what it's the same word the priest himself I'd be afther sayin' to you if you wor to ax his raverence consarnin' it, for it's plain to be seen it was nothing good you seen there, and there's neither luck nor grace about it."

Peter's adventure made no little noise in the neighbourhood, as the reader may well suppose; and a few evenings after it, being on an errand to old Major Vandeleur, who lived in a snug old-fashioned house, close by the river, under a perfect bower of ancient trees, he was called on to relate the story in the parlour.[161]

The Major was, as I have said, an old man; he was small, lean, and upright, with a mahogany complexion, and a wooden inflexibility of face; he was a man, besides, of few words, and if *he* was old, it follows plainly that his mother was older still. Nobody could guess or tell *how* old, but it was admitted that her own generation had long passed away, and that she had not a competitor left. She had French blood in her veins, and although she did not retain her charms quite so well as Ninon de l'Enclos, she was in full possession of all her mental activity, and talked quite enough for herself and the Major.

"So, Peter," she said, "you have seen the dear, old Royal Irish again in the streets of Chapelizod. Make him a tumbler of punch, Frank; and Peter, sit down, and while you take it let us have the story."

Peter accordingly, seated near the door, with a tumbler of the nectarian stimulant steaming beside him, proceeded with marvellous courage, considering they had no light but the uncertain glare of the fire, to relate with minute particularity his awful adventure. The old lady listened at first with a smile of good-natured incredulity; her cross-examination touching the drinking-bout at Palmerstown had been teazing, but as the narrative proceeded she became attentive, and at length absorbed, and once or twice she uttered ejaculations of pity or awe. When it was over, the old lady looked with a somewhat sad and stern abstraction on the table, patting her cat assiduously meanwhile, and then suddenly looking upon her son, the Major, she said—

"Frank, as sure as I live he has seen the wicked Captain Devereux."

The Major uttered an inarticulate expression of wonder.

[162]

"The house was precisely that he has described. I have told you the story often, as I heard it from your dear grandmother, about the poor young lady he ruined, and the dreadful suspicion about the little baby. *She*, poor thing, died in that house heartbroken, and you know he was shot shortly after in a duel."

This was the only light that Peter ever received respecting his adventure. It was supposed, however, that he still clung to the hope that treasure of some sort was hidden about the old house, for he was often seen lurking about its walls, and at last his fate overtook him, poor fellow, in the pursuit; for climbing near the summit one day, his holding gave way, and he fell upon the hard uneven ground, fracturing a leg and a rib, and after a short interval died, and he, like the other heroes of these true tales, lies buried in the little churchyard of Chapelizod.

8
WICKED CAPTAIN WALSHAWE, OF WAULING

Anonymous in the *Dublin University Magazine* (1869).

CHAPTER I.
PEG O'NEILL PAYS THE CAPTAIN'S DEBTS.

A very odd thing happened to my uncle, Mr. Watson, of Haddlestone; and to enable you to understand it, I must begin at the beginning.

In the year 1822, Mr. James Walshawe, more commonly known as Captain Walshawe, died at the age of eighty-one years. The Captain in his early days, and so long as health and strength permitted, was a scamp of the active, intriguing sort; and spent his days and nights in sowing his wild oats, of which he seemed to have an inexhaustible stock. The harvest of this tillage was plentifully interspersed with thorns, nettles, and thistles, which stung the husbandman unpleasantly, and did not enrich him.

Captain Walshawe was very well known in the neighbourhood of Wauling, and very generally avoided there. A "captain" by courtesy, for he had never reached that rank in the army list. He had quitted the service in[164] 1766, at the age of twenty-five; immediately previous to which period his debts had grown so troublesome, that he was induced to extricate himself by running away with and marrying an heiress.

Though not so wealthy quite as he had imagined, she proved a very comfortable investment for what remained of his shattered affections; and he lived and enjoyed himself very much in his old way, upon her income, getting into no end of scrapes and scandals, and a good deal of debt and money trouble.

When he married his wife, he was quartered in Ireland, at Clonmel, where was a nunnery, in which, as pensioner, resided Miss O'Neill, or as she was called in the country, Peg O'Neill—the heiress of whom I have spoken.

Her situation was the only ingredient of romance in the affair, for the young lady was decidedly plain, though good-humoured looking, with that style of features which is termed *potato*; and in figure she was a little too plump, and rather short. But she was impressible; and the handsome young English Lieutenant was too much for her monastic tendencies, and she eloped.

In England there are traditions of Irish fortune-hunters, and in Ireland of English. The fact is, it was the vagrant class of each country that chiefly visited the other in old times; and a handsome vagabond, whether at home or abroad, I suppose, made the most of his face, which was also his fortune.

At all events, he carried off the fair one from the sanctuary; and for some sufficient reason, I suppose, they took up their abode at Wauling, in Lancashire.

Here the gallant captain amused himself after his fashion, sometimes running up, of course on business, to London. I believe few wives have ever cried more in a given time than did that poor, dumpy, potato-faced[165] heiress, who got over the nunnery garden wall, and jumped into the handsome Captain›s arms, for love.

He spent her income, frightened her out of her wits with oaths and threats, and broke her heart.

Latterly she shut herself up pretty nearly altogether in her room. She had an old, rather grim, Irish servant-woman in attendance upon her. This domestic was tall, lean, and religious, and the Captain knew instinctively she hated him; and he hated her in return, and often threatened to put her out of the house, and sometimes even to kick her out of the window. And whenever a wet day confined him to the house, or the stable, and he grew tired of smoking, he would begin to swear and curse at her for a *diddled* old mischief-maker, that could never be easy, and was always troubling the house with her cursed stories, and so forth.

But years passed away, and old Molly Doyle remained still in her original position. Perhaps he thought that there must be somebody there, and that he was not, after all, very likely to change for the better.

CHAPTER II.
THE BLESSED CANDLE.

He tolerated another intrusion, too, and thought himself a paragon of patience and easy good-nature for so doing. A Roman Catholic clergyman, in a long black frock, with a low standing collar, and a little white muslin fillet round his neck—tall, sallow, with blue chin, and dark steady eyes—used to glide up and down the stairs, and through[166] the passages; and the Captain sometimes met him in one place and sometimes in another. But by a caprice incident to such tempers he treated this cleric exceptionally, and even with a surly sort of courtesy, though he grumbled about his visits behind his back.

I do not know that he had a great deal of moral courage, and the ecclesiastic looked severe and self-possessed; and somehow he thought he had no good opinion of him, and if a natural occasion were offered, might say extremely unpleasant things, and hard to be answered.

Well the time came at last, when poor Peg O'Neill—in an evil hour Mrs. James Walshawe—must cry, and quake, and pray her last. The doctor came from Penlynden, and was just as vague as usual, but more gloomy, and for about a week came and went oftener. The cleric in the long black frock was also daily there. And at last came that last sacrament in the gates of death, when the sinner is traversing those dread steps that never can be retraced; when the face is turned for ever from life, and we see a receding shape, and hear a voice already irrevocably in the land of spirits.

So the poor lady died; and some people said the Captain "felt it very much." I don't think he did. But he was not very well just then, and looked the part of mourner and penitent to admiration—being seedy and sick. He drank a great deal of brandy and water that night, and called in Farmer Dobbs, for want of better company, to drink with him; and told him all his grievances, and how happy he and "the poor lady up-stairs" might have been, had it not been for liars, and pick-thanks, and tale-bearers, and the like, who came between them—meaning Molly Doyle—whom, as he waxed eloquent over his liquor, he came at last to curse and rail at by[167] name, with more than his accustomed freedom. And he described his own natural character and amiability in such moving terms, that he wept maudlin tears of sensibility over his theme; and when Dobbs was gone, drank some more grog, and took to railing and cursing again by himself; and then mounted the stairs unsteadily, to see «what the devil Doyle and the other —— old witches were about in poor Peg›s room.»

When he pushed open the door, he found some half-dozen crones, chiefly Irish, from the neighbouring town of Hackleton, sitting over tea and snuff, etc., with candles lighted round the corpse, which was arrayed in a strangely cut robe of brown serge. She had secretly belonged to some order—I think the Carmelite, but I am not certain—and wore the habit in her coffin.

"What the d—— are you doing with my wife?" cried the Captain, rather thickly. "How dare you dress her up in this —— trumpery, you—you cheating old witch; and what's that candle doing in her hand?"

I think he was a little startled, for the spectacle was grisly enough. The dead lady was arrayed in this strange brown robe, and in her rigid fingers, as in a socket, with the large wooden beads and cross wound round it, burned a wax candle, shedding its white light over the sharp features of the corpse. Moll Doyle was not to be put down by the Captain, whom she hated, and accordingly, in her phrase, "he got as good as he gave." And the Captain's wrath waxed fiercer, and he chucked the wax taper from the dead hand, and was on the point of flinging it at the old serving-woman's head.

"The holy candle, you sinner!" cried she.

"I've a mind to make you eat it, you beast," cried the Captain.

But I think he had not known before what it was, for[168] he subsided a little sulkily, and he stuffed his hand with the candle (quite extinct by this time) into his pocket, and said he—

"You know devilish well you had no business going on with y-y-your d—— *witch*-craft about my poor wife, without my leave—you do—and you'll please to take off that d—— brown pinafore, and get her decently into her coffin, and I'll pitch your devil's waxlight into the sink."

And the Captain stalked out of the room.

"An' now her poor sowl's in prison, you wretch, be the mains o' ye; an' may yer own be shut into the wick o' that same candle, till it's burned out, ye savage."

"I'd have you ducked for a witch, for two-pence," roared the Captain up the staircase, with his hand on the banisters, standing on the lobby. But the door of the chamber of death clapped angrily, and he went down to the parlour, where he examined the holy candle for a while, with a tipsy gravity, and then with something of that reverential feeling for the symbolic, which is not uncommon in rakes and scamps, he thoughtfully locked it up in a press, where were accumulated all sorts of obsolete rubbish—soiled packs of cards, disused tobacco-pipes, broken powder-flasks, his military sword, and a dusky bundle of the "Flash Songster," and other questionable literature.

He did not trouble the dead lady's room any more. Being a volatile man it is probable that more cheerful plans and occupations began to entertain his fancy.

CHAPTER III.
MY UNCLE WATSON VISITS WAULING.

So the poor lady was buried decently, and Captain Walshawe reigned alone for many years at Wauling. He was too shrewd and too experienced by this time to run violently down the steep hill that leads to ruin. So there was a method in his madness; and after a widowed career of more than forty years, he, too, died at last with some guineas in his purse.

Forty years and upwards is a great *edax rerum*, and a wonderful chemical power. It acted forcibly upon the gay Captain Walshawe. Gout supervened, and was no more conducive to temper than to enjoyment, and made his elegant hands lumpy at all the small joints, and turned them slowly into crippled claws. He grew stout when his exercise was interfered with, and ultimately almost corpulent. He suffered from what Mr. Holloway calls "bad legs," and was wheeled about in a great leathern-backed chair, and his infirmities went on accumulating with his years.

I am sorry to say, I never heard that he repented, or turned his thoughts seriously to the future. On the contrary, his talk grew fouler, and his fun ran upon his favourite sins, and his temper waxed more truculent. But he did not sink into dotage. Considering his bodily infirmities, his energies and his malignities, which were many and active, were marvellously little abated by time. So he went on to the close. When his temper was stirred, he cursed and swore in a way that made decent people tremble. It was a word and a blow with him; the latter, luckily, not very sure now. But he would[170] seize his crutch and make a swoop or a pound at the offender, or shy his medicine-bottle, or his tumbler, at his head.

It was a peculiarity of Captain Walshawe, that he, by this time, hated nearly everybody. My Uncle, Mr. Watson, of Haddlestone, was cousin to the Captain, and his heir-at-law. But my uncle had lent him money on mortgage of his estates, and there had been a treaty to sell, and terms and a price were agreed upon, in "articles" which the lawyers said were still in force.

I think the ill-conditioned Captain bore him a grudge for being richer than he, and would have liked to do him an ill turn. But it did not lie in his way; at least while he was living.

My Uncle Watson was a Methodist, and what they call a "class-leader"; and, on the whole, a very good man. He was now near fifty—grave, as beseemed his profession—somewhat dry—and a little severe, perhaps— but a just man.

A letter from the Penlynden doctor reached him at Haddlestone, announcing the death of the wicked old Captain; and suggesting his attendance at the funeral, and the expediency of his being on the spot to look after things at Wauling. The reasonableness of this striking my good Uncle, he made his journey to the old house in Lancashire incontinently, and reached it in time for the funeral.

My Uncle, whose traditions of the Captain were derived from his mother, who remembered him in his slim, handsome youth—in shorts, cocked-hat and lace, was amazed at the bulk of the coffin which contained his mortal remains; but the lid being already screwed down, he did not see the face of the bloated old sinner.

CHAPTER IV.
IN THE PARLOUR.

What I relate, I had from the lips of my uncle, who was a truthful man, and not prone to fancies.

The day turning out awfully rainy and tempestuous, he persuaded the doctor and the attorney to remain for the night at Wauling.

There was no will—the attorney was sure of that; for the Captain's enmities were perpetually shifting, and he could never quite make up his mind, as to how best to give effect to a malignity whose direction was being constantly modified. He had had instructions for drawing a will a dozen times over. But the process had always been arrested by the intending testator.

Search being made, no will was found. The papers, indeed were all right, with one important exception: the leases were nowhere to be seen. There were special circumstances connected with several of the principal tenancies on the estate—unnecessary here to detail—which rendered the loss of these documents one of very serious moment, and even of very obvious danger.

My uncle, therefore, searched strenuously. The attorney was at his elbow, and the doctor helped with a suggestion now and then. The old serving-man seemed an honest deaf creature, and really knew nothing.

My Uncle Watson was very much perturbed. He fancied—but this possibly was only fancy—that he had detected for a moment a queer look in the attorney's face; and from that instant it became fixed in his mind that he knew all about the leases. Mr. Watson expounded that evening in the parlour to the doctor, the attorney,[172] and the deaf servant. Ananias and Sapphira figured in the foreground; and the awful nature of fraud and theft, or tampering in anywise with the plain rule of honesty in matters pertaining to estates, etc., were pointedly dwelt upon; and then came a long and strenuous prayer, in which he entreated with fervour and aplomb that the hard heart of the sinner who had abstracted the leases might be softened or broken in such a way as to lead to their restitution; or that, if he continued reserved and contumacious, it might at least be the will of Heaven to bring him to public justice and the documents to light. The fact is, that he was praying all this time at the attorney.

When these religious exercises were over, the visitors retired to their rooms, and my Uncle Watson wrote two or three pressing letters by the fire. When his task was done, it had grown late; the candles were flaring in their sockets, and all in bed, and, I suppose, asleep, but he.

The fire was nearly out, he chilly, and the flame of the candles throbbing strangely in their sockets shed alternate glare and shadow round the old wainscoted room and its quaint furniture. Outside were the wild thunder and piping of the storm; and the rattling of distant windows sounded through the passages, and down the stairs, like angry people astir in the house.

My Uncle Watson belonged to a sect who by no means reject the supernatural, and whose founder, on the contrary, has sanctioned ghosts in the most emphatic way. He was glad therefore to remember, that in prosecuting his search that day, he had seen some six inches of wax candle in the press in the parlour; for he had no fancy to be overtaken by darkness in his present situation. He had no time to lose; and taking the bunch of keys—of which he was now master—he soon fitted the lock, and[173] secured the candle—a treasure in his circumstances; and lighting it, he stuffed it into the socket of one of the expiring candles, and extinguishing the other, he looked round the room in the steady light reassured. At the same moment, an unusually violent gust of the storm blew a handful of gravel against the parlour window, with a sharp rattle that startled him in the midst of the roar and hubbub; and the flame of the candle itself was agitated by the air.

CHAPTER V.
THE BED-CHAMBER.

My Uncle walked up to bed, guarding his candle with his hand, for the lobby windows were rattling furiously, and he disliked the idea of being left in the dark more than ever.

His bedroom was comfortable, though old-fashioned. He shut and bolted the door. There was a tall looking-glass opposite the foot of his four-poster, on the dressing-table between the windows. He tried to make the curtains meet, but they would not draw; and like many a gentleman in a like perplexity, he did not possess a pin, nor was there one in the huge pincushion beneath the glass.

He turned the face of the mirror away therefore, so that its back was presented to the bed, pulled the curtains together, and placed a chair against them, to prevent their falling open again. There was a good fire, and a reinforcement of round coal and wood inside the fender. So he piled it up to ensure a cheerful blaze through the night,[174] and placing a little black mahogany table, with the legs of a Satyr, beside the bed, and his candle upon it, he got between the sheets, and laid his red night-capped head upon his pillow, and disposed himself to sleep.

The first thing that made him uncomfortable was a sound at the foot of his bed, quite distinct in a momentary lull of the storm. It was only the gentle rustle and rush of the curtains, which fell open again; and as his eyes opened, he saw them resuming their perpendicular dependence, and sat up in his bed almost expecting to see something uncanny in the aperture.

There was nothing, however, but the dressing-table, and other dark furniture, and the window-curtains faintly undulating in the violence of the storm. He did not care to get up, therefore—the fire being bright and cheery—to replace the curtains by a chair, in the position in which he had left them, anticipating possibly a new recurrence of the relapse which had startled him from his incipient doze.

So he got to sleep in a little while again, but he was disturbed by a sound, as he fancied, at the table on which stood the candle. He could not say what it was, only that he wakened with a start, and lying so in some amaze, he did distinctly hear a sound which startled him a good deal, though there was nothing necessarily supernatural in it. He described it as resembling what would occur if you fancied a thinnish table-leaf, with a convex warp in it, depressed the reverse way, and suddenly with a spring recovering its natural convexity. It was a loud, sudden thump, which made the heavy candlestick jump, and there was an end, except that my uncle did not get again into a doze for ten minutes at least.

The next time he awoke, it was in that odd, serene way that sometimes occurs. We open our eyes, we know not why, quite placidly, and are on the instant wide awake.[175] He had had a nap of some duration this time, for his candle-flame was fluttering and flaring, *in articulo*, in the silver socket. But the fire was still bright and cheery; so he popped the extinguisher on the socket, and almost at the same time there came a tap at his door, and a sort of crescendo "hush-sh-sh!" Once more my Uncle was sitting up, scared and perturbed, in his bed. He recollected, however, that he had bolted his door; and such inveterate materialists are we in the midst of our spiritualism, that this reassured him, and he breathed a deep sigh, and began to grow tranquil. But after a rest of a minute or two, there came a louder and sharper knock at his door; so that instinctively he called out, "Who's there?" in a loud, stern key. There was no sort of response, however. The nervous effect of the start subsided; and I think my uncle must have remembered how constantly, especially on a stormy night, these creaks or cracks which simulate all manner of goblin noises, make themselves naturally audible.

CHAPTER VI.
THE EXTINGUISHER IS LIFTED.

After a while, then, he lay down with his back turned toward that side of the bed at which was the door, and his face toward the table on which stood the massive old candlestick, capped with its extinguisher, and in that position he closed his eyes. But sleep would not revisit them. All kinds of queer fancies began to trouble him—some of them I remember.[176]

He felt the point of a finger, he averred, pressed most distinctly on the tip of his great toe, as if a living hand were between his sheets, and making a sort of signal of attention or silence. Then again he felt something as large as a rat make a sudden bounce in the middle of his bolster, just under his head. Then a voice said "Oh!" very gently, close at the back of his head. All these things he felt certain of, and yet investigation led to nothing. He felt odd little cramps stealing now and then about him; and then, on a sudden, the middle finger of his right hand was plucked backwards, with a light playful jerk that frightened him awfully.

Meanwhile the storm kept singing, and howling, and ha-ha-hooing hoarsely among the limbs of the old trees and the chimney-pots; and my Uncle Watson, although he prayed and meditated as was his wont when he lay awake, felt his heart throb excitedly, and sometimes thought he was beset with evil spirits, and at others that he was in the early stage of a fever.

He resolutely kept his eyes closed, however, and, like St. Paul's shipwrecked companions, wished for the day. At last another little doze seems to have stolen upon his senses, for he awoke quietly and completely as before—opening his eyes all at once, and seeing everything as if he had not slept for a moment.

The fire was still blazing redly—nothing uncertain in the light—the massive silver candlestick, topped with its tall extinguisher, stood on the centre of the black mahogany table as before; and, looking by what seemed a sort of accident to the apex of this, he beheld something which made him quite misdoubt the evidence of his eyes.

He saw the extinguisher lifted by a tiny hand, from beneath, and a small human face, no bigger than a thumb-nail, with nicely proportioned features peep from beneath[177] it. In this Lilliputian countenance was such a ghastly consternation as horrified my Uncle unspeakably. Out came a little foot then and there, and a pair of wee legs, in short silk stockings and buckled shoes, then the rest of the figure; and, with the arms holding about the socket, the little legs stretched and stretched, hanging about the stem of the candlestick till the feet reached the base, and so down the Satyr-like leg of the table, till they reached the floor, extending elastically, and strangely enlarging in all proportions as they approached the ground, where the feet and buckles were those of a well-shaped, full grown man, and the figure tapering upward until it dwindled to its original fairy dimensions at the top, like an object seen in some strangely curved mirror.

Standing upon the floor he expanded, my amazed uncle could not tell how, into his proper proportions; and stood pretty nearly in profile at the bedside, a handsome and elegantly shaped young man, in a bygone military costume, with a small laced, three-cocked hat and plume on his head, but looking like a man going to be hanged—in unspeakable despair.

He stepped lightly to the hearth, and turned for a few seconds very dejectedly with his back toward the bed and the mantelpiece, and he saw the hilt of his rapier glittering in the firelight; and then walking across the room he placed himself at the dressing-table, visible through the divided curtains at the foot of the bed. The fire was blazing still so brightly that my uncle saw him as distinctly as if half a dozen candles were burning.

CHAPTER VII.
THE VISITATION CULMINATES.

The looking-glass was an old-fashioned piece of furniture, and had a drawer beneath it. My Uncle had searched it carefully for the papers in the daytime; but the silent figure pulled the drawer quite out, pressed a spring at the side, disclosing a false receptacle behind it, and from this he drew a parcel of papers tied together with pink tape.

All this time my Uncle was staring at him in a horrified state, neither winking nor breathing, and the apparition had not once given the smallest intimation of consciousness that a living person was in the same room. But now, for the first time, it turned its livid stare full upon my Uncle with a hateful smile of significance, lifting up the little parcel of papers between his slender finger and thumb. Then he made a long, cunning wink at him, and seemed to blow out one of his cheeks in a burlesque grimace, which, but for the horrific circumstances, would have been ludicrous. My Uncle could not tell whether this was really an intentional distortion or only one of those horrid ripples and deflections which were constantly disturbing the proportions of the figure, as if it were seen through some unequal and perverting medium.

The figure now approached the bed, seeming to grow exhausted and malignant as it did so. My Uncle's terror nearly culminated at this point, for he believed it was drawing near him with an evil purpose. But it was not so; for the soldier, over whom twenty years seemed to have passed in his brief transit to the dressing-table and back again, threw himself into a great high-backed arm-chair of stuffed leather at the far side of the fire, and[179] placed his heels on the fender. His feet and legs seemed indistinctly to swell, and swathings showed themselves round them, and they grew into something enormous, and the upper figure swayed and shaped itself into corresponding proportions, a great mass of corpulence, with a cadaverous and malignant face, and the furrows of a great old age, and colourless glassy eyes; and with these changes, which came indefinitely but rapidly as those of a sunset cloud, the fine regimentals faded away, and a loose, gray, woollen drapery, somehow, was there in its stead; and all seemed to be stained and rotten, for swarms of worms seemed creeping in and out, while the figure grew paler and paler, till my Uncle, who liked his pipe, and employed the simile naturally, said the whole effigy grew to the colour of tobacco ashes, and the clusters of worms into little wriggling knots of sparks such as we see running over the residuum of a burnt sheet of paper. And so with the strong draught caused by the fire, and the current of air from the window, which was rattling in the storm, the feet seemed to be drawn into the fireplace, and the whole figure, light as ashes, floated away with them, and disappeared with a whisk up the capacious old chimney.

It seemed to my Uncle that the fire suddenly darkened and the air grew icy cold, and there came an awful roar and riot of tempest, which shook the old house from top to base, and sounded like the yelling of a blood-thirsty mob on receiving a new and long-expected victim.

Good Uncle Watson used to say, "I have been in many situations of fear and danger in the course of my life, but never did I pray with so much agony before or since; for then, as now, it was clear beyond a cavil that I had actually beheld the phantom of an evil spirit."

CONCLUSION.

Now there are two curious circumstances to be observed in this relation of my Uncle's, who was, as I have said, a perfectly veracious man.

First—The wax candle which he took from the press in the parlour and burnt at his bedside on that horrible night was unquestionably, according to the testimony of the old deaf servant, who had been fifty years at Wauling, that identical piece of "holy candle" which had stood in the fingers of the poor lady's corpse, and concerning which the old Irish crone, long since dead, had delivered the curious curse I have mentioned against the Captain.

Secondly—Behind the drawer under the looking-glass, he did actually discover a second but secret drawer, in which were concealed the identical papers which he had suspected the attorney of having made away with. There were circumstances, too, afterwards disclosed which convinced my Uncle that the old man had deposited them there preparatory to burning them, which he had nearly made up his mind to do.

Now, a very remarkable ingredient in this tale of my Uncle Watson was this, that so far as my father, who had never seen Captain Walshawe in the course of his life, could gather, the phantom had exhibited a horrible and grotesque, but unmistakeable resemblance to that defunct scamp in the various stages of his long life.

Wauling was sold in the year 1837, and the old house shortly after pulled down, and a new one built nearer to the river. I often wonder whether it was rumoured to be haunted, and, if so, what stories were current about it. It was a commodious and stanch old house, and withal rather handsome; and its demolition was certainly suspicious.

9
SIR DOMINICK'S BARGAIN

A LEGEND OF DUNORAN

Anonymous in *All the Year Round* (1872). The theme occurs first in «The Fortunes of Sir Robert Ardagh» (*Dublin University Magazine*, 1838), reprinted in the *Purcell Papers*. It is varied and elaborated in "The Haunted Baronet" (*Chronicles of Golden Friars*, vols. i. ii.).

In the early autumn of the year 1838, business called me to the south of Ireland. The weather was delightful, the scenery and people were new to me, and sending my luggage on by the mail-coach route in charge of a servant, I hired a serviceable nag at a posting-house, and, full of the curiosity of an explorer, I commenced a leisurely journey of five-and-twenty miles on horseback, by sequestered cross-roads, to my place of destination. By bog and hill, by plain and ruined castle, and many a winding stream, my picturesque road led me.

I had started late, and having made little more than half my journey, I was thinking of making a short halt at the next convenient place, and letting my horse have a rest and a feed, and making some provision also for the comforts of his rider.[182]

It was about four o'clock when the road, ascending a gradual steep, found a passage through a rocky gorge between the abrupt termination of a range of mountain to my left and a rocky hill, that rose dark and sudden at my right. Below me lay a little thatched village, under a long line of gigantic beech-trees, through the boughs of which the lowly chimneys sent up their thin turf-smoke. To my left, stretched away for miles, ascending the mountain range I have mentioned, a wild park, through whose sward and ferns the rock broke, time-worn and lichen-stained. This park was studded with straggling wood, which thickened to something like a forest, behind and beyond the little village I was approaching, clothing the irregular ascent of the hillsides with beautiful, and in some places discoloured foliage.

As you descend, the road winds slightly, with the grey park-wall, built of loose stone, and mantled here and there with ivy, at its left, and crosses a shallow ford; and as I approached the village, through breaks in the woodlands, I caught glimpses of the long front of an old ruined house, placed among the trees, about half-way up the picturesque mountain-side.

The solitude and melancholy of this ruin piqued my curiosity, and when I had reached the rude thatched public-house, with the sign of St. Columbkill, with robes, mitre, and crozier displayed over its lintel, having seen to my horse and made a good meal myself on a rasher and eggs, I began to think again of the wooded park and the ruinous house, and resolved on a ramble of half an hour among its sylvan solitudes.

The name of the place, I found, was Dunoran; and beside the gate a stile admitted to the grounds, through which, with a pensive enjoyment, I began to saunter towards the dilapidated mansion.[183]

A long grass-grown road, with many turns and windings, led up to the old house, under the shadow of the wood.

The road, as it approached the house skirted the edge of a precipitous glen, clothed with hazel, dwarf-oak, and thorn, and the silent house stood with its wide-open hall-door facing this dark ravine, the further edge of which was crowned with towering forest; and great trees stood about the house and its deserted courtyard and stables.

I walked in and looked about me, through passages overgrown with nettles and weeds; from room to room with ceilings rotted, and here and there a great beam dark and worn, with tendrils of ivy trailing over it. The tall walls with rotten plaster were stained and mouldy, and in some rooms the remains of decayed wainscoting crazily swung to and fro. The almost sashless windows were darkened also with ivy, and about the tall chimneys the jackdaws were wheeling, while from the huge trees that overhung the glen in sombre masses at the other side, the rooks kept up a ceaseless cawing.

As I walked through these melancholy passages—peeping only into some of the rooms, for the flooring was quite gone in the middle, and bowed down toward the centre, and the house was very nearly un-roofed, a state of things which made the exploration a little critical—I began to wonder why so grand a house, in the midst of scenery so picturesque, had been permitted to go to decay; I dreamed of the hospitalities of which it had long ago been the rallying place, and I thought what a scene of Redgauntlet revelries it might disclose at midnight.

The great staircase was of oak, which had stood the weather wonderfully, and I sat down upon its steps, musing vaguely on the transitoriness of all things under the sun.[184]

Except for the hoarse and distant clamour of the rooks, hardly audible where I sat, no sound broke the profound stillness of the spot. Such a sense of solitude I have seldom experienced before. The air was stirless, there was not even the rustle of a withered leaf along the passage. It was oppressive. The tall trees that stood close about the building darkened it, and added something of awe to the melancholy of the scene.

In this mood I heard, with an unpleasant surprise, close to me, a voice that was drawling, and, I fancied, sneering, repeat the words: "Food for worms, dead and rotten; God over all."

There was a small window in the wall, here very thick, which had been built up, and in the dark recess of this, deep in the shadow, I now saw a sharp-featured man, sitting with his feet dangling. His keen eyes were fixed on me, and he was smiling cynically, and before I had well recovered my surprise, he repeated the distich:

"If death was a thing that money could buy,The rich they would live, and the poor they would die.

"It was a grand house in its day, sir," he continued, "Dunoran House, and the Sarsfields. Sir Dominick Sarsfield was the last of the old stock. He lost his life not six foot away from where you are sitting."

As he thus spoke he let himself down, with a little jump, on to the ground.

He was a dark-faced, sharp-featured, little hunchback, and had a walking-stick in his hand, with the end of which he pointed to a rusty stain in the plaster of the wall.

"Do you mind that mark, sir?" he asked.

"Yes," I said, standing up, and looking at it, with a curious anticipation of something worth hearing.

"That's about seven or eight feet from the ground, sir, and you'll not guess what it is."[185]

"I dare say not," said I, "unless it is a stain from the weather."

"'Tis nothing so lucky, sir," he answered, with the same cynical smile and a wag of his head, still pointing at the mark with his stick. "That's a splash of brains and blood. It's there this hundhred years; and it will never leave it while the wall stands."

"He was murdered, then?"

"Worse than that, sir," he answered.

"He killed himself, perhaps?"

"Worse than that, itself, this cross between us and harm! I'm oulder than I look, sir; you wouldn't guess my years."

He became silent, and looked at me, evidently inviting a guess.

"Well, I should guess you to be about five-and-fifty."

He laughed, and took a pinch of snuff, and said:

"I'm that, your honour, and something to the back of it. I was seventy last Candlemas. You would not a' thought that, to look at me."

"Upon my word I should not; I can hardly believe it even now. Still, you don't remember Sir Dominick Sarsfield's death?" I said, glancing up at the ominous stain on the wall.

"No, sir, that was a long while before I was born. But my grandfather was butler here long ago, and many a time I heard tell how Sir Dominick came by his death. There was no masther in the great house ever sinst that happened. But there was two sarvants in care of it, and my aunt was one o' them; and she kep' me here wid her till I was nine year old, and she was lavin' the place to go to Dublin; and from that time it was let to go down. The wind sthript the roof, and the rain rotted the timber, and little by little, in sixty years' time, it kem to what[186] you see. But I have a likin› for it still, for the sake of ould times; and I never come this way but I take a look in. I don't think it's many more times I'll be turnin' to see the ould place, for I'll be undher the sod myself before long."

"You'll outlive younger people," I said.

And, quitting that trite subject, I ran on:

"I don't wonder that you like this old place; it is a beautiful spot, such noble trees."

"I wish ye seen the glin when the nuts is ripe; they're the sweetest nuts in all Ireland, I think," he rejoined, with a practical sense of the picturesque. "You'd fill your pockets while you'd be lookin' about you."

"These are very fine old woods," I remarked. "I have not seen any in Ireland I thought so beautiful."

"Eiah! your honour, the woods about here is nothing to what they wor. Al the mountains along here was wood when my father was a gossoon, and Murroa Wood was the grandest of them all. All oak mostly, and all cut down as bare as the road. Not one left here that's fit to compare with them. Which way did your honour come hither—from Limerick?"

"No. Killaloe."

"Well, then, you passed the ground where Murroa Wood was in former times. You kem undher Lisnavourra, the steep knob of a hill about a mile above the village here. 'Twas near that Murroa Wood was, and 'twas there Sir Dominick Sarsfield first met the devil, the Lord between us and harm, and a bad meeting it was for him and his."

I had become interested in the adventure which had occurred in the very scenery which had so greatly attracted me, and my new acquaintance, the little hunchback, was easily entreated to tell me the story, and spoke thus, so soon as we had each resumed his seat:[187]

"It was a fine estate when Sir Dominick came into it; and grand doings there was entirely, feasting and fiddling, free quarters for all the pipers in the counthry round, and a welcome for every one that liked to come. There was wine, by the hogshead, for the quality; and potteen enough to set a town a-fire, and beer and cidher enough to float a navy, for the boys and girls, and the likes o' me. It was kep' up the best part of a month, till the weather broke, and the rain spoilt the sod for the moneen jigs, and the fair of Allybally Killudeen comin' on they wor obliged to give over their divarsion, and attind to the pigs.

But Sir Dominick was only beginnin' when they wor lavin' off. There was no way of gettin' rid of his money and estates he did not try—what with drinkin', dicin', racin', cards, and all soarts, it was not many years before the estates wor in debt, and Sir Dominick a distressed man. He showed a bold front to the world as long as he could; and then he sould off his dogs, and most of his horses, and gev out he was going to thravel in France, and the like; and so off with him for awhile; and no one in these parts heard tale or tidings of him for two or three years. Till at last quite unexpected, one night there comes a rapping at the big kitchen window. It was past ten o'clock, and old Connor Hanlon, the butler, my grandfather, was sittin' by the fire alone, warming his shins over it. There was keen east wind blowing along the mountains that night, and whistling cowld enough, through the tops of the trees, and soundin' lonesome through the long chimneys.

(And the story-teller glanced up at the nearest stack visible from his seat.)

So he wasn't quite sure of the knockin' at the window, and up he gets, and sees his master's face.[188]

My grandfather was glad to see him safe, for it was a long time since there was any news of him; but he was sorry, too, for it was a changed place and only himself and old Juggy Broadrick in charge of the house, and a man in the stables, and it was a poor thing to see him comin' back to his own like that.

He shook Con by the hand, and says he:

"I came here to say a word to you. I left my horse with Dick in the stable; I may want him again before morning, or I may never want him."

And with that he turns into the big kitchen, and draws a stool, and sits down to take an air of the fire.

"Sit down, Connor, opposite me, and listen to what I tell you, and don't be afeard to say what you think."

He spoke all the time lookin' into the fire, with his hands stretched over it, and a tired man he looked.

"An' why should I be afeard, Masther Dominick?" says my grandfather. "Yourself was a good masther to me, and so was your father, rest his sould, before you, and I'll say the truth, and dar' the devil, and more than that, for any Sarsfield of Dunoran, much less yourself, and a good right I'd have."

"It's all over with me, Con," says Sir Dominick.

"Heaven forbid!" says my grandfather.

"'Tis past praying for," says Sir Dominick. "The last guinea's gone; the ould place will follow it. It must be sold, and I'm come here, I don't know why, like a ghost to have a last look round me, and go off in the dark again."

And with that he tould him to be sure, in case he should hear of his death, to give the oak box, in the closet off his room, to his cousin, Pat Sarsfield, in Dublin, and the sword and pistols his grandfather carried in Aughrim, and two or three thrifling things of the kind.[189]

And says he, "Con, they say if the divil gives you money overnight, you'll find nothing but a bagful of pebbles, and chips, and nutshells, in the morning. If I thought he played fair, I'm in the humour to make a bargain with him to-night."

"Lord forbid!" says my grandfather, standing up, with a start and crossing himself.

"They say the country's full of men, listin' sogers for the King o' France. If I light on one o' them, I'll not refuse his offer. How contrary things goes! How long is it since me an Captain Waller fought the jewel at New Castle?"

"Six years, Masther Dominick, and ye broke his thigh with the bullet the first shot."

"I did, Con," says he, "and I wish, instead, he had shot me through the heart. Have you any whisky?"

My grandfather took it out of the buffet, and the masther pours out some into a bowl, and drank it off.

"I'll go out and have a look at my horse," says he, standing up. There was sort of a stare in his eyes, as he pulled his riding-cloak about him, as if there was something bad in his thoughts.

"Sure, I won't be a minute running out myself to the stable, and looking after the horse for you myself," says my grandfather.

"I'm not goin' to the stable," says Sir Dominick; "I may as well tell you, for I see you found it out already—I'm goin' across the deer-park; if I come back you'll see me in an hour's time. But, anyhow, you'd better not follow me, for if you do I'll shoot you, and that 'id be a bad ending to our friendship."

And with that he walks down this passage here, and turns the key in the side door at that end of it, and out wid him on the sod into the moonlight and the cowld[190] wind; and my grandfather seen him walkin› hard towards the park-wall, and then he comes in and closes the door with a heavy heart.

Sir Dominick stopped to think when he got to the middle of the deer-park, for he had not made up his mind, when he left the house, and the whisky did not clear his head, only it gev him courage.

He did not feel the cowld wind now, nor fear death, nor think much of anything but the shame and fall of the old family.

And he made up his mind, if no better thought came to him between that and there, so soon as he came to Murroa Wood, he'd hang himself from one of the oak branches with his cravat.

It was a bright moonlight night, there was just a bit of a cloud driving across the moon now and then, but, only for that, as light a'most as day.

Down he goes, right for the wood of Murroa. It seemed to him every step he took was as long as three, and it was no time till he was among the big oak-trees with their roots spreading from one to another, and their branches stretching overhead like the timbers of a naked roof, and the moon shining down through them, and casting their shadows thick and twist abroad on the ground as black as my shoe.

He was sobering a bit by this time, and he slacked his pace, and he thought 'twould be better to list in the French king's army, and thry what that might do for him, for he knew a man might take his own life any time, but it would puzzle him to take it back again when he liked.

Just as he made up his mind not to make away with himself, what should he hear but a step clinkin' along the dry ground under the trees, and soon he sees a grand gentleman right before him comin' up to meet him.[191]

He was a handsome young man like himself, and he wore a cocked-hat with gold-lace round it, such as officers wears on their coats, and he had on a dress the same as French officers wore in them times.

He stopped opposite Sir Dominick, and he cum to a standstill also.

The two gentlemen took off their hats to one another, and says the stranger:

"I am recruiting, sir," says he, "for my sovereign, and you'll find my money won't turn into pebbles, chips, and nutshells, by to-morrow."

At the same time he pulls out a big purse full of gold.

The minute he set eyes on that gentleman, Sir Dominick had his own opinion of him; and at those words he felt the very hair standing up on his head.

"Don't be afraid," says he, "the money won't burn you. If it proves honest gold, and if it prospers with you, I'm willing to make a bargain. This is the last day of February," says he; "I'll serve you seven years, and at the end of that time you shall serve me, and I'll come for you when the seven years is over, when the clock turns the minute between February and March; and the first of March ye'll come away with me, or never. You'll not find me a bad master, any more than a bad servant. I love my own; and I command all the pleasures and the glory of the world. The bargain dates from this day, and the lease is out at midnight on the last day I told you; and in the year"—he told him the year, it was easy reckoned, but I forget it—"and if you'd rather wait," he says, "for eight months and twenty eight days, before you sign the writin', you may, if you meet me here. But I can't do a great deal for you in the mean time; and if you don't sign then, all you get from me, up to that time, will vanish away, and you'll be just as you are[192] to-night, and ready to hang yourself on the first tree you meet.»

Well, the end of it was, Sir Dominick chose to wait, and he came back to the house with a big bag full of money, as round as your hat a'most.

My grandfather was glad enough, you may be sure, to see the master safe and sound again so soon. Into the kitchen he bangs again, and swings the bag o' money on the table; and he stands up straight, and heaves up his shoulders like a man that has just got shut of a load; and he looks at the bag, and my grandfather looks at him, and from him to it, and back again. Sir Dominick looked as white as a sheet, and says he:

"I don't know, Con, what's in it; it's the heaviest load I ever carried."

He seemed shy of openin' the bag; and he made my grandfather heap up a roaring fire of turf and wood, and then, at last, he opens it, and, sure enough, 'twas stuffed full o' golden guineas, bright and new, as if they were only that minute out o' the Mint.

Sir Dominick made my grandfather sit at his elbow while he counted every guinea in the bag.

When he was done countin', and it wasn't far from daylight when that time came, Sir Dominick made my grandfather swear not to tell a word about it. And a close secret it was for many a day after.

When the eight months and twenty-eight days were pretty near spent and ended, Sir Dominick returned to the house here with a troubled mind, in doubt what was best to be done, and no one alive but my grandfather knew anything about the matter, and he not half what had happened.

As the day drew near, towards the end of October, Sir Dominick grew only more and more troubled in mind.[193]

One time he made up his mind to have no more to say to such things, nor to speak again with the like of them he met with in the wood of Murroa. Then, again, his heart failed him when he thought of his debts, and he not knowing where to turn. Then, only a week before the day, everything began to go wrong with him. One man wrote from London to say that Sir Dominick paid three thousand pounds to the wrong man, and must pay it over again; another demanded a debt he never heard of before; and another, in Dublin, denied the payment of a thundherin' big bill, and Sir Dominick could nowhere find the receipt, and so on, wid fifty other things as bad.

Well, by the time the night of the 28th of October came round, he was a'most ready to lose his senses with all the demands that was risin' up again him on all sides, and nothing to meet them but the help of the one dhreadful friend he had to depind on at night in the oak-wood down there below.

So there was nothing for it but to go through with the business that was begun already, and about the same hour as he went last, he takes off the little crucifix he wore round his neck, for he was a Catholic, and his gospel, and his bit o' the thrue cross that he had in a locket, for since he took the money from the Evil One he was growin' frightful in himself, and got all he could to guard him from the power of the devil. But to-night, for his life, he daren't take them with him. So he gives them into my grandfather's hands without a word, only he looked as white as a sheet o' paper; and he takes his hat and sword, and telling my grandfather to watch for him, away he goes, to try what would come of it.

It was a fine still night, and the moon—not so bright, though, now as the first time—was shinin' over heath and rock, and down on the lonesome oak-wood below him.[194]

His heart beat thick as he drew near it. There was not a sound, not even the distant bark of a dog from the village behind him. There was not a lonesomer spot in the country round, and if it wasn't for his debts and losses that was drivin' him on half mad, in spite of his fears for his soul and his hopes of paradise, and all his good angel was whisperin' in his ear, he would a' turned back, and sent for his clargy, and made his confession and his penance, and changed his ways, and led a good life, for he was frightened enough to have done a great dale.

Softer and slower he stept as he got, once more, in undher the big branches of the oak-threes; and when he got in a bit, near where he met with the bad spirit before, he stopped and looked round him, and felt himself, every bit, turning as cowld as a dead man, and you may be sure he did not feel much betther when he seen the same man steppin' from behind the big tree that was touchin' his elbow a'most.

"You found the money good," says he, "but it was not enough. No matter, you shall have enough and to spare. I'll see after your luck, and I'll give you a hint whenever it can serve you; and any time you want to see me you have only to come down here, and call my face to mind, and wish me present. You shan't owe a shilling by the end of the year, and you shall never miss the right card, the best throw, and the winning horse. Are you willing?"

The young gentleman's voice almost stuck in his throat, and his hair was rising on his head, but he did get out a word or two to signify that he consented; and with that the Evil One handed him a needle, and bid him give him three drops of blood from his arm; and he took them in the cup of an acorn, and gave him a pen, and bid him write some words that he repeated, and that Sir Dominick[195] did not understand, on two thin slips of parchment. He took one himself and the other he sunk in Sir Dominick›s arm at the place where he drew the blood, and he closed the flesh over it. And that›s as true as you›re sittin› there!

Well, Sir Dominick went home. He was a frightened man, and well he might be. But in a little time he began to grow aisier in his mind. Anyhow, he got out of debt very quick, and money came tumbling in to make him richer, and everything he took in hand prospered, and he never made a wager, or played a game, but he won; and for all that, there was not a poor man on the estate that was not happier than Sir Dominick.

So he took again to his old ways; for, when the money came back, all came back, and there were hounds and horses, and wine galore, and no end of company, and grand doin's, and divarsion, up here at the great house. And some said Sir Dominick was thinkin' of gettin' married; and more said he wasn't. But, anyhow, there was somethin' troublin' him more than common, and so one night, unknownst to all, away he goes to the lonesome oak-wood. It was something, maybe, my grandfather thought was troublin' him about a beautiful young lady he was jealous of, and mad in love with her. But that was only guess.

Well, when Sir Dominick got into the wood this time, he grew more in dread than ever; and he was on the point of turnin' and lavin' the place, when who should he see, close beside him, but my gentleman, seated on a big stone undher one of the trees. In place of looking the fine young gentleman in goold lace and grand clothes he appeared before, he was now in rags, he looked twice the size he had been, and his face smutted with soot, and he had a murtherin' big steel hammer, as heavy as a half[196] hundred, with a handle a yard long, across his knees. It was so dark under the tree, he did not see him quite clear for some time.

He stood up, and he looked awful tall entirely. And what passed between them in that discourse my grandfather never heered. But Sir Dominick was as black as night afterwards, and hadn't a laugh for anything nor a word a'most for any one, and he only grew worse and worse, and darker and darker. And now this thing, whatever it was, used to come to him of its own accord, whether he wanted it or no; sometimes in one shape, and sometimes in another, in lonesome places, and sometimes at his side by night when he'd be ridin' home alone, until at last he lost heart altogether and sent for the priest.

The priest was with him a long time, and when he heered the whole story, he rode off all the way for the bishop, and the bishop came here to the great house next day, and he gev Sir Dominick a good advice. He toult him he must give over dicin', and swearin', and drinkin', and all bad company, and live a vartuous steady life until the seven years bargain was out, and if the divil didn't come for him the minute afther the stroke of twelve the first morning of the month of March, he was safe out of the bargain. There was not more than eight or ten months to run now before the seven years wor out, and he lived all the time according to the bishop's advice, as strict as if he was "in retreat."

Well, you may guess he felt quare enough when the mornin' of the 28th of February came.

The priest came up by appointment, and Sir Dominick and his raverence wor together in the room you see there, and kep' up their prayers together till the clock struck twelve, and a good hour after, and not a sign of a dis[197]turbance, nor nothing came near them, and the priest slep' that night in the house in the room next Sir Dominick's, and all went over as comfortable as could be, and they shook hands and kissed like two comrades after winning a battle.

So, now, Sir Dominick thought he might as well have a pleasant evening, after all his fastin' and praying; and he sent round to half a dozen of the neighbouring gentlemen to come and dine with him, and his raverence stayed and dined also, and a roarin' bowl o' punch they had, and no end o' wine, and the swearin' and dice, and cards and guineas changing hands, and songs and stories, that wouldn't do any one good to hear, and the priest slipped away, when he seen the turn things was takin', and it was not far from the stroke of twelve when Sir Dominick, sitting at the head of his table, swears, "this is the best first of March I ever sat down with my friends."

"It ain't the first o' March," says Mr. Hiffernan of Ballyvoreen. He was a scholard, and always kep' an almanack.

"What is it, then?" says Sir Dominick, startin' up, and dhroppin' the ladle into the bowl, and starin' at him as if he had two heads.

"'Tis the twenty-ninth of February, leap year," says he. And just as they were talkin', the clock strikes twelve; and my grandfather, who was half asleep in a chair by the fire in the hall, openin' his eyes, sees a short square fellow with a cloak on, and long black hair bushin' out from under his hat, standin' just there where you see the bit o' light shinin' again' the wall.

(My hunchbacked friend pointed with his stick to a little patch of red sunset light that relieved the deepening shadow of the passage.)

"Tell your master," says he, in an awful voice, like the[198] growl of a baist, «that I›m here by appointment, and expect him down-stairs this minute.»

Up goes my grandfather, by these very steps you are sittin' on.

"Tell him I can't come down yet," says Sir Dominick, and he turns to the company in the room, and says he with a cold sweat shinin' on his face, "for God's sake, gentlemen, will any of you jump from the window and bring the priest here?" One looked at another and no one knew what to make of it, and in the meantime, up comes my grandfather again, and says he, tremblin', "He says, sir, unless you go down to him, he'll come up to you."

"I don't understand this, gentlemen, I'll see what it means," says Sir Dominick, trying to put a face on it, and walkin' out o' the room like a man through the press-room, with the hangman waitin' for him outside. Down the stairs he comes, and two or three of the gentlemen peeping over the banisters, to see. My grandfather was walking six or eight steps behind him, and he seen the stranger take a stride out to meet Sir Dominick, and catch him up in his arms, and whirl his head against the wall, and wi' that the hall-doore flies open, and out goes the candles, and the turf and wood-ashes flyin' with the wind out o' the hall-fire, ran in a drift o' sparks along the floore by his feet.

Down runs the gintlemen. Bang goes the hall-doore. Some comes runnin' up, and more runnin' down, with lights. It was all over with Sir Dominick. They lifted up the corpse, and put its shoulders again' the wall; but there was not a gasp left in him. He was cowld and stiffenin' already.

Pat Donovan was comin' up to the great house late that night and after he passed the little brook, that the carriage track up to the house crosses, and about fifty[199] steps to this side of it, his dog, that was by his side, makes a sudden wheel, and springs over the wall, and sets up a yowlin› inside you›d hear a mile away; and that minute two men passed him by in silence, goin› down from the house, one of them short and square, and the other like Sir Dominick in shape, but there was little light under the trees where he was, and they looked only like shadows; and as they passed him by he could not hear the sound of their feet and he drew back to the wall frightened; and when he got up to the great house, he found all in confusion, and the master›s body, with the head smashed to pieces, lying just on *that spot*.

The narrator stood up and indicated with the point of his stick the exact site of the body, and, as I looked, the shadow deepened, the red stain of sunlight vanished from the wall, and the sun had gone down behind the distant hill of New Castle, leaving the haunted scene in the deep grey of darkening twilight.

So I and the story-teller parted, not without good wishes on both sides, and a little "tip," which seemed not unwelcome, from me.

It was dusk and the moon up by the time I reached the village, remounted my nag, and looked my last on the scene of the terrible legend of Dunoran.

10
ULTOR DE LACY
A LEGEND OF CAPPERCULLEN

Anonymous in the *Dublin University Magazine* (1861).

CHAPTER I.
THE JACOBITE'S LEGACY.

In my youth I heard a great many Irish family traditions, more or less of a supernatural character, some of them very peculiar, and all, to a child at least, highly interesting. One of these I will now relate, though the translation to cold type from oral narrative, with all the aids of animated human voice and countenance, and the appropriate *mise en scéne* of the old-fashioned parlour fireside and its listening circle of excited faces, and, outside, the wintry blast and the moan of leafless boughs, with the occasional rattle of the clumsy old window-frame behind shutter and curtain, as the blast swept by, is at best a trying one.

About midway up the romantic glen of Cappercullen, near the point where the counties of Limerick, Clare, and Tipperary converge, upon the then sequestered and forest-bound range of the Slieve-Felim hills, there stood, in the reigns of the two earliest Georges, the picturesque[201] and massive remains of one of the finest of the Anglo-Irish castles of Munster—perhaps of Ireland.

It crowned the precipitous edge of the wooded glen, itself half-buried among the wild forest that covered that long and solitary range. There was no human habitation within a circle of many miles, except the half-dozen hovels and the small thatched chapel composing the little village of Murroa, which lay at the foot of the glen among the straggling skirts of the noble forest.

Its remoteness and difficulty of access saved it from demolition. It was worth nobody's while to pull down and remove the ponderous and clumsy oak, much less the masonry or flagged roofing of the pile. Whatever would pay the cost of removal had been long since carried away. The rest was abandoned to time—the destroyer.

The hereditary owners of this noble building and of a wide territory in the contiguous counties I have named, were English—the De Lacys—long naturalized in Ireland. They had acquired at least this portion of their estate in the reign of Henry VIII., and held it, with some vicissitudes, down to the establishment of the revolution in Ireland, when they suffered attainder, and, like other great families of that period, underwent a final eclipse.

The De Lacy of that day retired to France, and held a brief command in the Irish Brigade, interrupted by sickness. He retired, became a poor hanger-on of the Court of St. Germains, and died early in the eighteenth century—as well as I remember, 1705—leaving an only son, hardly twelve years old, called by the strange but significant name of Ultor.

At this point commences the marvellous ingredient of my tale.

When his father was dying, he had him to his bedside, with no one by except his confessor; and having told him,[202] first, that on reaching the age of twenty-one, he was to lay claim to a certain small estate in the county of Clare, in Ireland, in right of his mother—the title-deeds of which he gave him—and next, having enjoined him not to marry before the age of thirty, on the ground that earlier marriages destroyed the spirit and the power of enterprise, and would incapacitate him from the accomplishment of his destiny—the restoration of his family—he then went on to open to the child a matter which so terrified him that he cried lamentably, trembling all over, clinging to the priest›s gown with one hand and to his father›s cold wrist with the other, and imploring him, with screams of horror, to desist from his communication.

But the priest, impressed, no doubt, himself, with its necessity, compelled him to listen. And then his father showed him a small picture, from which also the child turned with shrieks, until similarly constrained to look. They did not let him go until he had carefully conned the features, and was able to tell them, from memory, the colour of the eyes and hair, and the fashion and hues of the dress. Then his father gave him a black box containing this portrait, which was a full-length miniature, about nine inches long, painted very finely in oils, as smooth as enamel, and folded above it a sheet of paper, written over in a careful and very legible hand.

The deeds and this black box constituted the most important legacy bequeathed to his only child by the ruined Jacobite, and he deposited them in the hands of the priest, in trust, till his boy, Ultor, should have attained to an age to understand their value, and to keep them securely.

When this scene was ended, the dying exile's mind, I suppose, was relieved, for he spoke cheerily, and said he believed he would recover; and they soothed the crying[203] child, and his father kissed him, and gave him a little silver coin to buy fruit with; and so they sent him off with another boy for a walk, and when he came back his father was dead.

He remained in France under the care of this ecclesiastic until he had attained the age of twenty-one, when he repaired to Ireland, and his title being unaffected by his father's attainder, he easily made good his claim to the small estate in the county of Clare.

There he settled, making a dismal and solitary tour now and then of the vast territories which had once been his father's, and nursing those gloomy and impatient thoughts which befitted the enterprises to which he was devoted.

Occasionally he visited Paris, that common centre of English, Irish, and Scottish disaffection; and there, when a little past thirty, he married the daughter of another ruined Irish house. His bride returned with him to the melancholy seclusion of their Munster residence, where she bore him in succession two daughters—Alice, the elder, dark-eyed and dark-haired, grave and sensible—Una, four years younger, with large blue eyes and long and beautiful golden hair.

Their poor mother was, I believe, naturally a light-hearted, sociable, high-spirited little creature; and her gay and childish nature pined in the isolation and gloom of her lot. At all events she died young, and the children were left to the sole care of their melancholy and embittered father. In process of time the girls grew up, tradition says, beautiful. The elder was designed for a convent, the younger her father hoped to mate as nobly as her high blood and splendid beauty seemed to promise, if only the great game on which he had resolved to stake all succeeded.

CHAPTER II.
THE FAIRIES IN THE CASTLE.

The Rebellion of '45 came, and Ultor de Lacy was one of the few Irishmen implicated treasonably in that daring and romantic insurrection. Of course there were warrants out against him, but he was not to be found. The young ladies, indeed, remained as heretofore in their father's lonely house in Clare; but whether he had crossed the water or was still in Ireland was for some time unknown, even to them. In due course he was attainted, and his little estate forfeited. It was a miserable catastrophe—a tremendous and beggarly waking up from a life-long dream of returning principality.

In due course the officers of the crown came down to take possession, and it behoved the young ladies to flit. Happily for them the ecclesiastic I have mentioned was not quite so confident as their father, of his winning back the magnificent patrimony of his ancestors; and by his advice the daughters had been secured twenty pounds a year each, under the marriage settlement of their parents, which was all that stood between this proud house and literal destitution.

Late one evening, as some little boys from the village were returning from a ramble through the dark and devious glen of Cappercullen, with their pockets laden with nuts and "frahans," to their amazement and even terror they saw a light streaming redly from the narrow window of one of the towers overhanging the precipice among the ivy and the lofty branches, across the glen, already dim in the shadows of the deepening night.[205]

"Look—look—look—'tis the Phooka's tower!" was the general cry, in the vernacular Irish, and a universal scamper commenced.

The bed of the glen, strewn with great fragments of rock, among which rose the tall stems of ancient trees, and overgrown with a tangled copse, was at the best no favourable ground for a run. Now it was dark; and, terrible work breaking through brambles and hazels, and tumbling over rocks. Little Shaeen Mull Ryan, the last of the panic rout, screaming to his mates to wait for him—saw a whitish figure emerge from the thicket at the base of the stone flight of steps that descended the side of the glen, close by the castle-wall, intercepting his flight, and a discordant male voice shrieked—

"I have you!"

At the same time the boy, with a cry of terror, tripped and tumbled; and felt himself roughly caught by the arm, and hauled to his feet with a shake.

A wild yell from the child, and a volley of terror and entreaty followed.

"Who is it, Larry; what's the matter?" cried a voice, high in air, from the turret window. The words floated down through the trees, clear and sweet as the low notes of a flute.

"Only a child, my lady; a boy."

"Is he hurt?"

"Are you hurted?" demanded the whitish man, who held him fast, and repeated the question in Irish; but the child only kept blubbering and crying for mercy, with his hands clasped, and trying to drop on his knees.

Larry's strong old hand held him up. He was hurt, and bleeding from over his eye.

"Just a trifle hurted, my lady!"

"Bring him up here."[206]

Shaeen Mull Ryan gave himself over. He was among "the good people," who he knew would keep him prisoner for ever and a day. There was no good in resisting. He grew bewildered, and yielded himself passively to his fate, and emerged from the glen on the platform above; his captor's knotted old hand still on his arm, and looked round on the tall mysterious trees, and the gray front of the castle, revealed in the imperfect moonlight, as upon the scenery of a dream.

The old man who, with thin wiry legs, walked by his side, in a dingy white coat, and blue facings, and great pewter buttons, with his silver gray hair escaping from under his battered three-cocked hat; and his shrewd puckered resolute face, in which the boy could read no promise of sympathy, showing so white and phantom-like in the moonlight, was, as he thought, the incarnate ideal of a fairy.

This figure led him in silence under the great arched gateway, and across the grass-grown court, to the door in the far angle of the building; and so, in the dark, round and round, up a stone screw stair, and with a short turn into a large room, with a fire of turf and wood, burning on its long unused hearth, over which hung a pot, and about it an old woman with a great wooden spoon was busy. An iron candlestick supported their solitary candle; and about the floor of the room, as well as on the table and chairs, lay a litter of all sorts of things; piles of old faded hangings, boxes, trunks, clothes, pewter-plates, and cups; and I know not what more.

But what instantly engaged the fearful gaze of the boy were the figures of two ladies; red drugget cloaks they had on, like the peasant girls of Munster and Connaught, and the rest of their dress was pretty much in keeping. But they had the grand air, the refined expression and[207] beauty, and above all, the serene air of command that belong to people of a higher rank.

The elder, with black hair and full brown eyes, sat writing at the deal table on which the candle stood, and raised her dark gaze to the boy as he came in. The other, with her hood thrown back, beautiful and *riant*, with a flood of wavy golden hair, and great blue eyes, and with something kind, and arch, and strange in her countenance, struck him as the most wonderful beauty he could have imagined.

They questioned the man in a language strange to the child. It was not English, for he had a smattering of that, and the man's story seemed to amuse them. The two young ladies exchanged a glance, and smiled mysteriously. He was more convinced than ever that he was among the good people. The younger stepped gaily forward and said—

"Do you know who *I* am, my little man? Well, I›m the fairy Una, and this is my palace; and that fairy you see there (pointing to the dark lady, who was looking out something in a box), is my sister and family physician, the Lady Graveairs; and these (glancing at the old man and woman), are some of my courtiers; and I›m considering now what I shall do with *you*, whether I shall send you to-night to Lough Guir, riding on a rush, to make my compliments to the Earl of Desmond in his enchanted castle; or, straight to your bed, two thousand miles under ground, among the gnomes; or to prison in that little corner of the moon you see through the window—with the man-in-the-moon for your gaoler, for thrice three hundred years and a day! There, don't cry. You only see how serious a thing it is for you, little boys, to come so near my castle. Now, for this once, I'll let you go. But, henceforward, any boys I, or my people, may[208] find within half a mile round my castle, shall belong to me for life, and never behold their home or their people more.»

And she sang a little air and chased mystically half a dozen steps before him, holding out her cloak with her pretty fingers, and courtesying very low, to his indescribable alarm.

Then, with a little laugh, she said—

"My little man, we must mend your head."

And so they washed his scratch, and the elder one applied a plaister to it. And she of the great blue eyes took out of her pocket a little French box of bon-bons and emptied it into his hand, and she said—

"You need not be afraid to eat these—they are very good—and I'll send my fairy, Blanc-et-bleu, to set you free. Take him (she addressed Larry), and let him go, with a solemn charge."

The elder, with a grave and affectionate smile, said, looking on the fairy—

"Brave, dear, wild Una! nothing can ever quell your gaiety of heart."

And Una kissed her merrily on the cheek.

So the oak door of the room again opened, and Shaeen, with his conductor, descended the stair. He walked with the scared boy in grim silence near half way down the wild hill-side toward Murroa, and then he stopped, and said in Irish—

"You never saw the fairies before, my fine fellow, and 'tisn't often those who once set eyes on us return to tell it. Whoever comes nearer, night or day, than this stone," and he tapped it with the end of his cane, "will never see his home again, for we'll keep him till the day of judgment; good-night, little gossoon—and away with you."

So these young ladies, Alice and Una, with two old servants, by their father's direction, had taken up their abode in a portion of that side of the old castle which overhung the glen; and with the furniture and hangings they had removed from their late residence, and with the aid of glass in the casements and some other indispensable repairs, and a thorough airing, they made the rooms they had selected just habitable, as a rude and temporary shelter.

CHAPTER III.
THE PRIEST'S ADVENTURES IN THE GLEN.

At first, of course, they saw or heard little of their father. In general, however, they knew that his plan was to procure some employment in France, and to remove them there. Their present strange abode was only an adventure and an episode, and they believed that any day they might receive instructions to commence their journey.

After a little while the pursuit relaxed. The government, I believe, did not care, provided he did not obtrude himself, what became of him, or where he concealed himself. At all events, the local authorities showed no disposition to hunt him down. The young ladies' charges on the little forfeited property were paid without any dispute, and no vexatious inquiries were raised as to what had become of the furniture and other personal property which had been carried away from the forfeited house.

The haunted reputation of the castle—for in those days, in matters of the marvellous, the oldest were children—secured the little family in the seclusion they coveted. Once, or sometimes twice a week, old Laurence, with a[210] shaggy little pony, made a secret expedition to the city of Limerick, starting before dawn, and returning under the cover of the night, with his purchases. There was beside an occasional sly moonlit visit from the old parish priest, and a midnight mass in the old castle for the little outlawed congregation.

As the alarm and inquiry subsided, their father made them, now and then, a brief and stealthy visit. At first these were but of a night's duration, and with great precaution; but gradually they were extended and less guarded. Still he was, as the phrase is in Munster, "on his keeping." He had firearms always by his bed, and had arranged places of concealment in the castle in the event of a surprise. But no attempt nor any disposition to molest him appearing, he grew more at ease, if not more cheerful.

It came, at last, that he would sometimes stay so long as two whole months at a time, and then depart as suddenly and mysteriously as he came. I suppose he had always some promising plot on hand, and his head full of ingenious treason, and lived on the sickly and exciting dietary of hope deferred.

Was there a poetical justice in this, that the little *ménage* thus secretly established, in the solitary and time-worn pile, should have themselves experienced, but from causes not so easily explicable, those very supernatural perturbations which they had themselves essayed to inspire?

The interruption of the old priest's secret visits was the earliest consequence of the mysterious interference which now began to display itself. One night, having left his cob in care of his old sacristan in the little village, he trudged on foot along the winding pathway, among the gray rocks and ferns that threaded the glen, intending a[211] ghostly visit to the fair recluses of the castle, and he lost his way in this strange fashion.

There was moonlight, indeed, but it was little more than quarter-moon, and a long train of funereal clouds were sailing slowly across the sky—so that, faint and wan as it was, the light seldom shone full out, and was often hidden for a minute or two altogether. When he reached the point in the glen where the castle-stairs were wont to be, he could see nothing of them, and above, no trace of the castle-towers. So, puzzled somewhat, he pursued his way up the ravine, wondering how his walk had become so unusually protracted and fatiguing.

At last, sure enough, he saw the castle as plain as could be, and a lonely streak of candle-light issuing from the tower, just as usual, when his visit was expected. But he could not find the stair; and had to clamber among the rocks and copse-wood the best way he could. But when he emerged at top, there was nothing but the bare heath. Then the clouds stole over the moon again, and he moved along with hesitation and difficulty, and once more he saw the outline of the castle against the sky, quite sharp and clear. But this time it proved to be a great battlemented mass of cloud on the horizon. In a few minutes more he was quite close, all of a sudden, to the great front, rising gray and dim in the feeble light, and not till he could have struck it with his good oak "wattle" did he discover it to be only one of those wild, gray frontages of living rock that rise here and there in picturesque tiers along the slopes of those solitary mountains. And so, till dawn, pursuing this mirage of the castle, through pools and among ravines, he wore out a night of miserable misadventure and fatigue.

Another night, riding up the glen, so far as the level way at bottom would allow, and intending to make his[212] nag fast at his customary tree, he hears on a sudden a horrid shriek at top of the steep rocks above his head, and something—a gigantic human form, it seemed—came tumbling and bounding headlong down through the rocks, and fell with a fearful impetus just before his horse›s hoofs and there lay like a huge palpitating carcass. The horse was scared, as, indeed, was his rider, too, and more so when this apparently lifeless thing sprang up to his legs, and throwing his arms apart to bar their further progress, advanced his white and gigantic face towards them. Then the horse started about, with a snort of terror, nearly unseating the priest, and broke away into a furious and uncontrollable gallop.

I need not recount all the strange and various misadventures which the honest priest sustained in his endeavours to visit the castle, and its isolated tenants. They were enough to wear out his resolution, and frighten him into submission. And so at last these spiritual visits quite ceased; and fearing to awaken inquiry and suspicion, he thought it only prudent to abstain from attempting them in the daytime.

So the young ladies of the castle were more alone than ever. Their father, whose visits were frequently of long duration, had of late ceased altogether to speak of their contemplated departure for France, grew angry at any allusion to it, and they feared, had abandoned the plan altogether.

CHAPTER IV.
THE LIGHT IN THE BELL TOWER.

Shortly after the discontinuance of the priest's visits, old Laurence, one night, to his surprise, saw light issuing from a window in the Bell Tower. It was at first only a tremulous red ray, visible only for a few minutes, which seemed to pass from the room, through whose window it escaped upon the courtyard of the castle, and so to lose itself. This tower and casement were in the angle of the building, exactly confronting that in which the little outlawed family had taken up their quarters.

The whole family were troubled at the appearance of this dull red ray from the chamber in the Bell Tower. Nobody knew what to make of it. But Laurence, who had campaigned in Italy with his old master, the young ladies' grandfather—"the heavens be his bed this night!"—was resolved to see it out, and took his great horse-pistols with him, and ascended to the corridor leading to the tower. But his search was vain.

This light left a sense of great uneasiness among the inmates, and most certainly it was not pleasant to suspect the establishment of an independent and possibly dangerous lodger or even colony, within the walls of the same old building.

The light very soon appeared again, steadier and somewhat brighter, in the same chamber. Again old Laurence buckled on his armour, swearing ominously to himself, and this time bent in earnest upon conflict. The young ladies watched in thrilling suspense from the great window in *their* stronghold, looking diagonally across the court. But as Laurence, who had entered the massive range of[214] buildings opposite, might be supposed to be approaching the chamber from which this ill-omened glare proceeded, it steadily waned, finally disappearing altogether, just a few seconds before his voice was heard shouting from the arched window to know which way the light had gone.

This lighting up of the great chamber of the Bell Tower grew at last to be of frequent and almost continual recurrence. It was, there, long ago, in times of trouble and danger, that the De Lacys of those evil days used to sit in feudal judgment upon captive adversaries, and, as tradition alleged, often gave them no more time for shrift and prayer, than it needed to mount to the battlement of the turret overhead, from which they were forthwith hung by the necks, for a caveat and admonition to all evil disposed persons viewing the same from the country beneath.

Old Laurence observed these mysterious glimmerings with an evil and an anxious eye, and many and various were the stratagems he tried, but in vain, to surprise the audacious intruders. It is, however, I believe, a fact that no phenomenon, no matter how startling at first, if prosecuted with tolerable regularity, and unattended with any new circumstances of terror, will very long continue to excite alarm or even wonder.

So the family came to acquiesce in this mysterious light. No harm accompanied it. Old Laurence, as he smoked his lonely pipe in the grass-grown courtyard, would cast a disturbed glance at it, as it softly glowed out through the darking aperture, and mutter a prayer or an oath. But he had given over the chase as a hopeless business. And Peggy Sullivan, the old dame of all work, when, by chance, for she never willingly looked toward the haunted quarter, she caught the faint reflection of its dull effulgence with the corner of her eye, would sign herself with the cross or fumble at her beads, and deeper furrows would gather in her forehead, and her face grow ashen and perturbed. And this was not mended by the levity with which the young ladies, with whom the spectre had lost his influence, familiarity, as usual, breeding contempt, had come to talk, and even to jest, about it.

CHAPTER V.
THE MAN WITH THE CLARET-MARK.

But as the former excitement flagged, old Peggy Sullivan produced a new one; for she solemnly avowed that she had seen a thin-faced man, with an ugly red mark all over the side of his cheek, looking out of the same window, just at sunset, before the young ladies returned from their evening walk.

This sounded in their ears like an old woman's dream, but still it was an excitement, jocular in the morning, and just, perhaps, a little fearful as night overspread the vast and desolate building, but still, not wholly unpleasant. This little flicker of credulity suddenly, however, blazed up into the full light of conviction.

Old Laurence, who was not given to dreaming, and had a cool, hard head, and an eye like a hawk, saw the same figure, just about the same hour, when the last level gleam of sunset was tinting the summits of the towers and the tops of the tall trees that surrounded them.

He had just entered the court from the great gate, when he heard all at once the hard peculiar twitter of alarm which sparrows make when a cat or a hawk invades[216] their safety, rising all round from the thick ivy that overclimbed the wall on his left, and raising his eyes listlessly, he saw, with a sort of shock, a thin, ungainly man, standing with his legs crossed, in the recess of the window from which the light was wont to issue, leaning with his elbows on the stone mullion, and looking down with a sort of sickly sneer, his hollow yellow cheeks being deeply stained on one side with what is called a «claret mark.»

"I have you at last, you villain!" cried Larry, in a strange rage and panic: "drop down out of that on the grass here, and give yourself up, or I'll shoot you."

The threat was backed with an oath, and he drew from his coat pocket the long holster pistol he was wont to carry, and covered his man cleverly.

"I give you while I count ten—one-two-three-four. If you draw back, I'll fire, mind; five-six—you'd better be lively—seven-eight-nine—one chance more; will you come down? Then take it—ten!"

Bang went the pistol. The sinister stranger was hardly fifteen feet removed from him, and Larry was a dead shot. But this time he made a scandalous miss, for the shot knocked a little white dust from the stone wall a full yard at one side; and the fellow never shifted his negligent posture or qualified his sardonic smile during the procedure.

Larry was mortified and angry.

"You'll not get off this time, my tulip!" he said with a grin, exchanging the smoking weapon for the loaded pistol in reserve.

"What are you pistolling, Larry?" said a familiar voice close by his elbow, and he saw his master, accompanied by a handsome young man in a cloak.

"That villain, your honour, in the window, there."[217]

"Why there's nobody there, Larry," said De Lacy, with a laugh, though that was no common indulgence with him.

As Larry gazed, the figure somehow dissolved and broke up without receding. A hanging tuft of yellow and red ivy nodded queerly in place of the face, some broken and discoloured masonry in perspective took up the outline and colouring of the arms and figure, and two imperfect red and yellow lichen streaks carried on the curved tracing of the long spindle shanks. Larry blessed himself, and drew his hand across his damp forehead, over his bewildered eyes, and could not speak for a minute. It was all some devilish trick; he could take his oath he saw every feature in the fellow's face, the lace and buttons of his cloak and doublet, and even his long finger nails and thin yellow fingers that overhung the cross-shaft of the window, where there was now nothing but a rusty stain left.

The young gentleman who had arrived with De Lacy, staid that night and shared with great apparent relish the homely fare of the family. He was a gay and gallant Frenchman, and the beauty of the younger lady, and her pleasantry and spirit, seemed to make his hours pass but too swiftly, and the moment of parting sad.

When he had departed early in the morning, Ultor De Lacy had a long talk with his elder daughter, while the younger was busy with her early dairy task, for among their retainers this *proles generosa* reckoned a «kind» little Kerry cow.

He told her that he had visited France since he had been last at Cappercullen, and how good and gracious their sovereign had been, and how he had arranged a noble alliance for her sister Una. The young gentleman was of high blood, and though not rich, had, nevertheless,[218] his acres and his *nom de terre*, besides a captain's rank in the army. He was, in short, the very gentleman with whom they had parted only that morning. On what special business he was now in Ireland there was no necessity that he should speak; but being here he had brought him hither to present him to his daughter, and found that the impression she had made was quite what was desirable.

"You, you know, dear Alice, are promised to a conventual life. Had it been otherwise—"

He hesitated for a moment.

"You are right, dear father," she said, kissing his hand, "I *am* so promised, and no earthly tie or allurement has power to draw me from that holy engagement.»

"Well," he said, returning her caress, "I do not mean to urge you upon that point. It must not, however, be until Una's marriage has taken place. That cannot be, for many good reasons, sooner than this time twelve months; we shall then exchange this strange and barbarous abode for Paris, where are many eligible convents, in which are entertained as sisters some of the noblest ladies of France; and there, too, in Una's marriage will be continued, though not the name, at all events the blood, the lineage, and the title which, so sure as justice ultimately governs the course of human events, will be again established, powerful and honoured in this country, the scene of their ancient glory and transitory misfortunes. Meanwhile, we must not mention this engagement to Una. Here she runs no risk of being sought or won; but the mere knowledge that her hand was absolutely pledged, might excite a capricious opposition and repining such as neither I nor you would like to see; therefore be secret."

The same evening he took Alice with him for a ramble[219] round the castle wall, while they talked of grave matters, and he as usual allowed her a dim and doubtful view of some of those cloud-built castles in which he habitually dwelt, and among which his jaded hopes revived.

They were walking upon a pleasant short sward of darkest green, on one side overhung by the gray castle walls, and on the other by the forest trees that here and there closely approached it, when precisely as they turned the angle of the Bell Tower, they were encountered by a person walking directly towards them. The sight of a stranger, with the exception of the one visitor introduced by her father, was in this place so absolutely unprecedented, that Alice was amazed and affrighted to such a degree that for a moment she stood stock-still.

But there was more in this apparition to excite unpleasant emotions, than the mere circumstance of its unexpectedness. The figure was very strange, being that of a tall, lean, ungainly man, dressed in a dingy suit, somewhat of a Spanish fashion, with a brown laced cloak, and faded red stockings. He had long lank legs, long arms, hands, and fingers, and a very long sickly face, with a drooping nose, and a sly, sarcastic leer, and a great purplish stain over-spreading more than half of one cheek.

As he strode past, he touched his cap with his thin, discoloured fingers, and an ugly side glance, and disappeared round the corner. The eyes of father and daughter followed him in silence.

Ultor De Lacy seemed first absolutely terror-stricken, and then suddenly inflamed with ungovernable fury. He dropped his cane on the ground, drew his rapier, and, without wasting a thought on his daughter, pursued.

He just had a glimpse of the retreating figure as it disappeared round the far angle. The plume, and the[220] lank hair, the point of the rapier-scabbard, the flutter of the skirt of the cloak, and one red stocking and heel; and this was the last he saw of him.

When Alice reached his side, his drawn sword still in his hand, he was in a state of abject agitation.

"Thank Heaven, he's gone!" she exclaimed.

"He's gone," echoed Ultor, with a strange glare.

"And you are safe," she added, clasping his hand.

He sighed a great sigh.

"And you don't think he's coming back?"

"He!—who?"

"The stranger who passed us but now. Do you know him, father?"

"Yes—and—no, child—I know him not—and yet I know him too well. Would to heaven we could leave this accursed haunt to-night. Cursed be the stupid malice that first provoked this horrible feud, which no sacrifice and misery can appease, and no exorcism can quell or even suspend. The wretch has come from afar with a sure instinct to devour my last hope—to dog us into our last retreat—and to blast with his triumph the very dust and ruins of our house. What ails that stupid priest that he has given over his visits? Are *my* children to be left without mass or confession—the sacraments which *guard* as well as save—because he once loses his way in a mist, or mistakes a streak of foam in the brook for a dead man›s face? D——n him!»

"See, Alice, *if* he won›t come,» he resumed, «you must only *write* your confession to him in full—you and Una. Laurence is trusty, and will carry it—and we›ll get the bishop›s—or, if need be, the Pope›s leave for him to give you absolution. I›ll move heaven and earth, but you *shall* have the sacraments, poor children!—and see him. I›ve been a wild fellow in my youth, and never pretended[221] to sanctity; but I know there›s but one safe way—and—and—keep you each a bit of this—(he opened a small silver box)—about you while you stay here—fold and sew it up reverently in a bit of the old psaltery parchment and wear it next your hearts—›tis a fragment of the consecrated wafer—and will help, with the saints› protection, to guard you from harm—and be strict in fasts, and constant in prayer—*I* can do nothing—nor devise any help. The curse has fallen, indeed, on me and mine.»

And Alice, saw, in silence, the tears of despair roll down his pale and agitated face.

This adventure was also a secret, and Una was to hear nothing of it.

CHAPTER VI.
VOICES.

Now Una, nobody knew why, began to lose spirit, and to grow pale. Her fun and frolic were quite gone! Even her songs ceased. She was silent with her sister, and loved solitude better. She said she was well, and quite happy, and could in no wise be got to account for the lamentable change that had stolen over her. She had grown odd too, and obstinate in trifles; and strangely reserved and cold.

Alice was very unhappy in consequence. What was the cause of this estrangement—had she offended her, and how? But Una had never before borne resentment for an hour. What could have altered her entire nature so? Could it be the shadow and chill of coming insanity?

Once or twice, when her sister urged her with tears and entreaties to disclose the secret of her changed spirits and demeanour, she seemed to listen with a sort of silent wonder and suspicion, and then she looked for a moment full upon her, and seemed on the very point of revealing all. But the earnest dilated gaze stole downward to the floor, and subsided into an odd wily smile, and she began to whisper to herself, and the smile and the whisper were both a mystery to Alice.

She and Alice slept in the same bedroom—a chamber in a projecting tower—which on their arrival, when poor Una was so merry, they had hung round with old tapestry, and decorated fantastically according to their skill and frolic. One night, as they went to bed, Una said, as if speaking to herself—

"'Tis my last night in this room—I shall sleep no more with Alice."

"And what has poor Alice done, Una, to deserve your strange unkindness?"

Una looked on her curiously, and half frightened, and then the odd smile stole over her face like a gleam of moonlight.

"My poor Alice, what have you to do with it?" she whispered.

"And why do you talk of sleeping no more with me?" said Alice.

"Why? Alice dear—no why—no reason—only a knowledge that it must be so, or Una will die."

"Die, Una darling!—what can you mean?"

"Yes, sweet Alice, die, indeed. We must all die some time, you know, or—or undergo a change; and my time is near—*very* near—unless I sleep apart from you.»

"Indeed, Una, sweetheart, I think you *are* ill, but not near death.»[223]

"Una knows what you think, wise Alice—but she's not mad—on the contrary, she's wiser than other folks."

"She's sadder and stranger too," said Alice, tenderly.

"Knowledge is sorrow," answered Una, and she looked across the room through her golden hair which she was combing—and through the window, beyond which lay the tops of the great trees, and the still foliage of the glen in the misty moonlight.

"'Tis enough, Alice dear; it must be so. The bed must move hence, or Una's bed will be low enough ere long. See, it shan't be far though, only into that small room."

She pointed to an inner room or closet opening from that in which they lay. The walls of the building were hugely thick, and there were double doors of oak between the chambers, and Alice thought, with a sigh, how completely separated they were going to be.

However she offered no opposition. The change was made, and the girls for the first time since childhood lay in separate chambers. A few nights afterwards Alice, awoke late in the night from a dreadful dream, in which the sinister figure which she and her father had encountered in their ramble round the castle walls, bore a principal part.

When she awoke there were still in her ears the sounds which had mingled in her dream. They were the notes of a deep, ringing, bass voice rising from the glen beneath the castle walls—something between humming and singing—listlessly unequal and intermittent, like the melody of a man whiling away the hours over his work. While she was wondering at this unwonted minstrelsy, there came a silence, and—could she believe her ears?—it certainly was Una's clear low contralto—softly singing a bar or two from the window. Then once more[224] silence—and then again the strange manly voice, faintly chaunting from the leafy abyss.

With a strange wild feeling of suspicion and terror, Alice glided to the window. The moon who sees so many things, and keeps all secrets, with her cold impenetrable smile, was high in the sky. But Alice saw the red flicker of a candle from Una's window, and, she thought, the shadow of her head against the deep side wall of its recess. Then this was gone, and there were no more sights or sounds that night.

As they sate at breakfast, the small birds were singing merrily from among the sun-tipped foliage.

"I love this music," said Alice, unusually pale and sad; "it comes with the pleasant light of morning. I remember, Una, when *you* used to sing, like those gay birds, in the fresh beams of the morning; that was in the old time, when Una kept no secret from poor Alice.»

"And Una knows what her sage Alice means; but there are other birds, silent all day long, and, they say, the sweetest too, that love to sing by *night* alone.»

So things went on—the elder girl pained and melancholy—the younger silent, changed, and unaccountable.

A little while after this, very late one night, on awaking, Alice heard a conversation being carried on in her sister's room. There seemed to be no disguise about it. She could not distinguish the words, indeed, the walls being some six feet thick, and two great oak doors intercepting. But Una's clear voice, and the deep bell-like tones of the unknown, made up the dialogue.

Alice sprung from her bed, threw her clothes about her, and tried to enter her sister's room; but the inner door was bolted. The voices ceased to speak as she knocked, and Una opened it, and stood before her in her night-dress, candle in hand.[225]

"Una—Una, darling, as you hope for peace, tell me who is here?" cried frightened Alice, with her trembling arms about her neck.

Una drew back, with her large, innocent blue eyes fixed full upon her.

"Come in, Alice," she said, coldly.

And in came Alice, with a fearful glance around. There was no hiding place there; a chair, a table, a little bed-stead, and two or three pegs in the wall to hang clothes on; a narrow window, with two iron bars across; no hearth or chimney—nothing but bare walls.

Alice looked round in amazement, and her eyes glanced with painful inquiry into those of her sister's. Una smiled one of her peculiar sidelong smiles, and said—

"Strange dreams! I've been dreaming—so has Alice. She hears and sees Una's dreams, and wonders—and well she may."

And she kissed her sister's cheek with a cold kiss, and lay down in her little bed, her slender hand under her head, and spoke no more.

Alice, not knowing what to think, went back to hers.

About this time Ultor de Lacy returned. He heard his elder daughter's strange narrative with marked uneasiness, and his agitation seemed to grow rather than subside. He enjoined her, however, not to mention it to the old servant, nor in presence of anybody she might chance to see, but only to him and to the priest, if he could be persuaded to resume his duty and return. The trial, however, such as it was, could not endure very long; matters had turned out favourably. The union of his younger daughter might be accomplished within a few months, and in eight or nine weeks they should be on their way to Paris.

A night or two after her father's arrival, Alice, in the[226] dead of the night, heard the well-known strange deep voice speaking softly, as it seemed, close to her own window on the outside; and Una›s voice, clear and tender, spoke in answer. She hurried to her own casement, and pushed it open, kneeling in the deep embrasure, and looking with a stealthy and affrighted gaze towards her sister›s window. As she crossed the floor the voices subsided, and she saw a light withdrawn from within. The moonbeams slanted bright and clear on the whole side of the castle overlooking the glen, and she plainly beheld the shadow of a man projected on the wall as on a screen.

This black shadow recalled with a horrid thrill the outline and fashion of the figure in the Spanish dress. There were the cap and mantle, the rapier, the long thin limbs and sinister angularity. It was so thrown obliquely that the hands reached to the window-sill, and the feet stretched and stretched, longer and longer as she looked, toward the ground, and disappeared in the general darkness; and the rest, with a sudden flicker, shot downwards, as shadows will on the sudden movement of a light, and was lost in one gigantic leap down the castle wall.

"I do not know whether I dream or wake when I hear and see these sights; but I will ask my father to sit up with me, and we *two* surely cannot be mistaken. May the holy saints keep and guard us!» And in her terror she buried her head under the bed-clothes, and whispered her prayers for an hour.

CHAPTER VII.
UNA'S LOVE.

"I have been with Father Denis," said De Lacy, next day, "and he will come to-morrow; and, thank Heaven! you may both make your confession and hear mass, and my mind will be at rest; and you'll find poor Una happier and more like herself."

But 'tween cup and lip there's many a slip. The priest was not destined to hear poor Una's shrift. When she bid her sister good-night she looked on her with her large, cold, wild eyes, till something of her old human affections seemed to gather there, and they slowly filled with tears, which dropped one after the other on her homely dress as she gazed in her sister's face.

Alice, delighted, sprang up, and clasped her arms about her neck. "My own darling treasure, 'tis all over; you love your poor Alice again, and will be happier than ever."

But while she held her in her embrace Una's eyes were turned towards the window, and her lips apart, and Alice felt instinctively that her thoughts were already far away.

"Hark!—listen!—hush!" and Una, with her delighted gaze fixed, as if she saw far away beyond the castle wall, the trees, the glen, and the night's dark curtain, held her hand raised near her ear, and waved her head slightly in time, as it seemed, to music that reached not Alice's ear, and smiled her strange pleased smile, and then the smile slowly faded away, leaving that sly suspicious light behind it which somehow scared her sister with an uncertain sense of danger; and she sang in tones so sweet and low that it seemed but a reverie of a song, recalling,[228] as Alice fancied, the strain to which she had just listened in that strange ecstasy, the plaintive and beautiful Irish ballad, "Shule, shule, shule, aroon," the midnight summons of the outlawed Irish soldier to his darling to follow him.

Alice had slept little the night before. She was now overpowered with fatigue; and leaving her candle burning by her bedside, she fell into a deep sleep. From this she awoke suddenly, and completely, as will sometimes happen without any apparent cause, and she saw Una come into the room. She had a little purse of embroidery—her own work—in her hand; and she stole lightly to the bedside, with her peculiar oblique smile, and evidently thinking that her sister was asleep.

Alice was thrilled with a strange terror, and did not speak or move; and her sister, slipped her hand softly under her bolster, and withdrew it. Then Una stood for a while by the hearth, and stretched her hand up to the mantelpiece, from which she took a little bit of chalk, and Alice thought she saw her place it in the fingers of a long yellow hand that was stealthily introduced from her own chamber-door to receive it; and Una paused in the dark recess of the door, and smiled over her shoulder toward her sister, and then glided into her room, closing the doors.

Almost freezing with terror, Alice rose and glided after her, and stood in her chamber, screaming—

"Una, Una, in heaven's name what troubles you?"

But Una seemed to have been sound asleep in her bed, and raised herself with a start, and looking upon her with a peevish surprise, said—

"What does Alice seek here?"

"You were in my room, Una, dear; you seem disturbed and troubled."[229]

"Dreams, Alice. My dreams crossing your brain; only dreams—dreams. Get you to bed, and sleep."

And to bed she went, but *not* to sleep. She lay awake more than an hour; and then Una emerged once more from her room. This time she was fully dressed, and had her cloak and thick shoes on, as their rattle on the floor plainly discovered. She had a little bundle tied up in a handkerchief in her hand, and her hood was drawn about her head; and thus equipped, as it seemed, for a journey, she came and stood at the foot of Alice›s bed, and stared on her with a look so soulless and terrible that her senses almost forsook her. Then she turned and went back into her own chamber.

She may have returned; but Alice thought not—at least she did not see her. But she lay in great excitement and perturbation; and was terrified, about an hour later, by a knock at her chamber door—not that opening into Una's room, but upon the little passage from the stone screw staircase. She sprang from her bed; but the door was secured on the inside, and she felt relieved. The knock was repeated, and she heard some one laughing softly on the outside.

The morning came at last; that dreadful night was over. But Una! Where was Una?

Alice never saw her more. On the head of her empty bed were traced in chalk the words—Ultor de Lacy, Ultor O'Donnell. And Alice found beneath her own pillow the little purse of embroidery she had seen in Una's hand. It was her little parting token, and bore the simple legend— "Una's love!"

De Lacy's rage and horror were boundless. He charged the priest, in frantic language, with having exposed his child, by his cowardice and neglect, to the machinations of the Fiend, and raved and blasphemed like a man demented.[230]

It is said that he procured a solemn exorcism to be performed, in the hope of disenthralling and recovering his daughter. Several times, it is alleged, she was seen by the old servants. Once on a sweet summer morning, in the window of the tower, she was perceived combing her beautiful golden tresses, and holding a little mirror in her hand; and first, when she saw herself discovered, she looked affrighted, and then smiled, her slanting, cunning smile. Sometimes, too, in the glen, by moonlight, it was said belated villagers had met her, always startled first, and then smiling, generally singing snatches of old Irish ballads, that seemed to bear a sort of dim resemblance to her melancholy fate. The apparition has long ceased. But it is said that now and again, perhaps once in two or three years, late on a summer night, you may hear—but faint and far away in the recesses of the glen—the sweet, sad notes of Una's voice, singing those plaintive melodies. This, too, of course, in time will cease, and all be forgotten.

CHAPTER VIII.
SISTER AGNES AND THE PORTRAIT.

When Ultor de Lacy died, his daughter Alice found among his effects a small box, containing a portrait such as I have described. When she looked on it, she recoiled in horror. There, in the plenitude of its sinister peculiarities, was faithfully portrayed the phantom which lived with a vivid and horrible accuracy in her remembrance. Folded in the same box was a brief narrative, stating that, "A.D. 1601, in the month of December, Walter de Lacy,[231] of Cappercullen, made many prisoners at the ford of Ownhey, or Abington, of Irish and Spanish soldiers, flying from the great overthrow of the rebel powers at Kinsale, and among the number one Roderic O›Donnell, an arch traitor, and near kinsman to that other O›Donnell who led the rebels; who, claiming kindred through his mother to De Lacy, sued for his life with instant and miserable entreaty, and offered great ransom, but was by De Lacy, through great zeal for the queen, as some thought, cruelly put to death. When he went to the tower-top, where was the gallows, finding himself in extremity, and no hope of mercy, he swore that though he could work them no evil before his death, yet that he would devote himself thereafter to blast the greatness of the De Lacys, and never leave them till his work was done. He hath been seen often since, and always for that family perniciously, insomuch that it hath been the custom to show to young children of that lineage the picture of the said O'Donnell, in little, taken among his few valuables, to prevent their being misled by him unawares, so that he should not have his will, who by devilish wiles and hell-born cunning, hath steadfastly sought the ruin of that ancient house, and especially to leave that *stemma generosum* destitute of issue for the transmission of their pure blood and worshipful name.»

Old Miss Croker, of Ross House, who was near seventy in the year 1821, when she related this story to me, had seen and conversed with Alice de Lacy, a professed nun, under the name of Sister Agnes, in a religious house in King-street, in Dublin, founded by the famous Duchess of Tyrconnell, and had the narrative from her own lips. I thought the tale worth preserving, and have no more to say.

11
THE VISION OF TOM CHUFF

Anonymous in *All the Year Round* (1870). A variation on «The Drunkard›s Dream» in *The Purcell Papers* (from *Dublin University Magazine*, 1838).

At the edge of melancholy Catstean Moor, in the north of England, with half-a-dozen ancient poplar-trees with rugged and hoary stems around, one smashed across the middle by a flash of lightning thirty summers before, and all by their great height dwarfing the abode near which they stand, there squats a rude stone house, with a thick chimney, a kitchen and bedroom on the ground-floor, and a loft, accessible by a ladder, under the shingle roof, divided into two rooms.

Its owner was a man of ill repute. Tom Chuff was his name. A shock-headed, broad-shouldered, powerful man, though somewhat short, with lowering brows and a sullen eye. He was a poacher, and hardly made an ostensible pretence of earning his bread by any honest industry. He was a drunkard. He beat his wife, and led his children a life of terror and lamentation, when he was at home. It was a blessing to his frightened little family when he absented himself, as he sometimes did, for a week or more together.[233]

On the night I speak of he knocked at the door with his cudgel at about eight o'clock. It was winter, and the night was very dark. Had the summons been that of a bogie from the moor, the inmates of this small house could hardly have heard it with greater terror.

His wife unbarred the door in fear and haste. Her hunchbacked sister stood by the hearth, staring toward the threshold. The children cowered behind.

Tom Chuff entered with his cudgel in his hand, without speaking, and threw himself into a chair opposite the fire. He had been away two or three days. He looked haggard, and his eyes were bloodshot. They knew he had been drinking.

Tom raked and knocked the peat fire with his stick, and thrust his feet close to it. He signed towards the little dresser, and nodded to his wife, and she knew he wanted a cup, which in silence she gave him. He pulled a bottle of gin from his coat-pocket, and nearly filling the teacup, drank off the dram at a few gulps.

He usually refreshed himself with two or three drams of this kind before beating the inmates of his house. His three little children, cowering in a corner, eyed him from under a table, as Jack did the ogre in the nursery tale. His wife, Nell, standing behind a chair, which she was ready to snatch up to meet the blow of the cudgel, which might be levelled at her at any moment, never took her eyes off him; and hunchbacked Mary showed the whites of a large pair of eyes, similarly employed, as she stood against the oaken press, her dark face hardly distinguishable in the distance from the brown panel behind it.

Tom Chuff was at his third dram, and had not yet spoken a word since his entrance, and the suspense was growing dreadful, when, on a sudden, he leaned back in[234] his rude seat, the cudgel slipped from his hand, a change and a death-like pallor came over his face.

For a while they all stared on; such was their fear of him, they dared not speak or move, lest it should prove to have been but a doze, and Tom should wake up and proceed forthwith to gratify his temper and exercise his cudgel.

In a very little time, however, things began to look so odd, that they ventured, his wife and Mary, to exchange glances full of doubt and wonder. He hung so much over the side of the chair, that if it had not been one of cyclopean clumsiness and weight, he would have borne it to the floor. A leaden tint was darkening the pallor of his face. They were becoming alarmed, and finally braving everything his wife timidly said, "Tom!" and then more sharply repeated it, and finally cried the appellative loudly, and again and again, with the terrified accompaniment, "He's dying—he's dying!" her voice rising to a scream, as she found that neither it nor her plucks and shakings of him by the shoulder had the slightest effect in recalling him from his torpor.

And now from sheer terror of a new kind the children added their shrilly piping to the talk and cries of their seniors; and if anything could have called Tom up from his lethargy, it might have been the piercing chorus that made the rude chamber of the poacher's habitation ring again. But Tom continued unmoved, deaf, and stirless.

His wife sent Mary down to the village, hardly a quarter of a mile away, to implore of the doctor, for whose family she did duty as laundress, to come down and look at her husband, who seemed to be dying.

The doctor, who was a good-natured fellow, arrived. With his hat still on, he looked at Tom, examined him, and when he found that the emetic he had brought with him, on conjecture from Mary's description, did not act,[235] and that his lancet brought no blood, and that he felt a pulseless wrist, he shook his head, and inwardly thought:

"What the plague is the woman crying for? Could she have desired a greater blessing for her children and herself than the very thing that has happened?"

Tom, in fact, seemed quite gone. At his lips no breath was perceptible. The doctor could discover no pulse. His hands and feet were cold, and the chill was stealing up into his body.

The doctor, after a stay of twenty minutes, had buttoned up his great-coat again and pulled down his hat, and told Mrs. Chuff that there was no use in his remaining any longer, when, all of a sudden, a little rill of blood began to trickle from the lancet-cut in Tom Chuff's temple.

"That's very odd," said the doctor. "Let us wait a little."

I must describe now the sensations which Tom Chuff had experienced.

With his elbows on his knees, and his chin upon his hands, he was staring into the embers, with his gin beside him, when suddenly a swimming came in his head, he lost sight of the fire, and a sound like one stroke of a loud church bell smote his brain.

Then he heard a confused humming, and the leaden weight of his head held him backward as he sank in his chair, and consciousness quite forsook him.

When he came to himself he felt chilled, and was leaning against a huge leafless tree. The night was moonless, and when he looked up he thought he had never seen stars so large and bright, or sky so black. The stars, too, seemed to blink down with longer intervals of darkness, and fiercer and more dazzling emergence, and something, he vaguely thought, of the character of silent menace and fury.[236]

He had a confused recollection of having come there, or rather of having been carried along, as if on men's shoulders, with a sort of rushing motion. But it was utterly indistinct; the imperfect recollection simply of a sensation. He had seen or heard nothing on his way.

He looked round. There was not a sign of a living creature near. And he began with a sense of awe to recognise the place.

The tree against which he had been leaning was one of the noble old beeches that surround at irregular intervals the churchyard of Shackleton, which spreads its green and wavy lap on the edge of the Moor of Catstean, at the opposite side of which stands the rude cottage in which he had just lost consciousness. It was six miles or more across the moor to his habitation, and the black expanse lay before him, disappearing dismally in the darkness. So that, looking straight before him, sky and land blended together in an undistinguishable and awful blank.

There was a silence quite unnatural over the place. The distant murmur of the brook, which he knew so well, was dead; not a whisper in the leaves above him; the air, earth, everything about and above was indescribably still; and he experienced that quaking of the heart that seems to portend the approach of something awful. He would have set out upon his return across the moor, had he not an undefined presentiment that he was waylaid by something he dared not pass.

The old grey church and tower of Shackleton stood like a shadow in the rear. His eye had grown accustomed to the obscurity, and he could just trace its outline. There were no comforting associations in his mind connected with it; nothing but menace and misgiving. His early training in his lawless calling was connected with this very[237] spot. Here his father used to meet two other poachers, and bring his son, then but a boy, with him.

Under the church porch, towards morning, they used to divide the game they had taken, and take account of the sales they had made on the previous day, and make partition of the money, and drink their gin. It was here he had taken his early lessons in drinking, cursing and lawlessness. His father's grave was hardly eight steps from the spot where he stood. In his present state of awful dejection, no scene on earth could have so helped to heighten his fear.

There was one object close by which added to his gloom. About a yard away, in rear of the tree, behind himself, and extending to his left, was an open grave, the mould and rubbish piled on the other side. At the head of this grave stood the beech-tree; its columnar stem rose like a huge monumental pillar. He knew every line and crease on its smooth surface. The initial letters of his own name, cut in its bark long ago, had spread out and wrinkled like the grotesque capitals of a fanciful engraver, and now with a sinister significance overlooked the open grave, as if answering his mental question, "Who for is t' grave cut?"

He felt still a little stunned, and there was a faint tremor in his joints that disinclined him to exert himself; and, further, he had a vague apprehension that take what direction he might, there was danger around him worse than that of staying where he was.

On a sudden the stars began to blink more fiercely, a faint wild light overspread for a minute the bleak landscape, and he saw approaching from the moor a figure at a kind of swinging trot, with now and then a zig-zag hop or two, such as men accustomed to cross such places make, to avoid the patches of slob or quag that meet them[238] here and there. This figure resembled his father›s, and like him, whistled through his finger by way of signal as he approached; but the whistle sounded not now shrilly and sharp, as in old times, but immensely far away, and seemed to sing strangely through Tom›s head. From habit or from fear, in answer to the signal, Tom whistled as he used to do five-and-twenty years ago and more, although he was already chilled with an unearthly fear.

Like his father, too, the figure held up the bag that was in his left hand as he drew near, when it was his custom to call out to him what was in it. It did not reassure the watcher, you may be certain, when a shout unnaturally faint reached him, as the phantom dangled the bag in the air, and he heard with a faint distinctness the words, "Tom Chuff's soul!"

Scarcely fifty yards away from the low churchyard fence at which Tom was standing, there was a wider chasm in the peat, which there threw up a growth of reeds and bulrushes, among which, as the old poacher used to do on a sudden alarm, the approaching figure suddenly cast itself down.

From the same patch of tall reeds and rushes emerged instantaneously what he at first mistook for the same figure creeping on all-fours, but what he soon perceived to be an enormous black dog with a rough coat like a bear's, which at first sniffed about, and then started towards him in what seemed to be a sportive amble, bouncing this way and that, but as it drew near it displayed a pair of fearful eyes that glowed like live coals, and emitted from the monstrous expanse of its jaws a terrifying growl.

This beast seemed on the point of seizing him, and Tom recoiled in panic and fell into the open grave behind him. The edge which he caught as he tumbled gave way, and down he went, expecting almost at the same instant to[239] reach the bottom. But never was such a fall! Bottomless seemed the abyss! Down, down, down, with immeasurable and still increasing speed, through utter darkness, with hair streaming straight upward, breathless, he shot with a rush of air against him, the force of which whirled up his very arms, second after second, minute after minute, through the chasm downward he flew, the icy perspiration of horror covering his body, and suddenly, as he expected to be dashed into annihilation, his descent was in an instant arrested with a tremendous shock, which, however, did not deprive him of consciousness even for a moment.

He looked about him. The place resembled a smoke-stained cavern or catacomb, the roof of which, except for a ribbed arch here and there faintly visible, was lost in darkness. From several rude passages, like the galleries of a gigantic mine, which opened from this centre chamber, was very dimly emitted a dull glow as of charcoal, which was the only light by which he could imperfectly discern the objects immediately about him.

What seemed like a projecting piece of the rock, at the corner of one of these murky entrances, moved on a sudden, and proved to be a human figure, that beckoned to him. He approached, and saw his father. He could barely recognise him, he was so monstrously altered.

"I've been looking for you, Tom. Welcome home, lad; come along to your place."

Tom's heart sank as he heard these words, which were spoken in a hollow and, he thought, derisive voice that made him tremble. But he could not help accompanying the wicked spirit, who led him into a place, in passing which he heard, as it were from within the rock, dreadful cries and appeals for mercy.

"What is this?" said he.[240]

"Never mind."

"Who are they?"

"New-comers, like yourself, lad," answered his father apathetically. "They give over that work in time, finding it is no use."

"What shall I do?" said Tom, in an agony.

"It's all one."

"But what shall I do?" reiterated Tom, quivering in every joint and nerve.

"Grin and bear it, I suppose."

"For God's sake, if ever you cared for me, as I am your own child, let me out of this!"

"There's no way out."

"If there's a way in there's a way out, and for Heaven's sake let me out of this."

But the dreadful figure made no further answer, and glided backwards by his shoulder to the rear; and others appeared in view, each with a faint red halo round it, staring on him with frightful eyes, images, all in hideous variety, of eternal fury or derision. He was growing mad, it seemed, under the stare of so many eyes, increasing in number and drawing closer every moment, and at the same time myriads and myriads of voices were calling him by his name, some far away, some near, some from one point, some from another, some from behind, close to his ears. These cries were increased in rapidity and multitude, and mingled with laughter, with flitting blasphemies, with broken insults and mockeries, succeeded and obliterated by others, before he could half catch their meaning.

All this time, in proportion to the rapidity and urgency of these dreadful sights and sounds, the epilepsy of terror was creeping up to his brain, and with a long and dreadful scream he lost consciousness.

When he recovered his senses, he found himself in a[241] small stone chamber, vaulted above, and with a ponderous door. A single point of light in the wall, with a strange brilliancy illuminated this cell.

Seated opposite to him was a venerable man with a snowy beard of immense length; an image of awful purity and severity. He was dressed in a coarse robe, with three large keys suspended from his girdle. He might have filled one's idea of an ancient porter of a city gate; such spiritual cities, I should say, as John Bunyan loved to describe.

This old man's eyes were brilliant and awful, and fixed on him as they were, Tom Chuff felt himself helplessly in his power. At length he spoke:

"The command is given to let you forth for one trial more. But if you are found again drinking with the drunken, and beating your fellow-servants, you shall return through the door by which you came, and go out no more."

With these words the old man took him by the wrist and led him through the first door, and then unlocking one that stood in the cavern outside, he struck Tom Chuff sharply on the shoulder, and the door shut behind him with a sound that boomed peal after peal of thunder near and far away, and all round and above, till it rolled off gradually into silence. It was totally dark, but there was a fanning of fresh cool air that overpowered him. He felt that he was in the upper world again.

In a few minutes he began to hear voices which he knew, and first a faint point of light appeared before his eyes, and gradually he saw the flame of the candle, and, after that, the familiar faces of his wife and children, and he heard them faintly when they spoke to him, although he was as yet unable to answer.

He also saw the doctor, like an isolated figure in the dark, and heard him say:[242]

"There, now, you have him back. He'll do, I think."

His first words, when he could speak and saw clearly all about him, and felt the blood on his neck and shirt, were:

"Wife, forgie me. I'm a changed man. Send for't sir."

Which last phrase means, "Send for the clergyman."

When the vicar came and entered the little bedroom where the scared poacher, whose soul had died within him, was lying, still sick and weak, in his bed, and with a spirit that was prostrate with terror, Tom Chuff feebly beckoned the rest from the room, and, the door being closed, the good parson heard the strange confession, and with equal amazement the man's earnest and agitated vows of amendment, and his helpless appeals to him for support and counsel.

These, of course, were kindly met; and the visits of the rector, for some time, were frequent.

One day, when he took Tom Chuff's hand on bidding him good-bye, the sick man held it still, and said:

"Ye'r vicar o' Shackleton, sir, and if I sud dee, ye'll promise me a'e thing, as I a promised ye a many. I a said I'll never gie wife, nor barn, nor folk o' no sort, skelp nor sizzup more, and ye'll know o' me no more among the sipers. Nor never will Tom draw trigger, nor set a snare again, but in an honest way, and after that ye'll no make it a bootless bene for me, but bein', as I say, vicar o' Shackleton, and able to do as ye list, ye'll no let them bury me within twenty good yerd-wands measure o' the a'd beech trees that's round the churchyard of Shackleton."

"I see; you would have your grave, when your time really comes, a good way from the place where lay the grave you dreamed of."

"That's jest it. I'd lie at the bottom o' a marl-pit liefer! And I'd be laid in anither churchyard just to be[243] shut o› my fear o› that, but that a› my kinsfolk is buried beyond in Shackleton, and ye›ll gie me yer promise, and no break yer word.»

"I do promise, certainly. I'm not likely to outlive you; but, if I should, and still be vicar of Shackleton, you shall be buried somewhere as near the middle of the churchyard as we can find space."

"That'll do."

And so content they parted.

The effect of the vision upon Tom Chuff was powerful, and promised to be lasting. With a sore effort he exchanged his life of desultory adventure and comparative idleness for one of regular industry. He gave up drinking; he was as kind as an originally surly nature would allow to his wife and family; he went to church; in fine weather they crossed the moor to Shackleton Church; the vicar said he came there to look at the scenery of his vision, and to fortify his good resolutions by the reminder.

Impressions upon the imagination, however, are but transitory, and a bad man acting under fear is not a free agent; his real character does not appear. But as the images of the imagination fade, and the action of fear abates, the essential qualities of the man reassert themselves.

So, after a time, Tom Chuff began to grow weary of his new life; he grew lazy, and people began to say that he was catching hares, and pursuing his old contraband way of life, under the rose.

He came home one hard night, with signs of the bottle in his thick speech and violent temper. Next day he was sorry, or frightened, at all events repentant, and for a week or more something of the old horror returned, and he was once more on his good behaviour. But in a little time came a relapse, and another repentance, and then a[244] relapse again, and gradually the return of old habits and the flooding in of all his old way of life, with more violence and gloom, in proportion as the man was alarmed and exasperated by the remembrance of his despised, but terrible, warning.

With the old life returned the misery of the cottage. The smiles, which had begun to appear with the unwonted sunshine, were seen no more. Instead, returned to his poor wife's face the old pale and heartbroken look. The cottage lost its neat and cheerful air, and the melancholy of neglect was visible. Sometimes at night were overheard, by a chance passer-by, cries and sobs from that ill-omened dwelling. Tom Chuff was now often drunk, and not very often at home, except when he came in to sweep away his poor wife's earnings.

Tom had long lost sight of the honest old parson. There was shame mixed with his degradation. He had grace enough left when he saw the thin figure of "t' sir" walking along the road to turn out of his way and avoid meeting him. The clergyman shook his head, and sometimes groaned, when his name was mentioned. His horror and regret were more for the poor wife than for the relapsed sinner, for her case was pitiable indeed.

Her brother, Jack Everton, coming over from Hexley, having heard stories of all this, determined to beat Tom, for his ill-treatment of his sister, within an inch of his life. Luckily, perhaps, for all concerned, Tom happened to be away upon one of his long excursions, and poor Nell besought her brother, in extremity of terror, not to interpose between them. So he took his leave and went home muttering and sulky.

Now it happened a few months later that Nelly Chuff fell sick. She had been ailing, as heartbroken people do, for a good while. But now the end had come.[245]

There was a coroner's inquest when she died, for the doctor had doubts as to whether a blow had not, at least, hastened her death. Nothing certain, however, came of the inquiry. Tom Chuff had left his home more than two days before his wife's death. He was absent upon his lawless business still when the coroner had held his quest.

Jack Everton came over from Hexley to attend the dismal obsequies of his sister. He was more incensed than ever with the wicked husband, who, one way or other, had hastened Nelly's death. The inquest had closed early in the day. The husband had not appeared.

An occasional companion—perhaps I ought to say accomplice—of Chuff's happened to turn up. He had left him on the borders of Westmoreland, and said he would probably be home next day. But Everton affected not to believe it. Perhaps it was to Tom Chuff, he suggested, a secret satisfaction to crown the history of his bad married life with the scandal of his absence from the funeral of his neglected and abused wife.

Everton had taken on himself the direction of the melancholy preparations. He had ordered a grave to be opened for his sister beside her mother's, in Shackleton churchyard, at the other side of the moor. For the purpose, as I have said, of marking the callous neglect of her husband, he determined that the funeral should take place that night. His brother Dick had accompanied him, and they and his sister, with Mary and the children, and a couple of the neighbours, formed the humble cortège.

Jack Everton said he would wait behind, on the chance of Tom Chuff coming in time, that he might tell him what had happened, and make him cross the moor with him to meet the funeral. His real object, I think, was to inflict upon the villain the drubbing he had so long wished[246] to give him. Anyhow, he was resolved, by crossing the moor, to reach the churchyard in time to anticipate the arrival of the funeral, and to have a few words with the vicar, clerk, and sexton, all old friends of his, for the parish of Shackleton was the place of his birth and early recollections.

But Tom Chuff did not appear at his house that night. In surly mood, and without a shilling in his pocket, he was making his way homeward. His bottle of gin, his last investment, half emptied, with its neck protruding, as usual on such returns, was in his coat-pocket.

His way home lay across the moor of Catstean, and the point at which he best knew the passage was from the churchyard of Shackleton. He vaulted the low wall that forms its boundary, and strode across the graves, and over many a flat, half-buried tombstone, toward the side of the churchyard next Catstean Moor.

The old church of Shackleton and its tower rose, close at his right, like a black shadow against the sky. It was a moonless night, but clear. By this time he had reached the low boundary wall, at the other side, that overlooks the wide expanse of Catstean Moor. He stood by one of the huge old beech trees, and leaned his back to its smooth trunk. Had he ever seen the sky look so black, and the stars shine out and blink so vividly? There was a death-like silence over the scene, like the hush that precedes thunder in sultry weather. The expanse before him was lost in utter blackness. A strange quaking unnerved his heart. It was the sky and scenery of his vision! The same horror and misgiving. The same invincible fear of venturing from the spot where he stood. He would have prayed if he dared. His sinking heart demanded a restorative of some sort, and he grasped the bottle in his coat-pocket. Turning to his left, as he did so, he saw the[247] piled-up mould of an open grave that gaped with its head close to the base of the great tree against which he was leaning.

He stood aghast. His dream was returning and slowly enveloping him. Everything he saw was weaving itself into the texture of his vision. The chill of horror stole over him.

A faint whistle came shrill and clear over the moor, and he saw a figure approaching at a swinging trot, with a zig-zag course, hopping now here and now there, as men do over a surface where one has need to choose their steps. Through the jungle of reeds and bulrushes in the foreground this figure advanced; and with the same unaccountable impulse that had coerced him in his dream, he answered the whistle of the advancing figure.

On that signal it directed its course straight toward him. It mounted the low wall, and, standing there, looked into the graveyard.

"Who med answer?" challenged the new-comer from his post of observation.

"Me," answered Tom.

"Who are you?" repeated the man upon the wall.

"Tom Chuff; and who's this grave cut for?" He answered in a savage tone, to cover the secret shudder of his panic.

"I'll tell you that, ye villain!" answered the stranger, descending from the wall, "I a' looked for you far and near, and waited long, and now you're found at last."

Not knowing what to make of the figure that advanced upon him, Tom Chuff recoiled, stumbled, and fell backward into the open grave. He caught at the sides as he fell, but without retarding his fall.

An hour after, when lights came with the coffin, the corpse of Tom Chuff was found at the bottom of the grave.[248] He had fallen direct upon his head, and his neck was broken. His death must have been simultaneous with his fall. Thus far his dream was accomplished.

It was his brother-in-law who had crossed the moor and approached the churchyard of Shackleton, exactly in the line which the image of his father had seemed to take in his strange vision. Fortunately for Jack Everton, the sexton and clerk of Shackleton church were, unseen by him, crossing the churchyard toward the grave of Nelly Chuff, just as Tom the poacher stumbled and fell. Suspicion of direct violence would otherwise have inevitably attached to the exasperated brother. As it was, the catastrophe was followed by no legal consequences.

The good vicar kept his word, and the grave of Tom Chuff is still pointed out by the old inhabitants of Shackleton pretty nearly in the centre of the churchyard. This conscientious compliance with the entreaty of the panic-stricken man as to the place of his sepulture gave a horrible and mocking emphasis to the strange combination by which fate had defeated his precaution, and fixed the place of his death.

The story was for many a year, and we believe still is, told round many a cottage hearth, and though it appeals to what many would term superstition, it yet sounded, in the ears of a rude and simple audience, a thrilling, and, let us hope, not altogether fruitless homily.

12
STORIES OF LOUGH GUIR

Anonymous in *All the Year Round* (1869-70). It differs from the other tales in this volume in being apparently a record of stories actually told to Le Fanu and not invented by him; and they purport to be, as the phrase goes, ‹veridical.›

When the present writer was a boy of twelve or thirteen, he first made the acquaintance of Miss Anne Baily, of Lough Guir, in the county of Limerick. She and her sister were the last representatives at that place, of an extremely good old name in the county. They were both what is termed "old maids," and at that time past sixty. But never were old ladies more hospitable, lively, and kind, especially to young people. They were both remarkably agreeable and clever. Like all old county ladies of their time, they were great genealogists, and could recount the origin, generations, and intermarriages, of every county family of note.

These ladies were visited at their house at Lough Guir by Mr. Crofton Croker; and are, I think, mentioned, by name, in the second series of his fairy legends; the series in which (probably communicated by Miss Anne Baily), he recounts some of the picturesque traditions of those beautiful lakes—lakes, I should no longer say, for the[250] smaller and prettier has since been drained, and gave up from its depths some long lost and very interesting relics.

In their drawing-room stood a curious relic of another sort: old enough, too, though belonging to a much more modern period. It was the ancient stirrup cup of the hospitable house of Lough Guir. Crofton Croker has preserved a sketch of this curious glass. I have often had it in my hand. It had a short stem; and the cup part, having the bottom rounded, rose cylindrically, and, being of a capacity to contain a whole bottle of claret, and almost as narrow as an old-fashioned ale glass, was tall to a degree that filled me with wonder. As it obliged the rider to extend his arm as he raised the glass, it must have tried a tipsy man, sitting in the saddle, pretty severely. The wonder was that the marvellous tall glass had come down to our times without a crack.

There was another glass worthy of remark in the same drawing-room. It was gigantic, and shaped conically, like one of those old-fashioned jelly glasses which used to be seen upon the shelves of confectioners. It was engraved round the rim with the words, "The glorious, pious, and immortal memory"; and on grand occasions, was filled to the brim, and after the manner of a loving cup, made the circuit of the Whig guests, who owed all to the hero whose memory its legend invoked.

It was now but the transparent phantom of those solemn convivialities of a generation, who lived, as it were, within hearing of the cannon and shoutings of those stirring times. When I saw it, this glass had long retired from politics and carousals, and stood peacefully on a little table in the drawing-room, where ladies' hands replenished it with fair water, and crowned it daily with flowers from the garden.

Miss Anne Baily's conversation ran oftener than her[251] sister›s upon the legendary and supernatural; she told her stories with the sympathy, the colour, and the mysterious air which contribute so powerfully to effect, and never wearied of answering questions about the old castle, and amusing her young audience with fascinating little glimpses of old adventure and bygone days. My memory retains the picture of my early friend very distinctly. A slim straight figure, above the middle height; a general likeness to the full-length portrait of that delightful Countess D›Aulnois, to whom we all owe our earliest and most brilliant glimpses of fairy-land; something of her gravely-pleasant countenance, plain, but refined and ladylike, with that kindly mystery in her sidelong glance and uplifted finger, which indicated the approaching climax of a tale of wonder.

Lough Guir is a kind of centre of the operations of the Munster fairies. When a child is stolen by the "good people," Lough Guir is conjectured to be the place of its unearthly transmutation from the human to the fairy state. And beneath its waters lie enchanted, the grand old castle of the Desmonds, the great earl himself, his beautiful young countess, and all the retinue that surrounded him in the years of his splendour, and at the moment of his catastrophe.

Here, too, are historic associations. The huge square tower that rises at one side of the stable-yard close to the old house, to a height that amazed my young eyes, though robbed of its battlements and one story, was a stronghold of the last rebellious Earl of Desmond, and is specially mentioned in that delightful old folio, the Hibernia Pacata, as having, with its Irish garrison on the battlements, defied the army of the lord deputy, then marching by upon the summits of the overhanging hills. The house, built under shelter of this stronghold of the once proud[252] and turbulent Desmonds, is old, but snug, with a multitude of small low rooms, such as I have seen in houses of the same age in Shropshire and the neighbouring English counties.

The hills that overhang the lakes appeared to me, in my young days (and I have not seen them since), to be clothed with a short soft verdure, of a hue so dark and vivid as I had never seen before.

In one of the lakes is a small island, rocky and wooded, which is believed by the peasantry to represent the top of the highest tower of the castle which sank, under a spell, to the bottom. In certain states of the atmosphere, I have heard educated people say, when in a boat you have reached a certain distance, the island appears to rise some feet from the water, its rocks assume the appearance of masonry, and the whole circuit presents very much the effect of the battlements of a castle rising above the surface of the lake.

This was Miss Anne Baily's story of the submersion of this lost castle:

THE MAGICIAN EARL.

It is well known that the great Earl of Desmond, though history pretends to dispose of him differently, lives to this hour enchanted in his castle, with all his household, at the bottom of the lake.

There was not, in his day, in all the world, so accomplished a magician as he. His fairest castle stood upon an island in the lake, and to this he brought his young and beautiful bride, whom he loved but too well; for she prevailed upon his folly to risk all to gratify her imperious caprice.

They had not been long in this beautiful castle, when she one day presented herself in the chamber in which[253] her husband studied his forbidden art, and there implored him to exhibit before her some of the wonders of his evil science. He resisted long; but her entreaties, tears, and wheedlings were at length too much for him and he consented.

But before beginning those astonishing transformations with which he was about to amaze her, he explained to her the awful conditions and dangers of the experiment.

Alone in this vast apartment, the walls of which were lapped, far below, by the lake whose dark waters lay waiting to swallow them, she must witness a certain series of frightful phenomena, which once commenced, he could neither abridge nor mitigate; and if throughout their ghastly succession she spoke one word, or uttered one exclamation, the castle and all that it contained would in one instant subside to the bottom of the lake, there to remain, under the servitude of a strong spell, for ages.

The dauntless curiosity of the lady having prevailed, and the oaken door of the study being locked and barred, the fatal experiments commenced.

Muttering a spell, as he stood before her, feathers sprouted thickly over him, his face became contracted and hooked, a cadaverous smell filled the air, and, with heavy winnowing wings, a gigantic vulture rose in his stead, and swept round and round the room, as if on the point of pouncing upon her.

The lady commanded herself through this trial, and instantly another began.

The bird alighted near the door, and in less than a minute changed, she saw not how, into a horribly deformed and dwarfish hag: who, with yellow skin hanging about her face and enormous eyes, swung herself on crutches toward the lady, her mouth foaming with fury, and her grimaces and contortions becoming more and more[254] hideous every moment, till she rolled with a yell on the floor, in a horrible convulsion, at the lady›s feet, and then changed into a huge serpent, with crest erect, and quivering tongue. Suddenly, as it seemed on the point of darting at her, she saw her husband in its stead, standing pale before her, and, with his finger on his lip, enforcing the continued necessity of silence. He then placed himself at his length on the floor, and began to stretch himself out and out, longer and longer, until his head nearly reached to one end of the vast room, and his feet to the other.

This horror overcame her. The ill-starred lady uttered a wild scream, whereupon the castle and all that was within it, sank in a moment to the bottom of the lake.

But, once in every seven years, by night, the Earl of Desmond and his retinue emerge, and cross the lake, in shadowy cavalcade. His white horse is shod with silver. On that one night, the earl may ride till day-break, and it behoves him to make good use of his time; for, until the silver shoes of his steed be worn through, the spell that holds him and his beneath the lake, will retain its power.

When I (Miss Anne Baily) was a child, there was still living a man named Teigue O'Neill, who had a strange story to tell.

He was a smith, and his forge stood on the brow of the hill, overlooking the lake, on a lonely part of the road to Cahir Conlish. One bright moonlight night, he was working very late, and quite alone. The clink of his hammer, and the wavering glow reflected through the open door on the bushes at the other side of the narrow road, were the only tokens that told of life and vigil for miles around.

In one of the pauses of his work, he heard the ring of many hoofs ascending the steep road that passed his[255] forge, and, standing in his doorway, he was just in time to see a gentleman, on a white horse, who was dressed in a fashion the like of which the smith had never seen before. This man was accompanied and followed by a mounted retinue, as strangely dressed as he.

They seemed, by the clang and clatter that announced their approach, to be riding up the hill at a hard hurry-scurry gallop; but the pace abated as they drew near, and the rider of the white horse who, from his grave and lordly air, he assumed to be a man of rank, and accustomed to command, drew bridle and came to a halt before the smith's door.

He did not speak, and all his train were silent, but he beckoned to the smith, and pointed down to one of his horse's hoofs.

Teigue stooped and raised it, and held it just long enough to see that it was shod with a silver shoe; which, in one place, he said, was worn as thin as a shilling. Instantaneously, his situation was made apparent to him by this sign, and he recoiled with a terrified prayer. The lordly rider, with a look of pain and fury, struck at him suddenly, with something that whistled in the air like a whip; and an icy streak seemed to traverse his body as if he had been cut through with a leaf of steel. But he was without scathe or scar, as he afterwards found. At the same moment he saw the whole cavalcade break into a gallop and disappear down the hill, with a momentary hurtling in the air, like the flight of a volley of cannon shot.

Here had been the earl himself. He had tried one of his accustomed stratagems to lead the smith to speak to him. For it is well known that either for the purpose of abridging or of mitigating his period of enchantment, he seeks to lead people to accost him. But what, in the[256] event of his succeeding, would befall the person whom he had thus ensnared, no one knows.

MOLL RIAL'S ADVENTURE.

When Miss Anne Baily was a child, Moll Rial was an old woman. She had lived all her days with the Bailys of Lough Guir; in and about whose house, as was the Irish custom of those days, were a troop of bare-footed country girls, scullery maids, or laundresses, or employed about the poultry yard, or running of errands.

Among these was Moll Rial, then a stout good-humoured lass, with little to think of, and nothing to fret about. She was once washing clothes by the process known universally in Munster as beetling. The washer stands up to her ankles in water, in which she has immersed the clothes, which she lays in that state on a great flat stone, and smacks with lusty strokes of an instrument which bears a rude resemblance to a cricket bat, only shorter, broader, and light enough to be wielded freely with one hand. Thus, they smack the dripping clothes, turning them over and over, sousing them in the water, and replacing them on the same stone, to undergo a repetition of the process, until they are thoroughly washed.

Moll Rial was plying her "beetle" at the margin of the lake, close under the old house and castle. It was between eight and nine o'clock on a fine summer morning, everything looked bright and beautiful. Though quite alone, and though she could not see even the windows of the house (hidden from her view by the irregular ascent and some interposing bushes), her loneliness was not depressing.

Standing up from her work, she saw a gentleman walking slowly down the slope toward her. He was a "grand-looking" gentleman, arrayed in a flowered silk dressing[257]-gown, with a cap of velvet on his head; and as he stepped toward her, in his slippered feet, he showed a very handsome leg. He was smiling graciously as he approached, and drawing a ring from his finger with an air of gracious meaning, which seemed to imply that he wished to make her a present, he raised it in his fingers with a pleased look, and placed it on the flat stones beside the clothes she had been beetling so industriously.

He drew back a little, and continued to look at her with an encouraging smile, which seemed to say: "You have earned your reward; you must not be afraid to take it."

The girl fancied that this was some gentleman who had arrived, as often happened in those hospitable and haphazard times, late and unexpectedly the night before, and who was now taking a little indolent ramble before breakfast.

Moll Rial was a little shy, and more so at having been discovered by so grand a gentleman with her petticoats gathered a little high about her bare shins. She looked down, therefore, upon the water at her feet, and then she saw a ripple of blood, and then another, ring after ring, coming and going to and from her feet. She cried out the sacred name in horror, and, lifting her eyes, the courtly gentleman was gone, but the blood-rings about her feet spread with the speed of light over the surface of the lake, which for a moment glowed like one vast estuary of blood.

Here was the earl once again, and Moll Rial declared that if it had not been for that frightful transformation of the water she would have spoken to him next minute, and would thus have passed under a spell, perhaps as direful as his own.

THE BANSHEE.

So old a Munster family as the Bailys, of Lough Guir, could not fail to have their attendant banshee. Every one attached to the family knew this well, and could cite evidences of that unearthly distinction. I heard Miss Baily relate the only experience she had personally had of that wild spiritual sympathy.

She said that, being then young, she and Miss Susan undertook a long attendance upon the sick bed of their sister, Miss Kitty, whom I have heard remembered among her contemporaries as the merriest and most entertaining of human beings. This light-hearted young lady was dying of consumption. The sad duties of such attendance being divided among many sisters, as there then were, the night watches devolved upon the two ladies I have named: I think, as being the eldest.

It is not improbable that these long and melancholy vigils, lowering the spirits and exciting the nervous system, prepared them for illusions. At all events, one night at dead of night, Miss Baily and her sister, sitting in the dying lady's room, heard such sweet and melancholy music as they had never heard before. It seemed to them like distant cathedral music. The room of the dying girl had its windows toward the yard, and the old castle stood near, and full in sight. The music was not in the house, but seemed to come from the yard, or beyond it. Miss Anne Baily took a candle, and went down the back stairs. She opened the back door, and, standing there, heard the same faint but solemn harmony, and could not tell whether it most resembled the distant music of instruments, or a choir of voices. It seemed to come through the windows of the old castle, high in the air. But when she approached the tower, the music, she thought, came from[259] above the house, at the other side of the yard; and thus perplexed, and at last frightened, she returned.

This aerial music both she and her sister, Miss Susan Baily, avowed that they distinctly heard, and for a long time. Of the fact she was clear, and she spoke of it with great awe.

THE GOVERNESS'S DREAM.

This lady, one morning, with a grave countenance that indicated something weighty upon her mind, told her pupils that she had, on the night before, had a very remarkable dream.

The first room you enter in the old castle, having reached the foot of the spiral stone stair, is a large hall, dim and lofty, having only a small window or two, set high in deep recesses in the wall. When I saw the castle many years ago, a portion of this capacious chamber was used as a store for the turf laid in to last the year.

Her dream placed her, alone, in this room, and there entered a grave-looking man, having something very remarkable in his countenance: which impressed her, as a fine portrait sometimes will, with a haunting sense of character and individuality.

In his hand this man carried a wand, about the length of an ordinary walking cane. He told her to observe and remember its length, and to mark well the measurements he was about to make, the result of which she was to communicate to Mr. Baily of Lough Guir.

From a certain point in the wall, with this wand, he measured along the floor, at right angles with the wall, a certain number of its lengths, which he counted aloud; and then, in the same way, from the adjoining wall he measured a certain number of its lengths, which he also counted distinctly. He then told her that at the point[260] where these two lines met, at a depth of a certain number of feet which he also told her, treasure lay buried. And so the dream broke up, and her remarkable visitant vanished.

She took the girls with her to the old castle, where, having cut a switch to the length represented to her in her dream, she measured the distances, and ascertained, as she supposed, the point on the floor beneath which the treasure lay. The same day she related her dream to Mr. Baily. But he treated it laughingly, and took no step in consequence.

Some time after this, she again saw, in a dream, the same remarkable-looking man, who repeated his message, and appeared displeased. But the dream was treated by Mr. Baily as before.

The same dream occurred again, and the children became so clamorous to have the castle floor explored, with pick and shovel, at the point indicated by the thrice-seen messenger, that at length Mr. Baily consented, and the floor was opened, and a trench was sunk at the spot which the governess had pointed out.

Miss Anne Baily, and nearly all the members of the family, her father included, were present at this operation. As the workmen approached the depth described in the vision, the interest and suspense of all increased; and when the iron implements met the solid resistance of a broad flagstone, which returned a cavernous sound to the stroke, the excitement of all present rose to its acme.

With some difficulty the flag was raised, and a chamber of stone work, large enough to receive a moderately-sized crock or pit, was disclosed. Alas! it was empty. But in the earth at the bottom of it, Miss Baily said, she herself saw, as every other bystander plainly did, the[261] circular impression of a vessel: which had stood there, as the mark seemed to indicate, for a very long time.

Both the Miss Bailys were strong in their belief hereafterwards, that the treasure which they were convinced had actually been deposited there, had been removed by some more trusting and active listener than their father had proved.

This same governess remained with them to the time of her death, which occurred some years later, under the following circumstances as extraordinary as her dream.

THE EARL'S HALL.

The good governess had a particular liking for the old castle, and when lessons were over, would take her book or her work into a large room in the ancient building, called the Earl's Hall. Here she caused a table and chair to be placed for her use, and in the chiaroscuro would so sit at her favourite occupations, with just a little ray of subdued light, admitted through one of the glassless windows above her, and falling upon her table.

The Earl's Hall is entered by a narrow-arched door, opening close to the winding stair. It is a very large and gloomy room, pretty nearly square, with a lofty vaulted ceiling, and a stone floor. Being situated high in the castle, the walls of which are immensely thick, and the windows very small and few, the silence that reigns here is like that of a subterranean cavern. You hear nothing in this solitude, except perhaps twice in a day, the twitter of a swallow in one of the small windows high in the wall.

This good lady having one day retired to her accustomed solitude, was missed from the house at her wonted hour of return. This in a country house, such as Irish houses Were in those days, excited little surprise, and no harm.[262] But when the dinner hour came, which was then, in country houses, five o›clock, and the governess had not appeared, some of her young friends, it being not yet winter, and sufficient light remaining to guide them through the gloom of the dim ascent and passages, mounted the old stone stair to the level of the Earl›s Hall, gaily calling to her as they approached.

There was no answer. On the stone floor, outside the door of the Earl's Hall, to their horror, they found her lying insensible. By the usual means she was restored to consciousness; but she continued very ill, and was conveyed to the house, where she took to her bed.

It was there and then that she related what had occurred to her. She had placed herself, as usual, at her little work table, and had been either working or reading—I forget which—for some time, and felt in her usual health and serene spirits. Raising her eyes, and looking towards the door, she saw a horrible-looking little man enter. He was dressed in red, was very short, had a singularly dark face, and a most atrocious countenance. Having walked some steps into the room, with his eyes fixed on her, he stopped, and beckoning to her to follow, moved back toward the door. About half way, again he stopped once more and turned. She was so terrified that she sat staring at the apparition without moving or speaking. Seeing that she had not obeyed him, his face became more frightful and menacing, and as it underwent this change, he raised his hand and stamped on the floor. Gesture, look, and all, expressed diabolical fury. Through sheer extremity of terror she did rise, and, as he turned again, followed him a step or two in the direction of the door. He again stopped, and with the same mute menace, compelled her again to follow him.

She reached the narrow stone doorway of the Earl's[263] Hall, through which he had passed; from the threshold she saw him standing a little way off, with his eyes still fixed on her. Again he signed to her, and began to move along the short passage that leads to the winding stair. But instead of following him further, she fell on the floor in a fit.

The poor lady was thoroughly persuaded that she was not long to survive this vision, and her foreboding proved true. From her bed she never rose. Fever and delirium supervened in a few days and she died. Of course, it is possible that fever, already approaching, had touched her brain when she was visited by the phantom, and that it had no external existence.

Milton Keynes UK
Ingram Content Group UK Ltd.
UKHW011019271123
433341UK00007B/657